Edward Robins

Echoes of the Playhouse

Reminiscences of Some Past Glories of the English Stage

Edward Robins

Echoes of the Playhouse
Reminiscences of Some Past Glories of the English Stage

ISBN/EAN: 9783337151775

Printed in Europe, USA, Canada, Australia, Japan

Cover: Foto ©Andreas Hilbeck / pixelio.de

More available books at **www.hansebooks.com**

MRS. ABINGTON.

AS "LADY SADLIFE" IN COLLEY CIBBER'S COMEDY, "THE DOUBLE GALLANT." FROM A
DRAWING BY ISAAC TAYLOR.

CONTENTS.

ILLUSTRATIONS.

[1] Reproduced from Lowndes's *British Theatre*, published in London,
1776-7.

[2] Reproduced from Bell's *British Theatre*, 1776.

ECHOES OF THE PLAYHOUSE

ECHOES OF THE PLAYHOUSE

CHAPTER I.

BY WAY OF PROLOGUE.

IT seems startling, not to say amusingly paradoxical, to think that the English and American drama of to-day, upon which a well-meaning clergyman occasionally pours forth a torrent of righteous indignation, and not always without reason, is the logical development of that most religious of dramatic institutions, the Miracle Play. The far-away period when pious compositions were acted in England under the patronage of the church authorities, with the object of pointing a moral by illustrating the virtues, temptations, and martyrdom of the saints, was simply the forerunner of an age when playwrights would concern themselves very little as to the holy men and women of old, but a great deal about heroes and heroines who, in some instances, would prove as unsaintlike as the most exacting admirer of *fin de siècle* realism could desire. From the

ecclesiastical, mediæval atmosphere of the Miracles,
and thence through a variety of transitions typified
by the Morals, Allegories, Masks, and Interludes of
Plantagenet times, the wonderful efforts of the Elizabethan authors, the brilliant but bad-tasting comedies
of the Stuart Restoration, and the more or less sententious, artificial, yet occasionally delightful pieces of the
Georgian era, is evolved what has been proudly spoken
of as the nineteenth century drama. A strange compound, certainly, to come down to us from the days of
cowled monk and princely bishop—a compound of good
and bad, of fine plays and trash, of innocent " rural " productions, and unhealthy studies in crime, of
thoughtful, sombre works, and of " farce-comedies "
more appropriate to the circus ring than the footlights.
These are the lineal descendants of so spiritual an
ancestor.

Without attempting to follow the researches of anti-
quarians as to the first appearance of Miracle Plays in
England, it may be noted that they were given in London in the twelfth century, according to the testimony
of William Fitzstephen, who refers, in his *Life of
Thomas à Becket*, to the performance in the metropolis
of " holy playes, representations of miracles, which
holy confessors have wrought, or representations of
torments." The subjects were not cheerful, from the
standpoint of the modern theatre-goer, who has even
been known to fall asleep over Shakespeare, but that
they were popular in different parts of the kingdom is

a matter of record. In Dunstable, for instance, a monk named Geoffrey superintended the presentation of a drama dealing with the life of St. Katherine, and evidently took upon himself the exacting duties of a stage manager. As a rule, however, such management was undertaken by laymen, the various trade guilds of important towns often being responsible for the proper introduction of the plays.

The performers generally appeared on movable scaffolds or stages placed in the open streets, or in the courtyard of an inn. Some of these scaffolds consisted of two compartments, one above the other, in the lower of which the *dramatis personæ* were obliged to dress, and while the arrangement must have had its inconveniences, more particularly for the audience, the actors possibly fared as comfortably as they would have done in the average dressing-room of the American theatre. Our auditoriums are fitted up like palaces, but alas! how much more like hovels oftentimes seem the quarters on the other side of the proscenium.

The Miracles were seldom acted in England after the middle of the sixteenth century, although they were not absolutely unknown during the reign of James I. Their place had gradually been taken by Moralities, plays that mark a distinct advance in dramatic construction, and a purpose on the part of the authors to get away from the purely sacred nature of the preceeding works. The characters of the Moralities were allegorical or symbolical, just as are those of some pantomimic piece where Good and Evil, Avarice, Generosity, and other abstract personages are represented, although it need hardly be added that the comparison goes no further. The Devil figured importantly in these outgrowths of the old Miracles, and entertainingly as well, as he has continued to do, in different guises, through a variety of stage literature. Whether posing as an out-and-out *Mephistopheles*, with cloven foot and horns, or hiding under the stylish clothes of the elegantly-gloved, polished villain of melodrama, Satan has always rejoiced the heart of the playwriter, and hundreds of years from now, no doubt, his crushing defeat in the last act, through the instrumentality of the hero, will be received with every manifestation of delight. In the Moralities the Devil was so represented that he might create amusement, and probably actual merriment, among the spectators, so that he may have been a comedian rather than the cynical, but gentlemanly, Evil One of the Goethe type, or the majestic personage pictured by Milton. There was one writer of the time of Henry VI. who evidently looked upon these plays as a work of this self-same Devil, for he cried out against the frequency of their performances, and set the pace for a host of agitators who have come after him, and to whom the existence of the stage seems one of the greatest evils of a world wherein they can at best see but little good.

Companies of strolling players had now become numerous, and as this "barnstorming" element increased there must have been a corresponding falling off in the one-time ecclesiastical spirit that imparted dignity and purity to the performances. With the change came greater license, but the breaking up of the old traditions proved beneficial in the end, paving the way, as it did, for the glorious Elizabethan epoch, when Shakespeare gave expression to developments and changes which had been gradually shaping themselves for three centuries.

Once that the sacerdotal character of the native drama was lost the English kings, who generally had a keen taste for the pleasures of life, began to directly encourage the showing of these Moralities, Interludes, or Masques. Henry VII. had two companies of players of his own ; Henry VIII., who placed the amusements of the Court on a very expensive footing, kept three companies, and one of the members of his household was John Heywood, the dramatic author and poet. At one time Heywood received the munificent salary of five pounds a quarter,* but that was a regal recompense compared to the three shillings and four pence paid to the writer of a piece played at Court in the year 1527. For the aforesaid shillings and pence, this unfortunate genius was not only required to put the dialogue into rhyme, but also had to have it both in English and Latin ! Surely, the commercial benefits

* Even allowing for the fact that this meant much more than a similar amount now-a-days, the wage was hardly a princely one.

of the playwright are greater than they were in the halcyon days of the Defender of the Faith.

The interludes of Heywood, which were more akin to modern comedy than to the old Miracles or Moralities ; *Gammer Gurton's Needle*, written by John Still (subsequently Bishop of Bath and Wells), and a play called *Ralph Roister Doister*, the work of Nicholas Udall, a master at Eton, mark a radical departure in the drama of the sixteenth century, and are really the first examples of a notable development from the ancient order of things. *Gammer Gurton's Needle* is generally regarded as the earliest regular English comedy, whatever may be the claims for the priority of Udall's production, and, as Schlegel well says : " However antiquated in language and versification, it possesses unequivocal merit in the low comic. The whole plot turns on a lost needle, the finding of which is pursued with the utmost assiduity ; the poverty of the persons of the drama, which this supposes, and the whole of their domestic conditions, is very amusingly portrayed, and the part of the cunning beggar especially is drawn with much humor."

A play having for the basis of its plot the search for a needle, suggests the epoch of Sardou's charming trifle, *A Scrap of Paper* (to use the Anglicized title), rather than the time when works about the saints or Bible characters were still familiar. But things moved quickly on, the tendency was less heavenly but none the less upward, and the religious controversies of the

Reformation were now reflected in some of the interludes in a way that would never have been dreamed of
in an earlier century. It is related that before Henry
VIII. separated from the Church of Rome he once entertained at Greenwich several French ambassadors,
for whose delectation he provided a Latin moral in
which the reformers were ridiculed and Luther and his
wife were represented. The latter wore a garment of
red silk, but whether it was thereby intended to represent her as a type of the scarlet woman further depo-
nent sayeth not. Morals espousing the Protestant
cause were written and played, however, with the
result that an Act of Parliament was passed setting
forth that no one should " play in interludes, sing or
rhyme any matter contrary to the doctrines of the
Church of Rome." For the first infringement of this
law a fine and a stay in jail of three months could be
imposed, while perpetual imprisonment was one of the
penalties meted out for a repetition of the offence. It
looks like the irony of fate, consequently, to read that
in the year 1551 the abandoned monastery of the Blackfriars, which had been surrendered to the Crown, or
confiscated, was turned into a sort of property-room,
where the dresses and appliances used in Court festivi-
ties could be stored.

During the reigns of Edward VI. and Queen Mary,
the drama had a rather precarious existence, and the
complete control the government exercised, at least
theoretically, over the players may be inferred from the

fact that in 1549 it had been determined, for political reasons, to put a temporary stop to public entertainments. On the accession of Queen Mary she forbade the introduction into the plays and interludes of sentiments favoring the Reformation, and one dramatist, ready to follow the changing tide, wrote a piece entitled *Respublica*, wherein the principles of Luther were held up to scorn and Mary was personified as *Queen Nemesis*. Under Elizabeth, who took so keen an interest in the drama, actors had still much to contend with, and the Virgin Queen herself issued stringent orders as to the licensing of performances, although there is good reason to believe that the strollers of her time stood in need of regulation. They were subjected, among other things, to the thunders of the reformed or Established Church, for the great plague of 1563, when so many citizens of London were stricken, was used by Archbishop Grindal as a proper excuse for launching forth an invective against the poor players. He called them an "idle sort of people, which had been infamous in all good Commonwealths," and advised the abolition of all dramatic entertainments for at least a year, on the ground that attendance at them was likely to spread the infection. He added that if the performances were forbidden for all time "it were not amiss." However, the plague ran its woeful course, the suggestion of the worthy Archbishop as to choking off the drama "forever and a day" was not taken, and several years later we find Elizabeth enjoying such compositions as *The Painful Pilgrimage, As Plain As Can Be* (which evidently had no reference to her personal appearance), *Six Fools, Orestes, King of Scots,* and a number of others, not forgetting one with the idyllic title of *Jack and Jill.*

But the patronage of royalty was not to save the Thespian from a legislative enactment which should put him in the same rank as a peddler, or a bear leader; indeed, the world moves so slowly that even yet virtuous persons can be found who, in the inmost recesses of their little minds, consider the actor scarcely better than a mountebank. Many of the nobility had from a by-gone period acted as sponsors for different companies of players who were looked upon in the light of servants by their respective patrons, and as the custom spread there came an abuse with it. Itinerants in no wise connected with any noble house wandered aimlessly from town to town, and their number finally became so great that in 1572 a law was passed providing that "all fencers, bearwards, *common players* in interludes and minstrels not belonging to any baron of this realm, or towards any other honorable personage of greater degree; all jugglers, peddlers, tinkers and petty chapmen, which said fencers, bearwards, common players in interludes and minstrels, etc. shall wander abroad and not have license of two justices of the peace at least shall be deemed and dealt with as rogues and vagabonds."

Yet, while the unlicensed player was labelled a vagrant, an incident occurred that was to signify much for the future respectability of his craft. This was the granting (1574) of the first royal patent ever given to a company of English actors. The latter were the servants of the ambitious Earl of Leicester, among them being James Burbage, the father of the more famous Richard Burbage of happy Shakespearian memory. The issuing of such a patent at once threw a sort of high official sanction about the company and the art it represented, although the whole circumstance is more important in the light of subsequent events than for any very substantial results accruing to Lord Leicester's dramatic henchmen. The Lord Mayor and Aldermen of London, who entertained rather puritanical ideas about the stage, and who practically had the power to prevent the giving of any play within their jurisdiction, did not show any enthusiasm for the troupe bearing the royal patent, and so James Burbage betook himself to the old monastic precinct of Blackfriars, then outside the limits of the city. He bought certain rooms in the neighborhood, and was having them altered into a permanent playhouse, when a number of unsympathetic but influential inhabitants of the district petitioned the Privy Council to put a peremptory stop to his enterprise. The remonstrants, highly indignant that their privacy should be invaded by anything so vulgar as a set of vagabond actors, royal patent nevertheless and notwithstanding, probably felt very much as might some rich residents of upper Fifth Avenue were an abattoir to be erected near their properties. The Black-friars tax-payers complained that Burbage's "common playhouse" would "grow to the very great annoyance and trouble, not only to all the nobelmen and gentlemen thereabouts inhabiting" but would also become a general inconvenience, "both by reason of the great resort and gathering together of all manner of vagrant and lewde persons that under color of resorting to the Playes will come thither and worke all manner of mischiefe."

The petition was not granted, and the indignation of the neighbors must only have increased on finding that Burbage's example was followed elsewhere. Indeed, two more places of dramatic amusement were erected about this period, one called "The Theatre," in Shoreditch, and the other, not far away, styled "The Curtain." This certain indication of public profligacy was too much for one learned divine, who preached a delightfully sensational sermon, wherein he wailed about the wickedness of London, which he stigmatized as "an abhominable and filthie citie," on the order of "Venus court and Bacchus kitchen," whatsoever that might be, and added : "Looke but upon the common playes in London, and see the multitude that flocketh to them and followeth them ; behold the sumptuous theatre houses, a continuall monument of London's prodigalitie and follie." From this horrible vista of sin he argued that : "The cause of plagues is sinne, if you look at it well, and the cause of sinne are playes ;

therefore, the cause of plagues are playes.'' All of which shows that the reverend gentleman had enough knowledge of logic to enunciate a syllogism, however defective might be his grammar or his common-sense.

While clergymen used the pulpit as a means of circumventing the wiles of his Satanic Majesty, insidiously spread through theatrical abomination, there were liberal-minded satirists who extracted humor from the protests of these nervous gentlemen. One writer of the day sings in this appreciative strain of the Philistianism of London's Mayor and Aldermen:

> " List unto my dittye
> Alas ! the more the pittye,
> From Troynovaunt's olde cittie
> The Aldermen and Maier
> Have drivn eche poore plaier :
> The cause I will declaier.
> They wisely doe complaine
> Of Wilson and Jack Lane,*
> And them who doe maintaine,
> And stablish as a rule
> Not one shall play the foole
> But they—a worthy schoole.
> Without a pipe and taber,
> They only meane to laber,
> To teche eche oxe-hed neyber,
> This is the cause and reason,
> At every tyme and season
> That Playes are worse than treason.''

Any impression that might have been produced by those who ridiculed the bigotry of an inartistic city corporation was in part dispelled by an accident which

* Two members of James Burbage's company.

occurred at a popular amusement resort of London, the "Paris Garden," about 1583. The Garden was then used for the baiting of wild beasts, but as the populace never saw much moral difference between the exhibition of bears, lions, and the like, and the presentation of plays, dramatic interests received a temporary set-back when, on a certain Sunday, a gallery of the building suddenly gave way and many of the occupants were injured. It was a judgment of God, said one puritanical preacher. A few weeks later, Elizabeth, nothing appalled, is choosing a company to be called the Queen's Players, and is enjoying the *Pastorall of Phillyda and Choryn*, the *History of Felix and Philomena*, and other interludes. So worldly a taste on the part of the sovereign must have been a cause of sadness to a retainer of Sir Francis Walsingham who wrote to the latter that "the daylie abuse of stage playes is such an offence to the Godly, and so great a hindrance to the Gospell, as the papists do exceeding rejoice at the bleamysh thereof, and not without cause, for every day in the weak the players' bills are sett up in sondry places of the cittie . . . whereas the wicked fation of Rome laugheth for joy, while the Godly weepe for sorrow. Woe is me ! the play houses are pestered when churches are naked ; at the one it is not possible to get a place, at the other voyde seates are plentie." Thus we see that the " wicked " Papists were not the only ones who laughed ; the worldly managers must have exulted as well.

Another proof of the popularity of the London theatre in the latter half of the sixteenth century is furnished, unwillingly enough, by the then rector of St. Botolph's Church, a clergyman named Gosson. He was the author of a book called *The School of Abuse*, in which he remarked, among sundry interesting things; "In our assemblies at plays in London you shall see such heaving and shouting, such pitching and shouldering to sit by women, such care for their garments, that they be not trodden, such eyes to their laps that no chips light on them, such pillows to their backs that they take no hurt, such masking in their ears, I know not what ; such giving their pippins to pass the time ; such playing at foot-saunt without cards, such ticking, such toying, such smiling, such winking and such manning them home when the sports are ended, that it is a right comedy to mark their behaviour."

Fair theatre-goers of the olden time, you must have had much more to answer for than the wearing of large hats !

All this while the profession of the player was approaching a more legitimate and enduring basis. Instead of inn-yards and open thoroughfares the actors now had regular houses in which to display their talents, and it is supposed that between the years 1570 and 1600 at least eleven places of amusement were constructed in London. The most important of these, from historic association, was the Globe Theatre, occupied, as it was, by the company of which Shakespeare was a member. Here and at the Blackfriars Theatre which was controlled by the same company, many of the poets' plays had their initial productions, under the direction of Richard Burbage. The latter was a much better actor than Shakespeare, who appears to have been a " utility man," rather than a leading one. Indeed, tradition has it that in *Hamlet* the author merely played the *Ghost*, and that in *As You Like It* he chose the faithful *Adam* rather than the attractive *Orlando*.

The Globe has been described as a massive structure, destitute of architectural ornament and without windows in the outer wall. The pit was open to the sky, and the actors performed by daylight ; the scene had no other decoration than wrought tapestry. In the background was a stage, a sort of balcony, which served for various purposes and signified all manner of things according to the circumstances. The players appeared, with rare exceptions, in the dress of their time, or at the most distinguished by high feathers on their hats or roses on their shoes. The chief means of disguise were false hair and beards and occasionally even masks. The famous playhouse was destroyed by fire in 1613, during the performance of *Henry VIII.*, presumably Shakespeare's play of that name. As Sir Henry Wotton related shortly after the event, in a letter to his nephew, " the King's players had a new play called *All Is True*, representing some principal pieces of the reign of Henry VIII., which was set forth with many extraordinary circumstances of pomp and majesty even to the matting of the stage ; the knights of the order, with their Georges and Garter, the guards with their embroidered coats and the like : sufficient, in truth, within a while, to make greatness very familiar, if not ridiculous. Now *King Henry* making a mask at the *Cardinal Wolsey's* house, and certain cannons being shot off at his entry, some of the paper or other stuff wherewith one of them was stopped, did light on the thatch, where, being thought at first but an idle smoke, and their eyes more attentive to the show, it kindled inwardly, and ran round like a train, consuming, within less than an hour, the whole house to the very grounds. This was the fatal period of that virtuous fabric wherein yet nothing did perish but wood and straw, and a few forsaken cloaks ; only one man had his breeches set on fire, that would perhaps have broiled him, if he had not, by the benefit of a provident wit, put it out with bottle ale."

Bottle ale saved the man's breeches, but it could not prevent the destruction of the Globe, which came to an untimely end through an excess of realistic display —a fact worth remembering in these later days, when stage pageants are looked upon as essentially modern innovations. "Rare" Ben Jonson, who is said to have been an eye-witness of the fire, thus alludes to it in his *Execration Upon Vulcan* :

" But, O, those reeds ! thy mere disdain of them
   Made thee beget that cruel stratagem,
   Which some are pleased to style but thy mad prank,

> Against the Globe, the glory of the Bank :
> Which, though it were the fort of the whole parish,
> Flanked with a ditch, and forc'd out of a marish,
> I saw with two poor chambers taken in,
> And raz'd, ere thought could urge, this might have been."

The theatre was rebuilt shortly afterward, but the historical memories cluster altogether about the old structure, rather than the new.

James I. showed a sincere interest in the drama, and had a decided admiration for Shakespeare, to whom he is believed to have addressed a letter with his own royal hand. Shortly after ascending the throne of England he granted a license to the actors of the Globe and Blackfriars, including by name Lawrence Fletcher, William Shakespeare, Richard Burbage, Augustine Phillippes, and others, whom he authorized to be known from that time as the King's Players. They were allowed to give " Comedies, tragedies, histories, interludes, morals, pastorals and stage plays " throughout the kingdom. James manifested his love of theatricals in many other ways, and his gay Queen, Anne of Denmark, was wont to act in, and manage, some of the masks held at Court, but his enthusiasm did not prevent his exercising a sort of censorship over the pieces that were brought out during his reign. On one occasion the drama of *Eastward, Ho !* gave offence to the King because several passages reflected on the Scotch, and the order went forth to arrest the authors. Ben Jonson had been concerned in the writing of the

2

inhibited play, and although he was not molested he took the ground that he was as guilty as the other two authors, whom he voluntarily accompanied to prison. The report went abroad that Jonson and his colleagues would have their ears cut off, and it is recorded that the poet's mother, at an entertainment given on their discharge from durance vile, showed her son "a paper which she designed, if the sentence had taken effect, to have mixed with his drink, and it was strong and lusty poison ; to show that she was no churl she designed to have first drank of it herself." What a grand tragedy the sensitive old dame would have evolved had the loyal Ben actually been deprived of his ears.

While there is good reason to believe that Shakespeare's comedies and tragedies were appreciated during his lifetime it is clear that the efforts of some of his contemporaries were not received with any vast amount of favor. Certainly it is safe to make such an inference from the critical sentiments of a theatre-goer of the time who writes to a friend : " They have plays at Court every night, both holidays and working days, wherein they show great patience, being for the most part such poor stuff that instead of delight they send the auditory away with discontent." The sentence may be involved, but it is to the point, as is also his further observation : " Indeed, our poet's brains and inventions are grown very dry, insomuch, that of five new plays there is not one that pleases, and therefore they are driven to furbish over their old, which stand them in best stead and bring them most profit." No wonder, if the old plays were those of Shakespeare, whose name never spelt ruin at that early period.

Charles I. was well disposed toward the drama, while the Puritans had anything but kindly feelings for it, and as a consequence its exponents had a peculiar time of it during the career of the ill-fated monarch and were, before his death, practically prevented from acting. Queen Henrietta Maria superintended the performance of a pastoral one Christmas tide and even condescended to take part therein herself, so that there was great indignation in royal circles shortly afterward when William Prynne published his celebrated tirade against the stage. *Histriomastix, the Player's Scourge*, was the awe-inspiring name of the book, and its author met with scant mercy at the hands of the government. He was brutally punished for his boldness in assailing a profession upon which royalty had smiled, being placed in the pillory, deprived of part of his ears, fined five thousand pounds, and, among incidental penalties, sentenced to imprisonment for life. Prynne was sent to the Fleet, where he seems to have accepted his fate with calmness and a moderate amount of *sang froid*. Later on he had his own triumph, for he was released by order of the Long Parliament and became, for the nonce, quite a hero. While in the Fleet he must have solaced himself with many comfortable reflections about the adversity attending upon the "rogues and

vagabonds" of the stage, and nothing, possibly, gave
him greater delight that the remembrance of the year
1629, when a company of French artists, men and
women, appeared at the Blackfriars Theatre.   This was
the first attempt made in England to popularize female
players, for all feminine parts were then taken by boys
or young men, and the innovation proved emphatically
unsuccessful, at least temporarily.   The adventurous
actresses, or " monsters "as Master Prynne ungallantly
calls them, were hissed off the stage, pelted with pippins, and otherwise poorly treated, and the author of
the *Histriomastix* has stigmatized the affair as " unwom-
anish," as well as " impudent, shameful " and " graceless."   It may have been impudent, seeing that the
British public is prone to look upon any change from
the established order of things as more or less of an
impertinence, but when you call a coterie of French
actresses " graceless " we must differ with you, Master
Prynne.

The day was now approaching when neither French
women nor English actors would be allowed to amuse
the public.   As early as 1642 Parliament ordered the
suppression of stage performances throughout the kingdom " during these calamitous times," and six years
later the House of Commons enacted that all players
were rogues, as defined by statutes of the reigns of
Elizabeth and James ; that the Lord Mayor, justices of
the peace, and sheriffs might demolish all stage galleries, seats, and boxes ; that players who persisted in fol-

lowing their profession should be publicly whipped ; and that any person witnessing a theatrical entertainment should be fined five shillings. As this Pharasaical process did not have all the results intended, a Provost Marshal was appointed for the purpose of seizing upon ballad-singers and prohibiting plays, in addition to other congenial duties.

And now the unfortunate actors, hounded, from pillar to post and unable to even acknowledge their calling, much less to pursue it, drifted into other occupations. Some of them became soldiers, some took up trades, and many of them, no doubt, were never more heard of or thought of by the public they had pleased so well. They had fallen upon evil days, these light-hearted mummers, and they would find that the Commonwealth did not mend matters, but a few of them would yet return to the boards in the merry beginning of the Restoration, and act as a connecting link between the ancient *régime* and the new.

CHAPTER II.

" LE ROI S'AMUSE."

DOUGHTY Oliver Cromwell struts his time upon the stage of history; his unambitious son Richard succeeds to the Protectorship and then gladly relinquishes the responsibility, and finally Charles II., "who never said a foolish thing nor ever did a wise one," has the good sense, nevertheless, to return to his kingdom at the right moment. The English people have tired of the Commonwealth, if, indeed, they ever cared for it, and the witty sovereign, with his brilliant, dissolute retinue of courtiers, is received with open arms. It is the honeymoon of the Restoration, when the jester, capped and belled, is abroad in the land, in spirit at least, and the nation, rebounding from the hypocrisy of the Roundheads, is waiting with childish eagerness to be amused. Men once more begin to think of the poor players who had been so ill bestowed during the past few years. Indeed Rhodes, the one-time prompter of the Blackfriars, and more lately a prosaic bookseller, had hastened off to General Monk in the latter part of 1659 and obtained permission to open a theatre in the Cockpit,

Drury Lane. But the keynote to the dramatic life of King Charles' reign is struck when, a little later, that mirth-loving monarch gives his sacred permission for the erection of two theatres, one in the self-same Drury Lane, under the management of Thomas Killigrew, who has what is known as the " King's Company," and the other in Salisbury Court, where Sir William Davenant directs the fortunes of the " Duke of York's Company." What a host of memories and anecdotes the names of these two famous troupes call up. Killigrew, who has been dubbed the jester of King Charles II., had been a page of the unfortunate Charles I., and accompanied the son into exile.* He had a merry wit, and became the boon companion of his new master when happier days dawned on the House of Stuart. What more appropriate, therefore, than that this purveyor to the royal amusement, this whimsical groom of the Bed Chamber, should undertake the direction of a theatre wherein the King was to pass many a pleasant hour and draw inspiration for some of his most serious amours. So we find that the " new Theatre in Drury Lane " was opened in 1663 by " His Majesty's Company of Comedians," when was enacted Beaumont and Fletcher's comedy of *The Humorous Lieutenant*, with a cast including Charles Hart, Major Mohun, Mr. Wintersel, Mr. Byrt, Mr. Clun, and Mrs.

* For some mysterious reason Dibdin insists that Killigrew the manager was Henry, and not Thomas Killigrew, but all the facts are against so wild a theory.

Marshall. It is interesting to note that the performance began at 3 P.M. "exactly" and that the prices of admission were : boxes, four shillings ; pit, two shillings six pence ; middle gallery, one shilling six pence, and upper gallery, one shilling.

The mention of Mistress Marshall as one of the company shows that the innovation of having women on the stage, which had been so frowned upon when the be-pippined French actresses had appeared a few years before, was now an accepted fact, and that the days when handsome youths played feminine roles were fast passing away. There was Charles Hart, for instance, who was now essaying the essentially masculine character of *Demetrius* in *The Humorous Lieutenant*, when as a boy this talented grandnephew of Shakespeare had impersonated women. Hereafter he was to figure in such roles as *Brutus, Othello*, and *Alexander the Great*, and to inspire the not very creditable affections of the notorious but beautiful Lady Castlemaine, to whom our old friend, Samuel Pepys, Esq., F. R. S., so often and lovingly refers in his diary.

"'To the King's playhouse," says Mr. Pepys, under date of April 7, 1668, "and there saw *The English Monsieur* (sitting for privacy sake in an upper box): the play hath much mirth in it as to that particular humor. After the play done I down to Knipp,* and did stay her undressing herself, and there saw the several players, men and women, go by ; and pretty to see

* An actress belonging to the King's Company.

how strange they are all, one to another, after the play is done. . . . Mrs. Knipp tells me that my Lady Castlemaine is mightily in love with Hart, of their house ; and he is much with her in private, and she goes to him and do give him many presents ; and that the thing is most certain, and Beck Marshall only privy to it, and the means of bringing them together, which is a very odd thing ; and by this means she is even with the King's love to Mrs. Davis."

A greater "boy actress" than Hart had ever been was Edward Kynaston, a member of the Duke of York's Company, and " the last beautiful youth who figured in petticoats on the stage." He was an unusually handsome man, even in old age, and appears to have made an admirable player of regal parts when he abandoned the line of acting in which he had once won such fame. " The loveliest lady that ever I saw in my life " is the way in which Pepys speaks of his performance in *The Loyall Subject*, and Colley Cibber says, in referring to him : " Though women were not admitted to the stage till the return of King Charles, yet it could not be so suddenly supplied with them but that there was still a necessity, for some time, to put the handsomest young men in petticoats—which Kynaston was then said to have worn with success, particularly in the part of Evadne in *The Maid's Tragedy*, which I have heard him speak of ; and which calls to my mind a ridiculous distress that arose from these sort of shifts which the stage was then put to. The King

coming a little before his usual time to a tragedy found
the actors not ready to begin, when his Majesty, not
choosing to have as much patience as his good subjects,
sent to them to know the meaning of it, upon which
the master of the company came to the box, and, rightly
judging that the best excuse for their default would be
the true one, fairly told his Majesty that the queen was
not shaved yet ; the King, whose good humor loved to
laugh at a jest as well as to make one, accepted the
excuse, which served to divert him till the male queen
could be effeminated.   In a word, Kynaston at that
time was so beautiful a youth that the ladies of quality
prided themselves in taking him with them in their
coaches to Hyde Park in his theatrical habit, after the
play ; which in those days they might have sufficient
time to do, because plays then were used to begin at
four o'clock, the hour that people of the same rank are
now going to dinner.''

As the boys in petticoats were disappearing, the
women, who sometimes acted in petticoats and as often
turned the tables on their masculine predecessors by
posing on the stage as elegant young men, were fast
giving to the theatre a prestige—and, in some instances,
an unsavory reputation—which it had never enjoyed
before.   One of the most notorious, and fascinating
actresses of that or later years was ''pretty witty Nell''
Gwynne, who first came into prominence in 1665, when
she appeared at Drury Lane in Dryden's play of *The
Indian Emperor*.   She was then but fifteen years old,

NELL GWYNNE.

FROM AN ENGRAVING BY WRIGHT, AFTER THE PAINTING BY SIR PETER LELY.

and had been brought out at the instigation of Hart, who finding her serving as an orange girl in the front of the house, was attracted by her beauty and charm of manner. So she was instructed in the rudiments of acting by Shakespeare's kinsman and the actor Lacey (who became so distinguished as a comedian that Charles II. had his portrait painted in three different characters) and soon showed herself to be an apt pupil. There have been many pictures of their *protégée*, but one representing her as a charming, fair-haired woman with blue eyes of the laughing order and a turned-up, piquante nose, seems to be most in accord with what one reads of this merry, kind-hearted creature, upon whom the frailties of human nature and the opinions of a world, which as often condemned as it admired her, weighed so lightly.

Poor Nell soon caught the fancy of the town, and heading the popular wave that wafted her so speedily into prosperity was the pleasure-seeking monarch himself, with whom the history of this actress is so inevitably associated. Her birth was obscure, her father had been either a fruiterer, as some say, or a captain, but be that as it may, Eleanor Gwynne became the ancestress of a semi-royal line represented by the Dukes of St. Albans, and was one of several famous players whose blood runs in the veins of English peers of the nineteenth century.

"To the King's House," writes the faithful Admiralty Secretary, "and there saw *The Humorous Lieutenant*, a silly play, I think; only the spirit in it that grows

very tall and then sinks again to nothing, having two
heads breeding upon one ; and then Knipp's singing did
please us.   Here in a box above we spied Mrs. Pierce,
and going out they called us, and so we staid for them,
and Knipp took us all in, and brought to us Nelly, a
most pretty woman, who acted the great part *Caelis* to-
day very fine, and did it pretty well ; I kissed her, and
so did my wife, and a mighty pretty soul she is."
And again, later on, we read :

" After dinner with my wife to the King's house,
to see *The Mayden Queene*, a new play of Dryden's,
mightily commended for the regularity of it, and the
strain and wit ; and the truth is, there is a comical part
done by Nell, which is *Florimel*, that I never can hope
ever to see the like done again by man or woman.
The King and Duke of York were at the play.   But so
great performance of a comical part was never, I believe, in the world before as Nell do this both as a mad
girle, then most and best of all when she comes in like
a young gallant ; and hath the motions and carriage of
a spark the most that ever I saw any man have.   It
makes me, I confess, admire her."   And Mr. Pepys keeps
on admiring her to the end of the chapter, with a keen
eye to her prettiness and an anecdote here and there
that makes her stand forth with all the Meissonier-like
clearness of a carefully executed picture.   He sees her
loitering at her lodging door in Drury Lane " in her
smock sleeves and bodice," and seeming " a mighty
pretty creature," and he meets her behind the scenes,

where her levity and looseness of conversation (once he heard her cursing at the smallness of the audience) leave a somewhat unpleasant impression on him. Yet he thinks her delightful, in spite of it all, and so did many more, including Charles Stuart, who doubtless saw in her worst phases only the subjects for half a dozen royal jests. He loved her in his careless, contemptuous way, and when he was dying prayed his brother not to let poor Nellie starve.

Rochester has summed up her life in these clever lines :

" The orange basket her fair arm did suit,
  Laden with pippins and Hesperian fruit ;
  This first step raised, to the wond'ring pit she sold
  The lovely fruit, smiling with streaks of gold.
  Fate now for her did its whole force engage,
  And from the pit she mounted to the stage ;
  There in full lustre did her glories shine,
  And long eclips'd, spread forth their light divine :
  There Hart * and Rowley's soul she did ensnare,
  And made a King a rival to a player."

What a company must have been the jesting Killigrew's, in those " palmy " seasons when ladies of quality often appeared at the theatre in masks, to avoid blushing over the positive indecencies in many of the comedies, and when Evelyn complains that " plays are now become with us a licentious excess, and a vice, and need severe censors." The moral atmosphere behind the scenes was stifling, and the conversation on the stage not a bit more healthy at times, but the lax-

* Hart was madly in love with his pupil.

ness of the age could not affect the genius or the fascination of the players. Take, for example, the beautiful
Mistress Hughes, who made her abode with Prince
Rupert, and who spent his money so lavishly that at
his death it was found necessary to sell his jewels by
lottery, in order to pay his debts. Then came Joseph
Haines, Cartwright, Clun, and others no less distinguished, not forgetting that "little man of mettle,"
Major Mohun, whose tragic flights of eloquence were
thought so much of by Court and town. Haines, who
appears to have been a man of considerable originality
and humor, was once ordered by Hart, as chief of the
house or stage manager, to dress for one of the senators,
in *Cataline's Conspiracy*. This was nothing more
or less than acting as a "super," and as Haines enjoyed the then lavish salary of fifty shillings a week,
he naturally considered himself exempt from any such
assignment. Hart ungenerously insisted, none the
less obstinate, no doubt, because he and Haines happened to be on bad terms, and so the latter had to obey
with the poorest kind of grace. But he was to be re-
venged for the slight put upon him. "He gets a
scaramouch dress, a large full ruff, makes himself
whiskers from ear to ear, puts on a large merry Andrew's
cap, a short pipe in his mouth, a little three-legged
stool in his hand, and in this manner follows Mr. Hart
on the stage, sets himself down behind him, and begins
to smoke his pipe, laugh and point at him, which comical figure put all the house in an uproar, some laugh-

ing, some clapping, and some hallooing. Now Mr. Hart, as those who knew him can aver, was a man of that exactness and grandeur on the stage, that let what would happen, he 'd never discompose himself or mind anything but what he then represented, and had a scene fallen behind him, he would not at that time look back to see what was the matter, which Joe knowing, remained still smoking ; the audience continued laughing, Mr. Hart acting and wondering at this unusual occasion of their mirth—sometimes thinking it some disturbance in the house ; again, that it might be something amiss in his dress. At last, turning himself towards the scenes, he discovered Joe in the aforesaid posture ; whereupon he immediately goes off the stage, swearing he would never set foot on it again unless Joe was immediately turned out of doors, which was no sooner spoke than put in practice."

Haines seems to have been everything from a scholar to a Bohemian of the most pronounced type. He held a position at Cambridge University at one stage of his career, but his chief claim to the consideration of posterity lies in the fact that he was a leading low comedian at Drury Lane from 1672 to 1701, and made his *Sparkish*, in *The Country Wife*, one of the most popular characters of the period. No one appreciated it more, possibly, than the elegant fellows about town whom he travestied. When James II. became King, Haines declared his conversion to the doctrines of the Roman Catholic Church, because the Virgin Mary had appeared to him in a vision and exclaimed, "Joe, arise!" but as this revelation was looked upon in the light of a joke and an amusing example of poor Joe's eccentricity, he was not allowed the benefit of his change of faith. He was actually made to recant on the stage, before a large audience, and announce his return to the Protestant fold. It must have been a remarkable scene, but then Haines was himself a re-markable man, and anything so bizarre was considered peculiarly fitting.

Yet a stranger member of the Drury Lane set was Cardell Goodman, who rejoiced under the not very savory nickname of "Scum." The checquered his-tory of "Scum" shows that he had once been a stu-dent at Cambridge, from which University he was expelled for mutilating a picture of the curious Chan-cellor of the institution, the picturesque Duke of Mon-mouth. Like others who have failed in some more prosaic profession he went on the stage, and made a great reputation for himself as a promising young fel-low who could play *Julius Cæsar* and *Alexander* with dignity and fervor. He complained that his salary was small, and that he could not dress as gallants of his time should, and so he actually took "to the road" and became a highwayman. The combination of art and robbery had its drawbacks, and Goodman would have ended his remarkable career on the gallows had it not been for the clemency of James II. The ex-highwayman was once heard to say that this act of

James' "was doing him so particular an honor, that no man could wonder if his acknowledgment had carried him a little further than ordinary in the interest of that prince. But as he had lately been out of luck in backing his old master, he had no way to get home the life he was out, upon his account, but by being under the same obligations to King William." This rather mysterious remark was taken to mean that Goodman having once volunteered to assassinate William of Orange, as a slight acknowledgment of the kindness of James, had now gone over heart and soul to the interests of the latter's son-in-law, in order to secure a pardon from the new sovereign. The rascality of this model player also included an attempt to kill two of the Duchess of Cleveland's (Lady Castlemaine's) children, by way of rewarding this fragile peeress for the attentions which she had showered upon him. The plot failed, and "Scum," who subsequently disappeared altogether, contrived to save his neck at the expense of a heavy fine.

They were an unprincipled crew, a few of these *protégés* of Court and people. Look at Moll Davis. She was a comedienne in the Duke's Company, a graceful dancer, and so fine a singer of the ditty, *My Lodging is on the Cold Ground*, that she attracted the amorous attention of King Charles. Mr. Pepys was pleased "mightily" at her "dancing in a shepherd's clothes," and he notes in one paragraph of that gossipy diary that "Miss Davis is for certain going away from the

Duke's house, the King being in love with her ; and a
house is taken for her, and furnishing ; and she hath
a ring given her already worth 600£." It is the old,
old story of Charles and his conquests, and so we are
not surprised to learn further on that once when Moll
played at Whitehall the Queen, Catharine of Braganza,
rose and left the house, or that the actress once made
Lady Castlemaine "look fire" when the two favorites
were together at the theatre. She had a daughter by
Charles who was named Mary Tudor, and whose son,
the third Earl of Derwentwater, lost his head for too
actively sympathizing with his relative, the Old Pre-
tender.

Clun, one of the best actors of the King's house, was
set upon and murdered one night while travelling out
of town to his country-place. " The house will have a
great miss of him," quaintly chronicles the ubiquitous
Pepys. Then there is Nokes, a natural actor of " plain
and palpable a simplicity " ; William Mountford, the
victim of the famous attempt to abduct Mrs. Bracegirdle ; Sanford, styled the " completest and most
natural performer of a villian that ever existed," and,
among others, John Lacey, a dancing-master by education, but comedian and playwright by selection.
This actor deeply offended his Majesty on one occasion by appearing in a comedy wherein the Court was
held up to contempt, and orders were given that the
troupe should stop performing. Charles relented, of
course (imagine him without his favorite theatre !), but

the comedy in question had to be withdrawn. "The King mightily angry," jots down Pepys, "and it was bitter indeed, but very fine and witty."

Of such material as this were the players who formed the two great theatrical troupes of the reign of Charles II., and among whom the brightest and most enduring light was the noble Betterton, to whose life the next chapter is devoted. The King's Company, (which had perhaps the greater prestige, because some of its members belonged to the sovereign's household establishment, wore an imposing scarlet uniform and were styled Gentlemen of the Grand Chamber) entered into practical competition with the Duke's Company. Both houses were under regulations of a strict order, and it was an understood thing that no play presented at one of them should be given at the rival theatre. Of course, frequent bickerings and internal dissensions occurred, and some of them were passed upon and dispelled by no less august a person than the King himself, who would doubtless have made a much better manager than he did a ruler. When it came to Davenant's forces, knotty problems were often decided by the Duke of York, that curious compound of ability and incompetency, youthful licentiousness and latter-day bigotry, who probably looked upon the stage as an attractive plaything, and nothing more. This toying with the drama must have been a delightful pastime for the two brothers, even if they had but little sympathy for the trials, privations, and struggles of the actors themselves.

So far as actual merit was in question the Duke's company, with the incomparable Betterton at its head, may have been the finer of the two organizations, all things taken into consideration, but merit is a quantity that does not always count in the success of stage performances, even in these enlightened times. Critics like to say that the best plays are the most paying to the manager, because the wish is more or less father to the thought, but the fact remains that some of the flimsiest of pieces have proved the more remunerative from the box-office standpoint. Sir William Davenant may have reasoned this way when he saw that the popularity of his players was on the wane, for money was a conspicuous factor in the theatre then, as it is now. Managers are not necessarily philanthropists ; they may often have artistic perceptions and ambitions, but without well-filled coffers schemes of elevating the stage are likely to degenerate into "such stuff as dreams are made on." Thoughtful youths who have started out to bring the world to their feet through the medium of Shakespearian tragedy have ended up by convulsing the town as *farceurs*, and more than one well-meaning theatre lessee has turned his house into a variety hall, and passed the rest of his life brooding over what he might have accomplished as a promoter of the legitimate.

At any rate, Davenant decided on introducing what the indignant Dibdin says "was then and is at this moment the disgrace and reproach of the theatre." In

other words "operas and masques took the place of
tragedies and comedies, and to Psyche and Circe yielded
Cleopatra and *Rosalind.* To see and to hear one thing,
and to think and to judge another, and nothing could
more completely verify the truth of this than what had
happened to the King's Company upon Davenant's
bringing forward these auxiliary helps ; for, though
they were composed of performers much superior to
those of the other they instantly experienced the most
cold and mortifying neglect, while the houses and the
coffers of the other house were completely filled ; nor
did they ever perfectly recover their estimation with
the public nor at all till they procured scenery and
decorations from France and attacked their opponents
with their own weapons."

Shakespeare and his less gifted companions had given
way, temporarily, to French gew-gaws and tinsel, and
the town went crazy over the importations from the
land of the hated Monsieur. Alas ! poor old Dibdin !
" Go for masques, go for operas, go for spectacles if you
will," he wails ; "let painting and music, those becoming attendants on poetry, aid the meritorious labours
of their lovely sister ; but let them keep within their
own province. Let us have magic and fairy-land, and
let fairies bring about these transformations to the
belief of which our minds are accommodated ; but do
not suffer stuffed elephants, pasteboard lions and leath-
ern tygers to train the car of a real hero. Let us remember that these tricks were borrowed from our

fantastic neighbors the French ; and that, even in France, Corneille with all his reputation never recovered the kick that was given to it by the necessity he was under of courting an auxiliary in the Flying Horse."

Sensitive Dibdin ! Could you revisit the glimpses of the moon you might take comfort in knowing that the *pros* and *cons* of stage realism have been argued ever since you left this sphere of action, and occasionally by men who look upon the whole question as essentially modern. The theatre of Shakespeare's time was not, to be sure, troubled with an excess of realism (to which fortunate circumstance we doubtless owe the introduction of so much beautiful imagery in his works), but scenic effects and gorgeous costumes, by no means unknown even then, were soon to play an important part in the drama.

There is no doubt that while the new entertainments proved a welcome change for a public which was pretty much like any other in its love of novelty, they distinctly tended to lower the tone of the stage, particularly at a season when morals on either side of the footlights were none too rigid, to speak politely, and when the new order of production gave such ample excuse for license. One writer, in comparing the times of Shakespeare with those of the Restoration, observes that once " many people thought a play an innocent diversion for an idle hour or two, the plays themselves being then more instructive and moral ; whereas of

late the playhouses are so extremely pestered with wiz-
ard masks, and their trade occasioning continual quarrels and abuses, that many of the more civilized part
of the town are uneasy in the company, and shun the
theatre as they would a house of scandal.''

The popularity of the Duke's house was not relished
by the King's Company, and an attempt was made to
stem the tide of success by producing, at Drury Lane,
parodies ridiculing the sumptuous affairs that were
turning the heads of the Londoners. But the audiences
insisted on having their heads turned, notwithstanding, and the '' Gentlemen of the Grand Chamber,''
with their lace and pretty scarlet uniforms, and their
fair companions, found themselves in the position of
dethroned favorites. But all this rivalry had an end,
for in 1682, when Killigrew and Davenant were both
dead, the two companies were united, through the instrumentality of Betterton, and began their joint season
at the new Drury Lane Theatre.

While these changes are going on Mr. Jeremy Collier,
M. A., is collecting material for his *Short View of the Im-
mortality and Profaneness of the English Stage*, which is
to create quite a stir and send the author's name down
to posterity—whereby he has an advantage over most of
the censors of the drama. In the preface of this volume
Mr. Collier announces his conviction that '' nothing has
gone farther in Debauching the Age than the Stage-
Poets and Play House.'' Further on he explains :
'' The business of plays is to recommend Vertue and

discountenance Vice ; To shew the Uncertainty of Humane Greatness, the suddain Turns of Fate, and the Unhappy Conclusions of Violence and Injustice. 'T is to expose the Singularities of Pride and Fancy, to make Folly and Falsehood contemptible, and to bring every thing that is Ill under Infamy and Neglect. This design has been oddly pursued by the English Stage. Our Poets write with a different view, and are gone into another Interest. 'T is true, were their intentions fair, they might be Serviceable to this Purpose. They have in a great measure the Springs of Thought and Inclination in their Power. Show, Musick, Action and Rhetorick, are moving Entertainments ; and, rightly employed, would be very significant. But Force and Motion are Things indifferent, and the Use lies chiefly in the Application. These Advantages are now, in the Enemies Hand, and under a very dangerous management. Like Cannon seized, they are pointed the wrong way ; and by the Strength of the Defence the Mischief is made the greater. That this complaint is not unreasonable, I shall endeavor to prove by shewing the Misbehaviour of the Stage, with respect to Morality and Religion. Their Liberties in the Following Particulars are intolerable, viz. : Their Smuttiness of Expression ; their Swearing Prophaneness, and Lewed Application of Scripture ; Their Abuse of the Clergy, Their making their top Characters Libertines, and giving them Success in their Debauchery."

There is warrant for some of the critical Jeremy's

Jeremiad, but we are about to see the stage enter upon an epoch whose glory shall not be dimmed for over a century, and in which there shall be a distinct improvement in some of the characteristics complained of in the *Short View*. Collier will be thought of simply as a literary freak, but the names of Betterton, of Oldfield, of Woffington, of Garrick, and of Kean will linger pleasantly in the world's memory for many a day.

CHAPTER III.

"THE ENGLISH ROSCIUS."

"AS it was said of Brutus and Cassius, that they were the last of the Romans; so may it be said of Mr. Betterton, that he was the last of our tragedians," * wrote one of his admirers and biographers, and his opinion was shared by many a theatre-goer who had so often delighted in the versatile genius of the greatest actor of his age. Thomas Betterton, the *English Roscius* as he was called by his contemporaries, began life under circumstances singularly in contrast with the distinction he was later to achieve. He was born in Westminster about 1635, his father, Matthew Betterton, holding the respectable but not particularly exalted position of an under-cook in the kitchen of Charles I. As a lad the future Roscius was quiet and studious, and received a fairly good education. Very little is known of his early years, however, and there has even been a dispute as to the bookseller to whom he was apprenticed. It was probably Rhodes, the whilom prompter and wardrobe-keeper of the Black-friars, who discreetly set up a book-shop at Charing

* Gildon's *Life of Betterton.*

Cross after the triumph of the Puritans had taken away the occupation of the players. According to Gildon, in his so-called *Life of Betterton*, that " which prepared Mr. Betterton and his fellow-prentice * for the stage was, that his master Rhodes having formerly been Wardrobe-keeper to the King's company of comedians in the Blackfriars, on General Monck's march to London, in 1659, with his Army, got a license from the Powers then in being, to set up a company of Players in the Cockpit in Drury Lane, and soon made his company complete, his apprentice, Mr. Betterton for Men's Parts, and Mr. Kynaston for Women's parts, being at the head of them. Mr. Betterton was now about twenty-two years of age,† when he got great applause by acting in the *Loyal Subject*, the *Wild Goose Chace*, the *Spanish Curate*, and many more. But while our young actor is thus rising under his master Rhodes, Sir William Davenant—getting a Patent of King Charles II. for erecting a company under the name of the Duke of York's Servants—took Mr. Betterton and all that acted under Mr. Rhodes into his company."

Davenant, after a more or less adventurous career which included imprisonment in the Tower and a narrow escape from being put to death for too much affection for the Royal cause, found himself during the final years of the Commonwealth in a melancholy condition as to purse, and so set about to fill the latter by means

* Kynaston.
† Betterton must have been about twenty-four years old.

of the drama. In other words, he wanted to start a theatre, and though the scheme was difficult of accomplishment, seeing that Parliament had formerly enacted such stringent laws against actors and those who patronized them, he obtained sufficient influence with Lord Whitlocke and other gentlemen to inaugurate a series of performances at Rutland House. This was in 1656, and, while the public was now ripe for such a return to first principles, a vast amount of tact and diplomacy had to be used by the venturesome Davenant, that the authorities should not put a stop to the enterprise. What he must observe was an apparent, if not an actual respect for the law, and so long as he would do this hundreds of Londoners, secretly worn out by the many absurd restrictions of the Puritans, were only too glad to attend his entertainments. The introductory piece "required all the author's wit to make it answer different intentions, for, first, it was to be so pleasing as to gain applause; and next, it was to be so remote from the very appearance of a play as not to give any offence to that pretended sanctity which was then in fashion. It began with music, then followed a prologue, in which the author banters the oddity of his own performance. The curtain being drawn up to the sound of slow and solemn music, there followed a grave declaration by one in a gilded rostrum, who personated *Diogenes*, and whose business it was to rail at and expose public entertainments. Then music in a lighter strain, after which a person in the character of *Aristophanes*, the old comic poet, answered *Diogenes*, and showed the use and excellency of dramatic entertainments. The whole of the grave entertainment was concluded by a song accompanied with music, to which the arguments on both sides are succinctly and elegantly stated. The second part of the entertainment consisted of two light declamations; the first by a citizen of Paris, who wittily rallies the follies of London; the other by a citizen of London, who takes the same liberty with Paris and its inhabitants. To this was tacked a song, and after that came a short epilogue: the music, which was very good, was composed by Dr. Coleman, Captain Cook, Mr. Harry Laws, and Mr. George Hudson." *

This was a mild sort of affair that would not satisfy modern theatre-goers, but the spectators were duly thankful for it, and their favor inspired Davenant to venture further and produce pieces of a bolder type. The theatre thus started under precarious auspices at Rutland House was practically the forerunner of the Duke's Theatre in Lincoln's Inn Fields, for the establishment of which he had received the royal patent. He was by no means without business sagacity, was Sir William, and the articles of agreement entered into between him and the players of the new company show that managerial contracts were in force over two centuries ago. These articles make interesting reading, something more than can be said for others of later origin. They are dated November 5, 1660, and are

* *Biographia Britannica.*

between Sir William Davenant, as party of the first
part, and Thomas Betterton (spelled Batterton), Thomas
Sheppey, Robert Nokes, James Noakes, Thomas Lo-
vell, John Moseley, Cave Underhill, Robert Turner,
and Thomas Lilleston, of the second part ; and Henry
Harris, painter, of the third part. It is provided that
during the occupation of temporary quarters the receipts accruing from the performances, after the payment for house-rent, supers and other necessary
expenses, shall be divided into fourteen shares,
whereof Davenant shall have four and the company
the remaining ten ; that " the said Thomas Batterton,
Thomas Sheppey, and the rest of the said company
shall admit such a consort of musicians into the said
playhouse for their necessary use, as the said Sir William shall nominate and provide, duringe their play-
inge in the said playhouse, not exceeding the rate of
30 s. the day " ; and that when the company shall
be quartered in the new house to be erected by Davenant the several receipts of the theatre are to be divided
into fifteen shares, two shares to be paid to the latter
towards " the house-rent, buildinge, scaffoldinge and
makinge of frames for scenes," one share for furnishing scenery, costumes, and properties, seven to Sir William " to maintaine all the women that are to performe
or represent women's parts in the aforesaid tragedies,
comedies, playes, or representations," and the other
five shares to be divided among Betterton and his companions.

One of the articles sets forth that Davenant shall not be responsible out of his shares " for the supplyeinge of cloathes, habitts, and scenes, to provide eyther hatts, feathers, gloves, ribbons, swordebelts, bands, stockings, or shoes " for any of the men actors, and it is further stipulated : " That a private boxe bee provided and established for the use of Thomas Killigrew, Esq., one of the groomes of his Majestie's bedchamber, sufficient to conteine sixe persons, into which the said Mr. Killigrew and such as he shall appoint, shall have liberty to enter without any salary or pay for their entrance into such a place of the said theatre as the said Sir Wm. Davenant, his heirs, etc. shall appoint."

The clause last quoted shows a commendable spirit of friendliness between rival managers, although the courtesy of the box was probably due to Killigrew's influence with the King. A man who could tell the latter with impunity that he was going " to fetch Oliver Cromwell from hell to take care of the affairs of the nation, for that his successor took no care of them at all " must have been of sufficient importance, independent of his theatrical pretensions, to receive the freedom of Sir William's house.

The theatre in Lincoln's Inn Fields designed for the Duke's Company, a playhouse altered and rearranged for the purpose, was opened in 1661 with an operatic piece styled *The Siege of Rhodes*. In this production Betterton played *Solomon, the Magnificent*, and Mistress Saunderson, whom he was afterward to marry, enacted

Ianthe. It enjoyed a run of twelve nights, and was followed by other successes, among them that historic revival of *Hamlet* with Betterton as the melancholy hero. "To the Opera," * writes Pepys, "and there saw *Hamlet*, Prince of Denmark done with scenes, very well; but above all, Betterton did the *Prince's* part beyond imagination." It was a performance well deserving a note in that voluminous diary, and one cannot but envy the good fortune of those who witnessed it. The attractive Mistress Saunderson, one of the first regular actresses on the English stage, and who was later to have the honor of instructing the Princesses Ma and Anne in the mysteries of elocution, was the fair *Ophelia*, Mrs. Davenport essayed the *Queen*, Harris was *Horatio*, and Lilleston the *King*. But the greatest of these was the *Hamlet* of Betterton, to which, however, one critic objected on the ground that it lacked originality. Whatever may have been the merits of this creation as compared with other *Hamlets* it can be taken for a certainty that Betterton played the role with wonderful effectiveness and that it proved one of his finest achievements. Colley Cibber, says in his *Apology* *apropos* to Betterton's appearance in the part in later years :

"You may have seen a *Hamlet* perhaps who on the first appearance of his father's spirit has thrown himself into all the straining vociferation requisite to express rage and fury ; and the house has thundered

* The Duke's Theatre was also known as the Opera.

CATHERINE CLIVE.

REPRODUCED FROM A FRAGMENT OF AN ENGRAVING BY J. FABER.

applause, though the misguided actor all the while was tearing a passion into rags. The late Mr. Addison, whilst I sate by him to see this scene acted, made the same observation, asking me with some surprise if I thought *Hamlet* should be in so violent a passion with the ghost, which though it might have astonished, had not provoked him. For you may observe that in this beautiful speech the passion never rises beyond an almost breathless astonishment, or an impatience limited only by filial reverence to inquire into the suspected wrongs that may have raised him from his peaceful tomb, and a desire to know what a spirit so seemingly distressed might wish or enjoin a sorrowful son to execute towards his future quiet in the grave. This was the light into which Betterton threw this scene, which he opened with a pause of mute amazement, then rising slowly to a solemn, trembling voice he made the ghost equally terrible to the spectators as to himself and in the descriptive part of the natural emotions which the ghostly vision gave him, the boldness of his expostulation was still governed by decency, manly, but not braving—his voice never rising into that seeming outrage or wild defiance of what he naturally revered."

Indeed, it is related that although Betterton's complexion was naturally ruddy, when, as *Hamlet*, he was confronted by the *Ghost* he "instantly turned as white as his neckcloth, while his whole body seemed to be affected with a strong tremor" ; had his father's

4

apparition actually risen before him he could not have displayed greater agony. The spectators shared the horror themselves, and so did Barton Booth on the memorable occasion of his first playing the *Ghost* to Betterton's *Hamlet* and being so awe-stricken that he could not speak his lines.

The man who was for half a century the most beloved figure on the English stage may not have possessed the extraordinary versatility of Garrick, yet he displayed remarkable variety in his art. One instance of this, in the early part of his career, is shown by his appearance in September, 1661, shortly after the revival of *Hamlet* (which was remunerative enough, by the way, to show that Shakespeare was the name to conjure by even during the careless, thoughtless reign of the second Charles) as *Sir Toby* in *Twelfth Night*. Poor Pepys could not enjoy the play because he went to see it "against my own mind and resolution," but his contemporaries who had no conscientious scruples of that kind found in the adventures of *Sir Toby* and the rest of that delightful company a generous entertainment. In a succeeding production of Davenant's *Love and Honor* Betterton played a certain *Prince Alvaro*, and had the honor of wearing the King's coronation clothes, while Mr. Harris, as another prince, donned a suit presented by the Duke of York, and Mr. Price, who did *Lionel*, was the recipient of a costume from Lord Oxford.

And so the "best actor in the world" goes on building up his reputation and adding to his already extensive repertoire. In the spring of 1662 we have him doing *Mercutio* in *Romeo and Juliet*, or more probably a garbled version of the tragedy, for it was the fashion in those days to lay violent hands on Shakespeare, altering, adapting, and ruining his masterpieces under the impression that they were made the more presentable and elegant thereby. Davenant went so far as to tamper with *Measure for Measure*, and actually interjected into it the characters of *Beatrice* and *Benedick*—an innovation that appears to have had the seal of approval put upon it by an unthinking public. Whether *Romeo and Juliet* was so roughly treated or not, it is at least very plain that Pepys, who had by this time recovered from his attack of righteousness, thought nothing of it. " My wife and I by coach first to see my little picture that is a drawing, and thence to the Opera, and there saw *Romeo and Juliet* the first time it was ever acted, but it is a play of itself the worst that ever I heard, and the worst acted that ever I saw these people do, and I am resolved to go no more to see the first time of acting, for they were all of them out more or less." The complainant might not have so keenly taken to heart the poorness of the acting could he have known how often *Romeo and Juliet* was to be slaughtered in future generations by companies far inferior to the Duke's.

Nor was Pepys much impressed with a subsequent Shakespearian performance wherein Betterton figured, namely *Henry the Eighth*. He refers to it as " the so much cried-up play," and writes it down as "so simple a thing, made up of a great many patches, that besides the shows and processions in it, there is nothing in the world good or well done." Nevertheless, the play was acted for fifteen consecutive days, and was evidently distinguished by an unusual exhibition of theatrical pomp. What is much more interesting is the fact that Betterton, who acted the *King*, had his inspiration, as it were, indirectly from Shakespeare himself. Sir William Davenant, who had coached his leading player in the part, had himself been instructed in it by old Mr. Lowen, who in his turn had been taught how to interpret it by no less a person than the immortal Bard of Avon. A few months later *Macbeth* was put on, and as the critical Samuel condescended to call it "a pretty good play, but admirably acted" we can comfort ourselves with the reflection that the beauties of the great poet were not altogether lost upon him.

As a transition from the gloom of *Macbeth* may be mentioned the performance of *The Rivals*, a probable adaptation of the *Two Noble Kinsmen* attributed to the authorship of Shakespeare and Fletcher. It introduced music and dancing of an agreeable character and had in it that famous song, "My Lodging is on the Cold Ground," which Moll Davis gave with sufficient charm to delight the King and excite the jealousy of the usually amiable Mistress Gwynne. Betterton, as *Philander*, made a fine impression and so did his rival by courtesy, Mr. Harris. The latter won considerable fame in these years, and had a more than ordinary amount of talent, but success turned his head and after demanding from Davenant a larger salary than that paid to Betterton, he left the theatre in Lincoln's Inn Fields, declaring that he would never act there more. He modified his vow, however, as the King did not encourage his attempt to join the other company, under Killigrew, and so he came back penitently to the fold, doubtless believing in his heart that he was far above the modest Betterton. To be sure, he was a "more ayery" man than his rival, and the oft-quoted but ever quaint and amusing Pepys held him in high esteem.

"Company at home," is the entry for January 24, 1666–7. "Amongst others, Captain Rolt. And anon, at about seven or eight o'clock comes Mr. Harris of the Duke's playhouse, and brings Mrs. Pierce with him, and also one dressed like a country maid with a straw hat on, and at first I could not tell who it was, though I expected Knipp; but it was she coming off the stage just as she acted this day in *The Goblins;* a merry jade. Now my house is full and four fiddlers that play well. Harris I first took to my closet: and I find him a very curious and understanding person in all pictures and other things [to find an actor understanding in other things must have been a revelation for the writer] and a man of fine conversation; and so is Rolt. Among other things, Harris sung his Irish song, the strangest in itself and the prettiest sung by him that ever I heard."

The great London plague of 1665 and the fire of 1666 put an end, for the time being, to all theatrical entertainments in the metropolis. When the horrors attendant upon these two calamities had passed away the theatres were re-opened. Betterton resumed his position at the Duke's house, acting in a round of characters well calculated to test his versatility and producing several of his own plays, incidentally showing thereby that he was more gifted as a creator of parts than of dramas. In the meanwhile Davenant had planned the erection of a new theatre in Dorset Gardens, Salisbury Court, and to this elaborate structure, designed by Sir Christopher Wren, and costing, with the scenery, some five thousand pounds, the Duke's Players moved in 1671. Sir William was then dead, and the royal patent was inherited by his wife and sons. One of the sons, Charles Davenant, took the ostensible direction of affairs, and Betterton had much to say in the management of the performances. To detail the various characters taken by the latter during the remaining years that the company existed is a matter for the historian of the stage, and can have no excuse in the present unpretentious memoirs. Let it suffice to say that by this time Betterton was at the height of a fame which was hardly to decrease with the approach of old age, and had received the popular recognition which he so richly deserved. "There are so many vouchers for the merit of this extraordinary actor," wrote Dibdin years after, "that there would be no great difficulty in ascertaining, or risk in asserting precisely what they were. I must content myself, however, with saying that it has been unanimously allowed, his personal and mental qualifications for the stage were correct to perfection, and that, after a variety of arguments to prove this, we are obliged to confess that he appears never to have been on the stage for a single moment the actor but the character he performed."

In 1682 was effected the union of the King's and the Duke's Company, the consolidated organization opening its season at the Theatre Royal, Drury Lane, which had been erected several years before under the supervision of Sir Christopher Wren. The list of players includes Betterton, and Mrs. Saunderson (now Mrs. Betterton), Kynaston, Mrs. Barry, Mountford, Smith, Underhill, and Sanford. Into this family was soon to come Colley Cibber, joining it as an humble but aspiring youth of nineteen, who for a while would simply be known as Master Colley. Thomas Davies, the actor and bookseller who "mouthed a sentence as curs mouth a bone," * was told by Cross, the prompter of the house, that after waiting a long time for some notice to be taken of him, Cibber obtained the honor of carrying a message in some play to Betterton. "Whatever was the cause, Master Colley was so terrified that the scene was disconcerted by him. Betterton asked in some anger who the young fellow was that

* Davies was fairly driven from the stage by this satirical line of Churchill's.

had committed the blunder. Downes replied : ' Master Colley.' ' Master Colley ! then forfeit him.' ' Why, sir,' said Downes, ' he has no salary.' ' No,' said Betterton, ' why, then, put him down ten shillings a week, and forfeit him five shillings.' To this good-natured adjustment of reward and punishment, Cibber owed the first money he ever received from the theatre.''

An incident like this was not likely to decrease the admiration of the young unsalaried performer for the great Betterton, and Cibber, when he came to write that delightful *Apology*, helped not a little to perpetuate the fame of a man who seems to have been as admirable in his personal relations as he was when treading the boards.

''Betterton was an actor,'' eloquently says Cibber, speaking *con amore*, ''as Shakespeare was an author, both without competitors ! formed for the mutual assistance and illustration of each other's genius ! How Shakespeare wrote, all men who have a taste for nature may read, and know—but, with what higher rapture would he still be read, could they conceive how Betterton played him. Then might they know, the one was born alone to speak what the other only knew to write. Pity it is that the momentary beauties flowing from an harmonious elocution, cannot like those of poetry, be their own record ! That the animated graces of the player can live no longer than the instant breath and motion that presents them ; or at best can but fairly glimmer through the memory or imperfect attestation of a few surviving spectators. Could *how Betterton* spoke be as easily known as *what* he spoke ; then might you see the Muse of *Shakespeare* in her triumph, with all her beauties in their best array, rising into real life, and charming her beholders. But alas! since all this is so far out of the reach of description, how shall I show you *Betterton*? Should I therefore tell you that all the *Othellos, Hamlets, Hotspurs, Macbeths*, and *Brutus's*, whom you may have seen since his time, have fallen far short of him ; this still would give you no idea of his particular excellence.'' Then Colley tries to give some idea of the hero whom he finds it so difficult to describe, and it is only to be regretted that space does not permit of further quotations from his enthusiastic estimate.

Anthony Aston, half-lawyer, half-actor, who travelled through the English provinces during the early Georgian era, giving a theatrical performance which he styled a medley, has left us the following graphic picture of the great actor.

'' Mr. Betterton (although a superlative good actor) labored under ill figure, being clumsily made, having a great head, a short thick neck, stooped into the shoulders, and had fat short arms, which he rarely lifted higher than his stomach. His left hand frequently lodged in his breast, between his coat and waistcoat, while, with his right, he prepared his speech. His actions were few, but just.—He had little eyes,

and a broad face, a little pock-fretten ; a corpulent
body, and thick legs, with large feet. He was better
to meet than to follow ; for his aspect was serious, venerable and majestic ; in his latter time a little paralytic.
His voice was low and grumbling ; yet he could tune
it by an artful *climax*, which enforced universal attention, even from fops and orange girls. He was inca-
pable of dancing, even in a country dance ; as was Mrs.
Barry ; but their good qualities were more than equal
to their deficiencies ; while Mrs. Bracegirdle sung
very agreeably in the Loves of Mars and Venus, and
danced in a country dance, as well as Mr. Wicks,
though not with so much art and foppery, but like a
well-bred gentlewoman. Mr. Betterton was the most
extensive actor, from *Alexander* or *Sir John Falstaff* ;
but in that last character, he wanted the waggery of
Estcourt, the drollery of Harper, and salaciousness of
Jack Evans. But then, Estcourt was too trifling ;
Harper had too much of the Bartholomew-fair ; and
Evans misplaced his humor.—Thus, you see what flaws
are in bright diamonds : and I have often wished that
Mr. Betterton would have resigned the part of *Hamlet*
to some young actor (who might have personated,
though not have acted it better) for, when he threw
himself at *Ophelia's* feet, he appeared a little too grave
for a young student, lately come from the University
of Wittenburg ; and his *repartees* seemed rather as
Apophthegms from a sage philosopher, then the sport-
ing flashes of a young *Hamlet* ; and no one else could

have pleased the town, he was so rooted in their opinion. His younger contemporary Powel attempted several of Betterton's parts as *Alexander*, *Jaffier*, etc., but lost his credit ; as in *Alexander*, he maintained not the dignity of a King, but out-Heroded Herod ; and in his poisoned mad scene, *out-raved* all probability ; while Betterton kept his passion under, and shewed it most (as fume smoakes most when stifled). Betterton from the time he was dressed, to the end of the play, kept his mind in the same temperament and adaptness as the present character required.—If I was to write of him all day I should still remember fresh matter in his behalf."

Here was what might be termed an unemotional critique, but it was probably a pretty just one excepting that Aston failed to grasp the achievements of the actor from every point of view, and has thus left us only half a picture, and not a flattered one at that.

Old Thomas might be drawing near the grave, but a grateful town, which has not always been so constant to its favorites, could never have too much of him. * Its appreciation was never more generously shown than at the historic benefit given in honor of the now venerable player, in April, 1709. *Love for Love* was the play, with the old man as *Valentine* ; the audience was large and particularly brilliant, and to crown the tri-

* Betterton only stayed at Drury Lane until 1695 ; then he and a number of his companions formed a company of their own in Lincoln's Inn Fields, and some years later they went over to the new Queen's Theatre, in the Haymarket.

umph of the evening Mrs. Barry delivered this epilogue
while she and lovely Mrs. Bracegirdle clasped him
about the waist :

> " So we to former leagues of Friendship true,
>   Have bid once more our peaceful homes adieu,
>   To aid old Thomas, and to pleasure you.
>   Like errant damsels boldly we engage,
>   Arm'd, as you see for the defenceless stage.
>   Time was when this good man no help did lack,
>   And scorned that any She should hold his Back.
>   But now, so age and frailty have ordained,
>   By two at once he 's forced to be sustained.
>   You see what failing nature brings man to,
>   And yet let none insult, for aught we know,
>   She may not bear so well with some of you :
>   Though old, you find his strength is not clean past,
>   But true as steel, he 's Mettle to the last.
>   If better he perform'd in days of yore,
>   Yet now he gives you all that 's in his power,
>   What can the youngest of you all do more ? "

After this royal ovation " old Thomas " will go on
playing for another year, exerting much of the customary charm in comedy, and surprising every one by flashes
of ancient fire in such characters as *Othello*, *Macbeth*, and
Lear. During the autumn of 1709 he will be found at
the Haymarket Theatre, a house established a short
time before ostensibly for the presentation of opera, and
it is here that his memorable farewell to the stage he
loved so well is to be made on April 13, 1710. " It is
his benefit night, and the tears are in his aged wife's
eyes and a painful sort of smile on her trembling lips,
for Betterton kisses her as he goes forth that afternoon

to take leave, as it proved, of the stage forever. He is in such pain from gout that he can scarcely walk to his carriage, and how is he to enact the noble and fiery *Melantius*, in that ill-named drama of horror, *The Maid's Tragedy*? Hoping for the best, the old player is conveyed to the theatre, built by Sir John Vanbrugh, in the Haymarket, the site of which is now occupied by the Opera House. Through the stage-door he is carried in loving arms to his dressing-room. At the end of an hour Wilks is there, and Pinkethman, and Mrs. Barry, all dressed for their parts, and agreeably disappointed to find the *Melantius* of the night robed, armored, and besworded, with one foot in a buskin, and the other in a slipper. To enable him even to wear the latter, he had first thrust his inflamed foot into water ; but stout as he seemed, trying his strength to and fro in the room, the hand of death was at that moment descending on the grandest of English actors.

" The house arose to receive him who had delighted themselves, their sires, and their grandsires. The audience were packed like Norfolk biffins. The edifice itself was only five years old, and when it was abuilding people laughed at the folly which reared a new theatre in the country, instead of in London ;—for in 1705 all beyond the rural haymarket was open field, straight away westward and northward. That such a house could ever be filled was set down as an impossibility ; the achievement was accomplished on this eventful benefit night ; when the popular favorite was about to utter his last words, and to belong thenceforward only to the history of the stage he had adorned.

" There was a shout which shook him, as *Lysippus* uttered the words ' Noble Melantius,' which heralded his coming. Every word which could be applied to himself was marked by a storm of applause, and when *Melantius* said of *Amintor :*

> ' His youth did promise much, and his ripe years
>   Will see it all performed '

a murmuring comment ran around the house, that this had been effected by Betterton himself. Again, when he bids *Amintor* ' hear thy friend, who has more years than thou ' there were probably few who did not wish that Betterton were as young as Wilks ; but when he subsequently thundered forth the famous passage ' My heart will never fail me ' there was a very tempest of excitement, which was carried to its utmost height, in thundering peal on peal of unbridled approbation, as the great Rhodian gazed full on the house, exclaiming :

> ' My heart
> And limbs are still the same : my will as great
> To do you service.' " *

Poor Betterton ! His heart and will may have been the same, but his gouty limbs were not, and he hastened the inevitable event when he put his feet in cold water, so that he might play at the benefit. Forty-eight hours after this final triumph he was dead, and a whole coun-

* Dr. Doran.

try mourned him as never actor had been mourned
before in England, and as perhaps none other, save
Garrick, has been since. He had lived to a fine old
age, great, lovable, and useful to the last ; smiled upon
by royalty as well as by the public and doubtless content in the feeling that though comparatively poor (a
foolish friend had helped to scatter his fortune by
unfortunate speculation) a grateful community would
never let him want. He was given an imposing burial
in Westminster Abbey, that historic resting-place for
the remains of so many who have contributed to Britain's greatness—among whom are none more deserving
of such honor than Thomas Betterton.

CHAPTER IV.

LIGHTS LONG SINCE EXTINGUISHED.

WE have seen that at the benefit given Betterton in 1709 the epilogue was spoken by a Mrs. Barry—"the famous Mrs. Barry," as she has been styled. Famous she was, indeed, while she lived, but the lustre of her achievements has diminished with time, and now her name conveys little or no idea to many who know the most minute detail in the career of several less powerful actresses. Her father, Edward Barry, a barrister, distinguished himself by raising a regiment for the support of Charles I., and his untimely death left the daughter dependent upon the charity of Lady Davenant. The Davenant family took a great interest in the girl's ambition to become celebrated, and through their influence she was brought out upon the stage, only to prove a comparative failure. In the meantime, the Earl of Rochester fell madly in love with her and undertook her tuition, with the result that though her morals were not improved by the kindness of this noble patron her art gained materially. It is related how the Earl boasted that he would make a great actress of her in six months, and the brilliant reputation she afterward gained certainly justified his confidence in her natural qualifications, as well as in the excellence of his own instruction. Her first hit, as we would express it now, was made in Lord Orrery's drama of *Mustapha*, wherein she figured as the *Queen of Hungary*, and her advancement after that event was rapid, even phenomenal. She created a deep impression in Otway's *Alcibiades*, especially on the heart of the author himself, who cherished for this gifted woman a love that she hardly deserved. He conceived the parts of *Monimia*, in *The Orphan* and of *Belvidera*, in *Venice Preserved*, that she might play them, and thus added to her renown; indeed, the title given her of " the famous Mrs. Barry " dates from her appearance in the last-named piece.

In characters of greatness, according to Dibdin, she was " graceful, noble, and dignified," no violence of passion was beyond the reach of her feelings, and in " the most melting distress and tenderness she was exquisitely affecting. Thus she was equally admirable in *Cassandra*, *Cleopatra*, *Roxana*, *Monimia*, or *Belvidera*." The mention of the part of *Roxana* suggests an anecdote of Mrs. Barry that is hardly creditable to the personal character of the best actress Dryden ever saw. *Roxana* is one of the two leading feminine rôles of *The Rival Queens, or the Death of Alexander the Great*. This tragedy was once a favorite, but is now only remembered in connection with the untimely fate of its talented author, Lee, whose career ended with insanity. It so happened that when Barry was cast for *Roxana* a Mrs. Boutelle whom she detested as a dangerous rival, quite unnecessarily, as it seems, was assigned the part of *Statira*. In one scene *Roxana* is called upon to engage in a deadly struggle with *Statira*, and to this episode, exciting enough when simply acted, Mrs. Barry once gave a tinge of realism that set the town agog for several days and put poor Mrs. Boutelle in a tremor of horror. With a cry of " Die, sorceress, die, and all my wrongs die with thee "— lines into which she put even more than the usual force—Mistress Barry sent her dagger completely through the armor worn by the detested *Statira*. There was a shriek from the slightly scratched Boutelle, and no little commotion ; but the episode was soon hushed up, after *Roxana* duly apologized and explained that she had been carried away by the illusion of the moment. The uncharitable supposition was privately expressed that temper rather than artistic feeling had carried away the impetuous Barry, but she was publicly given the benefit of the doubt.

This *contretemps* does not appear to have detracted from the popularity of the celebrated *Roxana*, nor was her private life, (anything but a decorous one,) a hindrance to her career on the stage. The world was much the same then as now. Cibber had a thorough appreciation of her genius, for he refers to her " presence of elevated dignity," with her " Mien and motion superb, and gracefully majestic ; and " her voice full, clear and strong, so that no violence of passion could be too much for her." He adds that "when distress or tenderness possessed her, she subsided into the most affecting melody and softness. In the art of exciting pity she had a power beyond all the actresses I have yet seen, or what your imagination can conceive. Of the former of these two great excellencies, she gave the most delightful proofs in almost all the heroic plays of Dryden and Lee; and of the latter, in the softer passions of Otway's *Monimia* and *Belvidera*. In scenes of anger, defiance, or resentment, while she was impetuous, and terrible, she poured out the sentiment with an enchanting harmony; and it was this particular excellence, for which Dryden made her the above recited compliment, upon her acting *Cassandra* in his *Cleomenes*. But here, I am apt to think his partiality for that character may have tempted his judgment to let it pass for her masterpiece; when he could not but know there were several other characters in which her action might have given her a fairer pretence to the praise he had bestowed on her, for *Cassandra;* for in no part of that is there the least ground for compassion, as in *Monimia;* nor equal cause for admiration, as in the noble love of *Cleopatra*, or the tempestuous jealousy of *Roxana*. 'T was in these lights I thought Mrs. Barry shone with a much brighter excellence than in *Cassandra*. She was the first person whose merit was distinguished by the indulgence of having an annual Benefit-Play, which was granted to her alone, if I mistake not, first in King James's time, and which became not common to others, 'till the division of this company,* after the death of King William's Queen, Queen Mary. This great actress dy'd of a fever toward the latter end of Queen Anne ; the year I have forgot ; but perhaps you will recollect it, by an Expression that fell from her in blank Verse, in her last hours, when she was delirious, viz. : 'Ha, ha ! and so they make us Lords, by dozens !' ''

Cibber places the date of her death upon her supposed utterance of a verse referring to an increase of the peerage for political reasons, during the reign of Queen Anne ; he had forgotten that Mrs. Barry died in 1713, after having lived in retirement since her farewell appearance on the stage in 1710. That she has not come down to posterity with the same *éclat* as two or three other actresses long since departed is really curious, for there has never been any difference of opinion regarding her wonderful abilities as a tragedienne. The only disagreement seems to have been as to her personal appearance, and the probabilities are that while she was not handsome she had great fascination, not only for Rochester and poor Otway, but for every one else. '' With all her enchantment,'' Anthony Aston records, '' this fine creature was not handsome ; her mouth opening most on the right side, which she strove to draw the other way ; and at times composing her face as if to have her picture drawn. She was

* Drury Lane.

middle-sized, had darkish hair, light eyes, and was indifferent plump. In tragedy she was solemn and august; in comedy alert, easy and genteel; pleasant in her face and manner, and filling the stage with a variety of action." Yet Aston sadly adds that "she could not sing, nor dance; no, not even in a country dance."

Of far different character was that "darling of the theatre," Mistress Anne Bracegirdle, a contemporary of Barry, and an actress at whose pretty feet all the gallants in town were ready to drop. But they would have dropped in vain, for she would have none of them, even though her admirers numbered the Dukes of Devonshire and Dorset, the Earl of Halifax, Congreve, and Lord Lovelace. Her virtue was extolled as much as her talents, and so deep an impression did she make by the possession of the former quality—not a very common one for the actresses who surrounded her— that Lord Halifax and his friends made up a purse of 800 guineas, which they presented to her as a slight testimonial of their regard—and surprise. Macauley has taken a rather cynical view of this "Diana of the stage!" (as Doctor Doran calls her), relating that "those who are acquainted with the parts which she was in the habit of saying, and with the epilogue which it was her special business to recite, will not give her credit for any extraordinary measure of virtue or delicacy. She seemed to have been a cold, vain, interested coquette who perfectly understood how much the influence of her charms was increased by the fame of a severity which cost her nothing, and who could venture to flirt with a succession of admirers in the just confidence that no flame which she might kindle in them would thaw her own ice."

Macauley's theory may be taken with the traditional grain of salt, for his prejudices were so pronounced that he was forced to give them to the world, even at the expense of a woman's character. That the free-and-easy people about her believed in her professions is a very good indication of the sincerity of the heroine of Congreve's famous lines:

> " Would she could make of me a saint,
>   Or I of her a sinner."

But in the role of heroine Mrs. Bracegirdle never appeared under more exciting auspices than on the memorable night when an attempt was made to carry off the unwilling charmer. Among her string of hopeless, sighing admirers, was a certain Captain Hill, who determined to obtain possession by force of the lovely object of his passion, and for this purpose enlisted the services of the notorious Lord Mohun, a ruffianly aristocrat quite ready for such a scheme. About ten o'clock one night, when the unconscious Bracegirdle and her mother were supping at the home of a Mr. Page in Drury Lane, the two conspirators, assisted by several soldiers whom they had bribed, attempted to smuggle the actress into a carriage, as she was leaving the house. The lady naturally protested, and her

ANNE BRACEGIRDLE.

FROM AN OLD PRINT.

screams soon brought assistance ; an angry mob gathered, and Lord Mohun and the Captain were only too glad to take themselves off. The affair had a fatal ending for poor Will Mountford, a graceful, handsome actor who used to play anything from a seventeenth century fop to *Alexander* in the *Rival Queens*. This playing of *Alexander* really cost him his life, as events turned out, for Mrs. Bracegirdle was the *Statira*, and Hill accordingly became absurdly jealous of the young actor. When the attempted abduction had such an unexpected ending the Captain met Mountford on the street; an altercation ensued and Hill ran his rival through the body with his sword, inflicting a fatal wound. The murderer fled from England, the delectable Mohun was tried for his life, but acquitted on the ground that there was not sufficient evidence to connect him with the crime, and Mountford's disconsolate widow subsequently married another actor, Verbruggen. This gallant second husband was the gentleman who loved to say : " Damn me, though I don't much value my wife, yet nobody shall abuse her."

Mrs. Bracegirdle left the stage during the reign of Queen Anne, when the younger charms of Nance Oldfield were beginning to make her own position insecure, and she lived to a good old age, dying as late as 1748.* She must have read Cibber's *Apology*, and have taken keen interest in the description of herself as it is here repeated.

* She was born in 1663.

" I come now to the last and only living person of all those theatrical characters I have promised you, Mrs. Bracegirdle ; who, I know, would rather pass her remaining days forgotten as an actress, than to have her youth recollected in the most favorable light I am able to place it ; yet, as she is essentially necessary to my theatrical history, and as I only bring her back to the company of those with whom she passed the spring and summer of her life, I hope it will excuse the liberty I take, in commemorating the delight which the publick received from her appearance, while she was an ornament to the theatre.

" Mrs. Bracegirdle was, now, but just blooming to her maturity ; her reputation as an actress, gradually rising with that of her person ; never any woman was in such general favor of her spectators, which to the last scene of her dramatic life, she maintained by not being unguarded in her private character. This dis-cretion contributed, not a little, to make her the Cara, the Darling of the Theatre :   For it will be no extrava-gant thing to say, scarce an audience saw her, that were less than half of them lovers, without a suspected favorite among them ; and tho' she might be said to have been the universal passion, and under the highest temptations, her constancy in resisting them served but to increase the number of her admirers.   And this perhaps you will more easily believe, when I extend not my encomiums on her person, beyond a sincerity that can be suspected ; for she had no greater claim to beauty than what the most desirable brunette might pretend to. But her youth, and lively aspect threw out such a glow of health, and cheerfulness, that on the stage few spectators that were not past it, could behold her without desire. It was even the fashion among the gay, and young, to have a taste or *tendre* for Mrs. Bracegirdle. She inspired the best authors to write for her, and two of them, when they gave her a lover in a play, seem'd palpably to plead their own passions, and make their private court to her in fictitious characters. In all the chief parts she acted, the desirable was so predominant, that no judge could be cold enough to consider, from what other particular excellence, she became delightful. To speak critically of an actress, that was extremely good were as hazardous as to be positive in one's opinion of the best opera singer. People often judge by comparison, where there is no similitude, in the performance. So that, in this case, we have only taste to appeal to, and of taste there can be no disputing. I shall therefore only say of Mrs. Bracegirdle, that the most eminent authors always chose her for their favorite character, and shall leave that uncontestable proof of her merit to its own value. Yet let me say, that there were two very different characters in which she acquitted herself with no common applause. If anything could excuse that desperate extravagance of love, that almost frantic passion of Lee's *Alexander the Great*, it must have been when Mrs. Bracegirdle was his *Statira ;* as when she acted *Millamant,* all the faults, follies, and affectations of that agreeable tyrant were venially melted down into so many charms, and attractions of a conscious beauty. In other characters, where singing was a necessary part of them, her voice and action gave a pleasure which good sense, in those days, was not ashamed to give praise to.

"She retired from the stage in the height of her favor from the publick, when most of her contemporaries, whom she had been bred up with, were declining, in the year 1710, nor could she be persuaded to return to it, under new masters, upon the most advantageous terms that were offered her; excepting one day, about a year after, to assist her good friend, Mr. Betterton, when she played *Angelica*, in *Love for Love*, for his benefit. She has still the happiness to retain her usual cheerfulness, to be, without the transitory charms of youth, agreeable."

The unfortunate Mountford, of whose death the icilly moral Bracegirdle was the innocent cause, stands out as one of the most attractive figures of the early days of King William's reign. He was impressive in tragedy, irresistible as a lover, and brilliant as a comedian; his appearance was handsome and his voice a marvel of melody. He made vice so alluring, did this "Prince Charming" of the stage, that Queen Mary thought it was dangerous to see him act the unprincipled *Rover* in one of the licentious Mrs. Behn's most famous plays, and he was known to be the "glass of fashion" and the "mould of form" which so inspired the great Mr. Wilks with the desire of imitation. " In comedy," Cibber notes, " he gave the truest life to what we call the fine gentleman ; his spirit shone the brighter for being polished with decency : in scenes of gaiety he never broke into the regard that was due to the presence of equal, or superior characters, tho' inferior actors played them ; he filled the stage, not by elbowing and crossing it before others, or disconcerting their action, but by surpassing them in true and masterly touches of nature.* He never laughed at his own jest, unless the point of his raillery upon another required it. He had a particular talent, in giving life to *bon mots* and repartees ; the wit of the poet seem'd always to come from his extempore, and sharpened into more wit from his brilliant manner of delivering it. . . . The agreeable was so natural to him, that even in that dissolute character of the *Rover* he seem'd to wash off the guilt from vice, and gave it charm and merit."

Dashing Will's no less dashing wife Susannah, afterward to be Mrs. Verbruggen, was inimitable as a coquette of the type then known on the stage, and could play a male coxcomb with remarkable humor and abandon. To again quote Cibber, whose cameo-like sketches are often so delightful that to reproduce them requires no apology, it appears that she was " mistress of more variety of humor than I ever knew in any one woman

---

* This is a lesson that a few modern players might take to heart.

actress. This variety, too, was attended with an equal vivacity, which made her excellent in characters extremely different. . . . Nor was her humor limited to her sex, for while her shape permitted she was a more adroit pretty fellow than is usually seen upon the stage : her easy air, action, mien, and gesture quite changed from the quoif, to the cock'd hat, and cavalier in fashion. People were so fond of seeing her a man, that when the part of *Bays* in the *Rehearsal* had for some time lain dormant she was desired to take it up, which I have seen her act with all the true, coxcombly spirit, and humor, that the sufficiency of the character required."

Of her *Melantha* in *Marriage à la Mode* the same critic chronicles that it was "as finished an impertinence as ever fluttered in a drawing-room, and seems to contain the most complete system of female foppery that could possibly be crowded into the tortured form of a fine lady. Her language, dress, motion, manners, soul, and body are in a continual hurry to be something more than is necessary or commendable. And though I doubt it will be a vain labor to offer you a just likeness of Mrs. Mountford's action, yet the fantastick impression is still so strong in my memory, that I cannot help saying something tho' fantastically, about it. The first ridiculous airs that break from her are upon a gallant, never seen before, who delivers her a letter from her father, recommending him to her good graces, as an honorable lover. Here now, one would think she might naturally show a little of the sex's decent reserve, tho' never so slightly covered! No, sir ; not a tittle of it ; modesty is the virtue of a poor-soul'd country gentlewoman ; she is too much a court lady to be under so vulgar a confusion ; she reads the letter, therefore, with a careless, dropping lip, and an erected brow, humming it hastily over, as if she were impatient to outgo her father's commands, by making a complete conquest of him at once ; and that the letter might not embarrass her attack, crack ! she crumbles it at once into her palm and pours upon him the whole artillery of airs, eyes, and motion ; down goes her dainty, diving body to the ground, as if she were sinking under the conscious load of her own attractions ; then launches into a flood of fine language, and compliment, still playing her chest forward, in fifty falls and risings, like a swan upon the waving water ; and, to complete her impertinence, she is so rapidly fond of her own wit, that she will not give her lover leave to praise it : silent, assenting bows, and vain endeavors to speak, are all the share of the conversation he is admitted to, which, at last, he is relieved from by her engagement to half a score visits, which she swims from him to make, with a promise to return in a twinkling."

With due allowance for eighteenth century affectation, this is as speaking a criticism as one could wish for, even in this epoch of analytical discussion, when the charms of an actress are put under the dramatic editor's microscope and described in cold type with as much minuteness as though Mr. Howells were dissecting one of his commonplace heroines. But to dispose of the blithesome Mountford, let it be added that in her last years* she became mildly deranged. It is related that one day, when her mind was clearer than usual, she demanded to know what play was to be performed at Drury Lane that evening, and showed unusual interest on hearing that it was to be *Hamlet.* The gentle *Ophelia* had been one of her favorite parts, curiously enough, and as the thought of past triumphs awoke her dormant intellect she determined to play the character once again. She contrived to escape from her attendants, hurried to the theatre, and concealing herself there until the cue for *Ophelia's* appearance in the mad scene, she suddenly pushed by the actress to whom the role was assigned, stepped upon the stage and represented the distraught heroine with an effectiveness and wild realism that electrified the audience. It was her farewell to the boards ; she was taken home, and died soon after. The story is a trifle theatrical, and may be apocryphal, but who cares to question it? The idea of a demented actress representing with horrible power the insanity of *Ophelia* is in itself essentially dramatic, and no one should grudge Mrs. Mountford the benefit of so unconventional an exit.

Among others in the talented company at Drury Lane whom the invaluable Colley has painted for the edification of succeeding generations, was that "cor-

* She died about 1703.

rect and natural comedian," Cave Underhill. He seems to have been a first-class actor consigned to second-class roles; "his particular excellence was in characters that may be called still-life," otherwise the "stiff, the heavy and the stupid." He was especially admired for his *Grave-digger* in *Hamlet*, and "the author of the *Tatler* recommends him to the favor of the town upon that play's being acted for his benefit, wherein, after his age had some years obliged him to leave the stage, he came on again, for that day, to perform his old part; but, alas! so worn, and disabled as if himself was to have lain in the grave he was digging; when he could no more excite laughter, his infirmities were dismissed with pity."

There was Tony Leigh, too, of whom the appreciative Charles II. used to speak as "My actor," and the natural Nokes. "I saw him once," says Cibber of the latter, "giving an account of some table talk to another actor behind the scenes, which a man of quality, accidentally listening to, was so deceived by his manner that he asked him if that was a new play he was rehearsing?" This anecdote was related to show that Nokes had the same manner on and off the stage. "His person was of the middle size, his voice clear and audible; his natural countenance grave and sober; but the moment he spoke the settled seriousness of his features was utterly discharg'd, and a dry drolling or laughing levity took such full possession of him, that I can only refer the idea of him to your imagination. In some of his low characters, that became it, he had a shuffling shamble in his gait, with so contented an ignorance in his aspect and an awkward absurdity in his gesture, that had you not known him, you could not have believ'd that naturally he could have had a grain of common sense. In a word, I am tempted to sum up the character of Nokes as a comedian, in a parodie of what Shakespeare's *Mark Antony* says of *Brutus* as a hero :

> ' His life was laughter, and the ludicrous
> So mixt, in him, that nature might stand up,
> And say to all the world,—this was an actor.' "

In a far different line of work was Sanford, who is said to have been the best impersonator of stage villains ever known. So thoroughly was he identified with such parts that the audiences would tolerate him in none others, and on one occasion the house became very indignant because he ventured to appear as an honest man. His private character was amiable, but a wicked person they would have him on the stage. Physical defects had not a little to do with the accident that first cast him for this kind of parts ; he had a deformed body, and it can readily be imagined that he could have made a highly popular *Richard III.* " Had Sandford lived in Shakespeare's time," according to Cibber, " his judgment must have chose him, above all other actors, to have played his *Richard the Third ;* I leave his person out of the question, which, tho' naturally made for it, yet that would have been the least part of his recommendation ; Sandford had stronger claims to it ; he had sometimes an uncouth stateliness in his motion, a harsh and sullen pride of speech, a meditating brow, a stern aspect, occasionally changing into an almost ludicrous triumph over all goodness and virtue : from thence falling into the most assuasive gentleness, and soothing candor of a designing heart. These, I say, must have preferred him to it ; these would have been colors so essentially shining in that character that it will be no dispraise to that great author to say, Sanford must have shewn as many masterly strokes in it (had he ever acted it) as are visible in the writing it.''

If Sanford entertained London by his heavy villains Richard Estcourt was no less acceptable from his wonderful powers as a mimic. His life was a curious one, beginning as it did on the stage and all but ending in a tavern of which he was the proprietor. He was born in 1668 at Tewkesbury, and received his education in the Latin school at that place, only to hurry off as soon as he could to act with a lot of strolling comedians. It is said that he made his *début* with these wanderers in the feminine role of *Roxana* in the *Rival Queens*, choosing this part so as to conceal his identity. But he was unable to escape detection, and, after being obliged to return to his home he had the supreme mortification of seeing himself apprenticed to a London apothecary. Medicine bottles, mortars, and pestles were by no means to young Estcourt's taste, so he took French leave of his master, drifted about England and Ireland and finally brought up at Drury Lane. Here his powers as a mimic brought him into favorable notice ; he imitated the voices, gestures, and methods of prominent actors, and earned the friendship of such men as the Duke of Marlborough and Sir Richard Steele. Steele helped to immortalize his friend by writing of him and contended that "the best man he knew of for heightening the revel-gaiety of a company was Dick Estcourt. Merry tales, accompanied with apt gestures and lively representations of circumstances and persons beguile the gravest mind into a consent to be as humorous as himself. Add to this that when a man is in his good grace, he has a mimickry that does not debase the person he represents, but which, taking from the gravity of the character, adds to the agreeableness of it."

The death of Estcourt was soon followed by that of George Powell, whose name will be found opposite the part of *Portius* in the original programme for Addison's *Cato*. Addison has thus alluded in the *Spectator* to the first *Portius*, in a way that indicates the thorough knowledge, on the part of this actor, of the advantages of theatrical clap-trap : "The warm and passionate parts of tragedy are always the most taking with the audience ; for which reason we often see the players pronouncing in all the violence of action several parts of the tragedy which the author writ with great temper, and designed that they should have been so acted. I have seen Powell very often raise himself a loud clap by this artifice." The author of *Cato* admits, however, that Powell " is excellently formed for a tragedian, and, when he pleases, deserves the admiration of the best judges."

This player never occupied a position of the commanding sort, although he appears to have had a very clear belief that he was the equal of Betterton. When the latter had become old and gouty, Powell announced that he would play *Falstaff* after the exact manner of the great actor, and he not only mimicked the style and voice of the original but also had the brutality to burlesque his infirmities. Consequently we can hardly wax sentimental in learning that his career was ruined by intemperance or that he died in poverty, with the bailiffs pursuing him to the grave.

With Powell must come to a close this brief sketch of the brightest lights among the remarkable players who acted as a connecting link between the end of the seventeenth and the beginning of the eighteenth century. While they dominate the scene changes are taking place in the drama ; the old order of things is vanishing, new faces are appearing, and the theatre of the Restoration has already passed into history, to be condemned for its licentiousness but lovingly remembered for the sake of the gifted men and charming women who gave it such brilliance. We are now in the reign of " good Queen Anne " ; let us tarry for a chapter to glance at theatrical conditions during the golden era of this amiable but commonplace sovereign.

CHAPTER V.

THE OLD RÉGIME AND THE NEW.

"HOW do you employ your time now?" a lady of quality is asked in the early days of the eighteenth century.

"I lie in bed," she says, "till noon, dress all the afternoon, dine in the evening, and play at cards till midnight."

"How do you spend the Sabbath?"

"In chit-chat."

"What do you talk of?"

"New fashions and new plays."

"How often do you go to Church?"

"Twice a year or oftener, according as my husband gives me new clothes."

"Why do you go to church when you have new clothes?"

"To see other people's finery, and to show my own, and to laugh at those scurvy, out-of-fashion creatures that come there for devotion."

"Pray, Madam, what books do you read?"

"I read lew'd plays and winning romances." *

* From the *English Lady's Catechism*, first published in 1703.

84

This very truthful lady whose frankness gives a fairly correct idea of the daily habits of contemporary women of fashion, might have added that she went to the theatre, presumably Drury Lane or Lincoln's Inn Fields, on the two or three evenings in the week when performances were given, and that when she saw a "lew'd play" she was better pleased than if the bill were Shakespearian. In all probability she belonged to the bevy of coquettish damsels whom Addison has immortalized in one of his brightest essays.

"Some years ago," he relates in the *Spectator*,* "I was at the tragedy of *Macbeth*, and unfortunately placed myself under a woman of quality that is since dead, who, as I found by the noise she made, was newly re-turned from France.† A little before the rising of the curtain, she broke out into a loud soliloquy, 'When will the dear witches enter?' and immediately upon their first appearance, asked a lady that sat three boxes from her on her right hand, if those witches were not charming creatures. A little after, as Betterton was in one of the finest speeches of the play, she shook her fan at another lady who sat as far on the left hand, and told her with a whisper that might be heard all over the pit, 'we must not expect to see Balloon to-night.' Not long after, calling out to a young baronet by his name, who sat three seats before me, she asked him

* No. 45, April 21, 1711.

† A trip to France was considered very *comme il faut* in Addison's day.

whether *Macbeth's* wife was still alive ; and before he could give an answer, fell a talking of the ghost of *Banquo.* She had by this time formed a little audience to herself, and fixed the attention of all about her. But as I had a mind to hear the play, I got out of the sphere of her impertinence, and planted myself in one of the most remotest corners of the pit.''

Addison was not the only unfortunate who had experiences of this sort—for the matter of that, the gentle art of talking, in and out of the boxes, and drawing attention from the stage, is still cultivated in some quarters—and it must have been a hard thing in those days to keep the uninterrupted run of a performance. There seems to have been a charming absence of self-restraint among the patrons of the drama, between the disturbances so often created in the upper gallery by the servants of the aristocratic visitors, and the talking, walking about the theatre, and general want of consideration among the '' quality '' themselves. The '' plain people '' in the middle class of life, who were given to neither coquetry, gallantry, nor good clothes, and their quiet, studious superiors who went to the play for the play's sake, must have launched many a secret, but nevertheless fervent anathema against the frivolous disturbers of their peace. But democracy was not as potent a factor in the theatre as out of it, and the noisy airs and graces of the women, the staring, the drivelling gossip and impertinences of the men, the flirting with the pretty orange girls,* and the general arrogance of upper-tendom, went on unchecked.

But the greatest confusion came from a custom which Anne, who was no enthusiastic admirer of the theatre, but who had a keen sense of decorum and decency, tried hard to correct. This was in allowing members of the audience to sit on the stage during a performance, mingle with the actors, stroll behind the scenes, and even penetrate into the dressing-rooms of the actresses. It is hard to picture such a helter-skelter state of affairs in the nineteenth century, when even the meanest theatre has stringent regulations as to the admission of outsiders into the quarters of the performers. Imagine Mr. Irving acting *Hamlet* with some of his audience nonchalantly reclining on chairs or sofas placed near the wings ; or worse still, think of empty-headed specimens of the *jeuness dorée* calmly walking around the players and almost jostling them, while the latter were speaking their lines ; then stumbling out among the scene-shifters, and finally ending by superintending the toilets and make-up of the feminine members of the company. Yet an anomaly like this was patiently endured when Anne came to the throne, probably because the public was hardened to the whole wretched business. But the incongruity of it gradually dawned upon the theatre-goers, and the

---

* The ostensible duty of the orange girls was to serve refreshments between the acts.

Queen herself undertook to institute a much-needed reform in this direction.

Whatever may have been the virtues of the sovereign she had no very clear perception of the artistic, and it is evident that her action came from a desire to prevent immorality rather than from any hope to preserve harmony and realism on the stage. That the abuse referred to was calculated to foster a looseness and want of decency in the relation between the actresses and the gentlemen who haunted their apartments is a fact that requires no elaboration. Fully conscious of this, Anne issued a proclamation setting forth that "no person of what quality soever" should " presume to go behind the stage, either before, or during the acting of any play." It was further ordered "that no woman be allowed or presume to wear a vizard mask in either of the theatres. And that no person come into either house without paying the prices established for their respective places."

The beaux who thought half the fun of going to the theatre consisted in ogling the actresses behind the scenes or boldly surveying the audience in front, were loth to obey the royal commands. They died hard, as it were, and it was not until about 1712, after another proclamation had been issued, that the practice was discontinued. The brilliant "Dick" Steele must have been delighted when the end came, for he has something to say in a number of the *Spectator* about the unsolicited performance of a young person who assisted in presenting the play of *Philaster*. This was " a very lusty fellow, but withal a sort of beau, who getting into one of the side-boxes in the stage before the curtain drew, was disposed to show the whole audience his activity by leaping over the spikes: he passed from thence to one of the entering doors, where he took snuff with tolerable good grace, displayed his fine clothes, made two or three feint passes at the curtain with his cane, and faced about and appeared at t'other door. Here he affected to survey the whole house, bowed and smiled at random, and then showed his teeth, which were some of them indeed very white. After this he retired behind the curtain, and obliged us with several views of his person from every opening. During the time of acting he appeared frequently in the prince's apartment, [one of the scenes of *Philaster*] made one at the hunting match, and was very forward in the rebellion."

Once that these gentlemen so "very forward" had to retire from the unwilling gaze of the audience one of the most striking differences between the old-fashioned theatre and that of to-day was removed. In some respects the conditions were very much the same then as now. Actors often ranted in a way to make the judicious grieve (this sorrow we shall have always with us); there was the inevitable amount of sham, fustian, and clap-trap about many things theatrical, and the gallery was appealed to with an eagerness worthy of a modern "ham-fatter," who will tear the proverbial passion into as many tatters as physical strength and an unmerciful Providence will allow. There were no melodramas, so called, but the mouths of heroes were filled with bombast, producing "such sentiments as proceed rather from a swelling than a greatness of mind," and "unnatural exclamations, curses, vows, blasphemies, a defiance of mankind, and an outraging of the gods" frequently passed upon the audience for "towering thoughts," and accordingly met "with infinite applause." * There were "blood and thunder" dramas, in which a general killing of the principal characters formed an agreeable feature; plays in which the enforced use of the handkerchief by tearful females was aimed at, and comedies constructed, as the play-bills would now put it, for laughing purposes only. Vaudeville, (whereby is meant variety entertainment) alleged "farce-comedy" (which is really not farce-comedy at all) and dime museums were unknown, but their places were well supplied by puppet shows, wax works, including the image of a certain countess who had "three hundred and sixty-five children, all born at one birth," tight-rope walking, acrobatic display, a gentleman without arms or hands, who wrote "very fine with his mouth," a lad covered with hog bristles, and any quantity of freaks, wild beasts, and diverse objects of curious interest.

The scheme of interjecting a little dancing and singing, or, rather, a great deal of it, into a performance of

* Addison.

the lighter vein, which is really the basis of the modern farce-comedy, had exemplification even then, as the following advertisement from the London *Daily Courant** plainly shows :

"At the Theatre in Dorset Gardens, this day being Friday the 30th of April, will be presented a farce call'd *The Cheats of Scapin*. And a comedy of two acts only, call'd *The Comical Rivals*, or the *School Boy*. With several Italian Sonatas by Signior Gasperini and others. And the Devonshire Girl being now upon her return to the City of Exeter, will perform three different dances, particularly her last new entry in imitation of Mademoiselle Subligni, and the Whip of Dunboyne by Mr. Claxton her Master, being the last time of their performance till winter. And at the desire of several persons of quality (hearing that Mr. Pinkethman hath hired the two famous French girls lately arrived from the Emperor's Court). They will perform several dances on the rope upon the stage, being improved to that degree, far exceeding all others in that art. And their Father presents you with the Newest Humors of Harlequin as performed by him before the Grand Signior at Constantinople. Also the famous Mr. Evans, lately arrived from Vienna, will show you wonders of another kind, vaulting on the manag'd horse, being the greatest master of that kind in the world. To begin at Five so that all may be done by Nine a Clock."

They did some things better in that quaint period.

* April 30, 1703.

The manager might furnish one with farce, comedy, and specialties all in the same evening, but he kept one distinct from the other ; at present the dancing, the singing, the horse-vaulting, et cætera, are integral parts of the " play," with the result that the spectator, however much he may enjoy the incidental features, is generally in a state of hopeless bewilderment as to the nature or plot of the farce itself.

So far as the morals of the plays go, the stage has greatly altered for the better. Even during Anne's time much improvement in tone was to be noted, but the foul atmosphere of the Restoration still pervaded the theatres and spoiled many a fine work, whose author, yielding to the taste of the age, tarnished the brilliancy of his wit by the introduction of nastiness and innuendo. So deeply rooted had become this habit of catering to the worst feeling of the audience that when Colley Cibber (whose career will be dwelt upon later) sought to get out of the beaten path by writing so comparatively clean a comedy as *The Careless Husband* the town was almost nonplussed. The hero, *Lord Morelove*, was not the licentious lover of old, with the manners of a gentleman and the heart of a libertine ; on the contrary he proved honest, without being prudish, and it may well be imagined how disappointed were certain frequenters of the theatre at such a change of treatment.

In one of Steele's comedies, however, exception was taken to a sentiment put into the mouth of a certain character, and some time later Sir Richard very sensibly modified the passage which had proved so objectionable even to several among his well-seasoned *clientelle*. The play was *The Funeral, or Grief à la Mode*, wherein those very necessary and respectable persons, the undertakers, were satirized with a delightful humor and originality that contributed largely to its success. Steele himself apologized, through the medium of the Spectator,* for the offending lines—which were by no means out of the way as things went in those easy-going days, and pleaded in extenuation that " if the audience would but consider the difficulty of keeping up a sprightly dialogue for five acts together, they would allow a writer, when he wants wit, and cannot please any otherwise, to help it out with a little smuttiness. . . . When the author cannot strike out of himself any more of that which he has superior to those who make up the bulk of his audience, his natural recourse is to that which he has in common with them ; and a description which gratifies a sensual appetite will please when the author has nothing about him to delight a refined imagination."

A plausible excuse, especially for Dick, but think of a dramatist being so frank in this year of grace, 1895.

Addison took a much higher view of the moral phase of playwriting. " It is one of the most unaccountable things in our age," he mourns, " that the lewedness of our theatre, should be so much complained of,

* No. 51, April 28, 1711.

and so little redressed. It is to be hoped, that some time or other we may be at leisure to restrain the licentiousness of the theatre, and make it contribute its assistance to the advancement of morality and to the reformation of the age.* As matters stand at present, multitudes are shut out from this noble diversion by reason of those abuses and corruptions that accompany it. A father is often afraid that his daughter should be ruined by these entertainments, which were invented for the accomplishment and refining of human nature. The Athenian and Roman plays were written with such a regard to morality, that Socrates used to frequent the one and Cicero the other. . . . On the contrary, cuckoldom is the basis of most of our modern plays. If an alderman appears upon the stage, you may be sure it is to be cuckolded. An husband that is a little grave or elderly generally meets with the same fate. Knights and baronets, country squires, and justices of the quorum, come up to town for no other purpose. I have seen poor Dogget cuckolded in all his capacities. In short our English writers are as frequently severe upon this innocent, unhappy creature commonly known by the name of a cuckold as the ancient comic writers were upon an eating parasite, or a vainglorious soldier.

" At the same time the poet so contrives matters that

* Addison says in a foot-note concerning the reformation of the age : "Impossible. No play will take, that is not adapted to the prevailing manners. But to flatter the age is not the way to reform it."

the two criminals are the favorites of the audience. We sit still, and wish well to them through the whole play, are pleased when they meet with proper opportunities, and are out of humor when they are disappointed. The truth of it is, the accomplished gentleman upon the English stage is the person that is familiar with other men's wives and indifferent to his own; as the fine woman is generally a composition of sprightliness and falsehood."

When Addison thus wailed over the degeneracy of the drama better times were coming; the curious mingling of wit, sparkle, and undisguised obscenity was giving way to a more sedate and classic style of composition, and morality was to be the gainer, even though one might often miss the *abandon* and unconventionality of the old-fashioned school. It would be like the transition from an unrestrained, free-and-easy country dance to the stately, dignified, and not always exciting minuet.

Dryden, one of the greatest offenders against good taste, was now dead, although his plays, poor stuff that some of them seem, in the light of modern standards, were still regarded with favor.

Congreve, whose epigrammatic wit and artificial yet none the less undeniable charm were often disgraced by the most unblushing ribaldry, had practically ceased to write for the stage, and evinced more anxiety to be regarded as a private gentleman than as a dramatist or *littérateur*. Possibly he regretted some of his broadness of expression, and foresaw that the eighteenth century, which had come in like a young rake, would go out as a very proper, punctilious old gentleman, primed with nice sentiments and abhorring vulgarity and bluntness. Whatever may have been his feelings on so delicate a subject we find him, some years later, rebuking the admiring Voltaire for having paid homage to him as an author. "Mr. Congreve," relates the great French skeptic, "had one defect, which was his entertaining too mean an idea of his own first profession, that of a writer, though it was to this he owed his fame and fortune. He spoke of his works as trifles that were beneath him, and hinted to me in our first conversation, that I should visit him upon no other footing than that of a gentleman who led a life of plainness and simplicity. I answered that had he been so unfortunate as to be a mere gentleman, I should never have come to see him ; and I was very much disgusted at so unseasonable a piece of vanity."

Voltaire's disgust did not interfere with his love of Congreve's work, for he pays the author of the *Double Dealer* a remarkable tribute in one of his "Letters Concerning the English Nation." He thinks that "Mr. Congreve raised the glory of comedy to a greater heighth than any English writer before or since his time. He wrote only a few plays, but they are excellent in their kind. The laws of the drama are strictly observed in them." It is added that all the characters are "shadowed with the utmost delicacy, and we *don't meet with so much as one low or coarse jest*," a curious criticism that is somewhat modified when we learn that "the language is everywhere that of men of fashion, but their actions are those of Knaves, a proof that he was perfectly well acquainted with human nature, and frequented what we call polite company."

And so we see Congreve cheerfully but goutily going down to his grave as a well-to-do gentleman might (not as a poor scribe, be it remembered), beloved by his distinguished friends and rejoicing in the affections of his very particular *chère amie*, Henrietta, Duchess of Marlborough. After he died the Duchess, to whom the great man had bequeathed the bulk of his fortune, put a marble tablet near his resting-place in Westminster Abbey, upon which she set forth, for the edification of posterity, "the happiness and honor she enjoyed in the sincere friendship of so worthy and honest a man, whose virtue, candor, and wit gained him the love and esteem of the present age, and whose writings will be the admiration of the future." When Sarah, the old Duchess of Marlborough, read the inscription she remarked with characteristic venom : " I know not what pleasure she might have had in his company, but I am sure it was no honor."

Congreve's plays are now as mouldy as that once plump, handsome body of his which lies in the great Abbey ; the student of the stage may know them, but the theatre-goer will never see them more. After all, it is only as he may have wished in those final days, as he approached the Great Beyond with a genteel air of patience and philosophy that so keenly stirred the admiration and sympathy of his associates. If in his inner consciousness he felt that the age was improving he never said so, for only a short time before his death he wrote :

> " Come see thy friend, retired without regret,
> Forgetting care, or striving to forget,
> In easy contemplation soothing time,
> With morals much, and now and then with rhyme.
> Not so robust in body as in mind,
> And always undejected, tho' declined ;
> Not wondering at the world's new wicked ways,
> Compared with those of our forefathers' days,
> For virtue now is neither more nor less,
> And vice is only varied in the dress.
> Believe it, men have ever been the same,
> And Ovid's Golden Age is but a dream." *

The long-since-forgotten plays of early eighteenth century celebrity would, for the most part, seem stupid enough and horridly archaic were they to be revived. Yet many of them delighted large audiences and inspired the finest efforts of players whose names will never be forgotten while there is interest in the history of the English stage. There was *The Provoked Wife* by Sir John Vanbrugh, a licentious comedy in which Betterton created, with great success, the role of *Sir John Brute*, and which was later to be revived by Garrick so that he might delight his admirers in the same character. It was a scandalous piece, yet it had so much genuine humor that Garrick ventured to add it

* *Epistle of Improving the Present Time.*

to his repertoire, with some of the original grossness left out, but as its heroine, *Lady Brute*, not content with being a wanton herself, actually connived at the ruin of her own niece, the oblivion that afterward overtook it is a matter for congratulation rather than regret.

Unlike the *Provoked Wife* and nearly all of its contemporaries, *The Inconstant* has survived to the present day, and was re-produced only a few seasons ago by Augustin Daly, with John Drew and Ada Rehan in the cast. Poor Farquhar, its author, wrote plays that had greater runs than the *Inconstant*, but they have been on the theatrical shelf many a long year. His first effort was suggestively styled *Love in a Bottle*, brought out when he was but twenty-one years old, and which was received with such favor that he soon produced the *Constant Couple*. Even in this era of lengthy runs a series of fifty-three performances in one season is not to be despised, while the fact that this was the record of the *Constant Couple* in 1700 was then something phenomenal, and clearly indicates the measure of its popularity. His remarkable list included the *Recruiting Officer* (wherein he depicted his own image as *Captain Plume* and mirrored several of his companions) and ended with perhaps the best of all, *The Beaux Stratagem*. The latter was written under peculiar conditions that contrasted in a pathetic way with the triumphant reception accorded it. The comedy was the product of six miserable weeks of worry and poverty, during which Farquhar lay dying of a lingering illness, wondering how the members of his family were to be fed, and seeing no happier prospect before them than starvation. These were the circumstances under which one of the most felicitous plays of the last century was conceived and developed, the author even then predicting that he would not live to see the end of its run.

From the very first Farquhar had encountered an unusually checquered experience. When a mere youth he took to the stage, where he chiefly distinguished himself by accidentally wounding a fellow-performer with his sword. He was a man of marked sensitiveness, and as a result of this unpleasant *contretemps* he gave up any ambition to shine in the profession. Wilks, however, advised him to write for the boards which he could no longer adorn by his presence, " and in return," says Dibdin, " Farquhar made his friend the hero of his pieces, which, however, he is said to have drawn as portraits of himself, having got a commission in the army, and being a young man greatly esteemed by the gay world ; young, volatile, and wild, but polished, sensible, and honorable." This " wild " but " sensible " young fellow always had before his eyes the awful spectre of poverty, and in his frantic effort to vanquish it so overreached himself that the phantom became a reality. He solemnly declared that he must marry a rich woman, and a lady who happened to be rich in nothing save her love for him, deceived this frank fortune-hunter into the belief that she was wealthy in money as well as affection. So Farquhar wed her, "without examining rent rolls or title deeds," and was much disappointed on finding that his wife's purse was no fuller than his own. He resigned his army commission, on the supposition that an influential nobleman would take care of him ; this anticipation, too, had no realization, and the dramatist, with that awful fear of a pauper's grave before his eyes, got poorer and poorer. His wife, to whom, to do him justice, he was sincerely attached, and his two little children were in actual want, for his dramatic work brought but few pounds into the household, and the misery of it all so preyed on his mind that he fell ill and died before he reached the age of thirty.

"Dear Bob," he wrote to Wilks just before his death, "I have not anything to leave thee, to perpetuate my memory but two helpless girls ; look upon them sometimes and think of him who was to the last moment of his life thine—G. Farquhar." Wilks did what he could for the unfortunate children, but their mother soon died, and the daughters of one of the greatest of English playwrights were allowed by an ungrateful public to eke out a precarious livelihood.

A writer who flourished after the manner of a green bay tree in Queen Anne's reign was Nicholas Rowe, over whose sentimental tragedies it became the fashion to weep profusely. One of them that enjoyed a great vogue was *Tamerlane*, in which the characters of King

William and Louis XIV. were depicted under the respective guises of *Tamerlane* and *Bajazet;* and others included the *Fair Penitent* and *Jane Shore.* Upon his trying comedy he met with dismal failure, which does not seem to have disconcerted him much, for when *The Biter* was brought out in 1705 Rowe sat in the front of the house and laughed, while all around him were hissing and hooting.

Of women dramatists there appears a curious array. Aphra Behn, who had varied her discreditable career by acting as a spy for the English Government, was no longer alive to invent filthy plays, but Mrs. Centlivre was writing, and so were Mrs. Pix, Mrs. Manley, and Mrs. Trotter (alias Cockburne). The last three, as Dibdin contemptuously observes, "made up a triumvirate of lady wits who enjoyed a great deal the admiration of the namby-pamby critics, and the indifference, and sometimes the ridicule of those whom heaven had vouchsafed to endow with taste and judgment." To dwell upon the effusions of these aspirants, or upon the more important work of several of their masculine colleagues, would take up two or three chapters, and so we will dismiss the plays of the period by mentioning one which, though no longer acted, is still remembered because it happens to be from the polished pen of Addison. *Cato* was the name of the tragedy, and it has been aptly described as "a compound of transcendant beauties and absurdities." It had its day of prosperity upon the stage ; indeed, it supplied the model for many a later example of less scholarly writers, and now it enjoys the somewhat dubious honor of being bound as part of Addison's Works—and frequently skipped in the reading thereof. Viewed from the present standpoint it seems prosy and lacking in situation, but Mr. Addison's contemporaries thought otherwise and quickly put upon his drama the mark of emphatic approval.

Steele, who had dedicated his *Tender Husband* to his *collaborateur* on the *Spectator*, addressed some "verses to the Author of the Tragedy of *Cato*," to the effect that

> " While you the fierce divided Britons awe,
> And *Cato* with an equal virtue draw.
> While envy is itself in wonder lost,
> And factions strive who shall applaud you most ;
> Forgive the fond ambition of a friend,
> Who hopes himself, not you, to recommend,
> And join th' applause which all the learn'd bestow
> On one, to whom a perfect work they owe.
> To my light scenes I once inscrib'd your name,
> And impotently strove to borrow fame :
> Soon will that die, which adds thy name to mine ;
> Let me, then, live, join'd to a work of thine."

Pope wrote a prologue for *Cato* and took care to get in a good word for home drama, as opposed to French adaptations and the Italian opera, fast becoming quite the rage. He concludes by calling upon Britons to approve the play, and pointed out that

> " With honest scorn the first-fam'd Cato viewed
> Rome learning arts from Greece, whom she subdued :
> Our scene precariously subsists too long
> On French translation and Italian song :
> Dare to have sense yourselves ; assert the stage,
> Be justly warm'd with your own native rage.
> Such plays alone should please a British ear,
> As Cato's self had not disdained to hear."

The mention of these productions recalls the fact that one of the homes of the drama at this time was the Theatre Royal, Drury Lane, which was managed by Christopher Rich, a lawyer, from 1690 to 1710, and subsequently by Collier, Wilks, Dogget, and Cibber. In the year 1712 Dogget retired from the partnership, and Barton Booth took his place, while two years later we find Steele becoming its proprietor by virtue of a life-patent granted to him. Henri Misson, the observant French traveller who visited England about the end of the seventeenth century, naturally attended performances at Drury Lane, and in his memoirs gives a graphic idea of the interior of the house.* "The pit is an amphitheatre fill'd with benches without back boards, and adorn'd and cover'd with green cloth. Men of quality, particularly the younger sort, some ladies of reputation and vertue, and abundance of damsels that hunt for prey, sit all together in this place, higgledy-piggledy; chatter, toy, play, hear, hear not. Farther up, against the wall, under the first gallery, and just opposite to the stage, rises another amphitheatre, which is taken up by persons of the best quality, among whom are generally very few men. The galleries, whereof there are only two rows, are fill'd with none but ordinary people, particularly the upper one."

The Dorset Gardens Theatre, in Salisbury Court, originally occupied by the defunct Duke of York's

* These *Memoirs* were translated into English in 1719.

Company, now seemed in a languishing condition. From being a temple for the muses of Tragedy and Comedy it gradually sank to the meanest uses until it was razed to the ground, in 1709. The house in Lincoln's Inn Fields had a fair amount of prosperity during its occupancy by Betterton and his company, who had revolted from the management of Rich, at Drury Lane, but for some time previous to Anne's death it remained untenanted.

London had at least one theatre too many, but a company was formed, notwithstanding, to build a new one in the Haymarket, where that novel and popular form of entertainment, Italian opera, might be presented. "Of this theatre," says Cibber, "I saw the first stone laid, on which was inscribed *The Little Whig*, in honor to a lady of extraordinary beauty,* then the celebrated toast and pride of that party." The house was opened with a great flourish of trumpets on an Easter Monday, 1705, with a performance of *The Triumph of Love,* otherwise "a translated opera, to Italian musick." Sir John Vanbrugh and Congreve, who directed the enterprise, hardly met with the expected success, although they were joined by Betterton and his associates, who came over from Lincoln's Inn Fields. But as Cibber has pointed out, the company was no longer what it had been. "Several of them, excellent in their different talents, were now dead, as Smith, Kynaston, Sandford, and Leigh, Mrs.

* Lady Sunderland, a daughter of the Duke of Marlborough.

Betterton and Underhill being, at this time, superannu-
ated pensioners, whose places were generally but ill supplied.   Nor could it be expected that Betterton himself,
at past seventy, could retain his former force and spirit,
though he was yet far distant from any competitor.
Thus, then, were these remains of the best set of actors
that I believe were ever known, at once in England, by
time, death, and the satiety of their hearers, mould-
'ring to decay."

Like equally sanguine managers of later years Congreve and Sir John gave up their new venture as soon
as they conveniently could, and one Owen Swiney, engaged to watch over the destinies of the theatre whose

> " Majestic columns stand where dung hills lay,
> And cars triumphal rise from carts of hay."

GENTLEMAN SMITH.

AS "PLUME" IN "THE RECRUITING OFFICER."   FROM A DRAWING BY ISAAC TAYLOR.

CHAPTER VI

CIBBER AND HIS "APOLOGY."

ONE of the most interesting figures of the eighteenth century stage, a man whose career makes
a bridge between the halcyon days of Betterton, Kynaston, and Barry and those of the incomparable Garrick
(whom he contemptuously called "the prettiest little
creature") now claims attention. This is none other
than Colley Cibber, whose want of genius was atoned
for by an "infinite variety" which enabled him to become actor, manager, dramatist, man about town and,
by some inscrutable dispensation of Providence and
royal favor, Poet Laureate of the English nation. As
an actor he was a success in characters of the light
foppish variety, yet he convulsed his friends, in a way
not intended, by his penchant for tragedy ; as a manager, he showed great administrative capacity, while he
could be overbearing and unpleasant ; as a dramatist
he wrote some popular, sprightly comedies, and as a
poet he seems to have been "one of the worst on record." "Colley Cibber, Sir," pompously said Dr. Johnson to the admiring Boswell, "was by no means a
blockhead ; but by arrogating to himself too much, he

was in danger of losing that degree of estimation to
which he was entitled."

The weighty Doctor, with all his prejudices and arrogance, had an elephantine way of hitting the bull's
eye of truth about men and things, and he never gauged
a nature better than he did in this instance. When,
however, he called Cibber a "Poor creature," he shot
wide of the mark, for while the volatile Colley had a
thousand faults he accomplished too much to deserve
so mean a description. Yet it would have been expect-
ing the impossible to ask that the man who insolently
referred to Garrick, even before his face, as "Punch,"
and who looked upon players as little more or less than
disreputable puppets, should find any great compliment
for a butterfly like the Laureate. Butterflies have their
uses, the one in this case writing an autobiography that
is now a theatrical classic, but Johnson could find no
health in them, particularly if their wings were singed
by the footlights.

Whatever was artistic in the temperament of this au-
thor-actor must have been inherited from his father,
Caius Gabriel Cibber, a native of Holstein who emi-
grated to England prior to the Restoration and afterwards acquired considerable fame as a sculptor. His
figures are now forgotten, but the dandified form of his
son seems a reality even yet ; we can picture him flit-
ting about among the coxcombs of his time ; then rushing to the theatre to play some character dear to his
heart, or hurrying home to compose a wretched ode

over which his friends were to laugh, and perhaps have for a sharer in their merriment the complaisant Colley himself.

In 1682, when little more than ten years old, the young Cibber was sent to a school in Lincolnshire, where his life seems to have been neither more brilliant nor less lazy than that of the average boy. "Even there," he remembers, "I was the same inconsistent creature I have been ever since! always in full spirits, in some small capacity to do right, but in a more frequent alacrity to do wrong ; and consequently often under a worse character than I wholly deserved." He writes an ode, later on, and gets the ill-will of his fellow-students for his pains, not so much because the poetry was bad, (although to judge by his subsequent efforts in this direction it must have been a curiosity,) as on account, very possibly, of his characteristic vanity at having perpetrated it.

Next the father tries to get his son admitted to Winchester College, but the fact that the lad is descended, on his mother's side, from the founder of the institution, William of Wickham, is not sufficient for the purpose, and so we shortly find Colley taking up arms in the interests of William of Orange, among the troops collected by his father's patron, the Earl of Devonshire, to accomplish the ruin of the obstinate James II. The peaceful establishment of King William on the English throne put a stop to any budding desire on the youth's part to become a great warrior, and now his tastes begin to incline toward the stage. He goes up to London, ostensibly to await an appointment in the Secretary of State's office, but the delay in the arrival of the preferment is as balm to his soul, or, to use his own quaint explanation : " The distant hope of a reversion was too cold a temptation for a spirit impatient as mine, that wanted immediate possession of what my heart was so differently set upon. The allurements of a theatre are still so_strong in my memory that perhaps few, except those who have felt them, can conceive : And I am yet so far willing to excuse my folly that I am convinc'd, were it possible to take off that disgrace and prejudice which custom has thrown upon the profession of an actor, many a well-born younger brother and beauty of low fortune would gladly have adorn'd the theatre, who by their not being able to brook such dishonor to their birth, have pass'd away their lives decently unheeded and forgotten."

All thoughts of settling down to a Government clerkship were finally thrown to the winds, and in 1690 the aspiring young fellow became an humble actor, strictly on probation, in the united company formed by Betterton, Mountford, Kynaston, Barry, Bracegirdle, and their associates. He was to receive no pay until that fortunate incident, already narrated, should bring him to the attention of Betterton, but he looked upon the privilege of witnessing gratis all the performances at the theatre as a sufficient reward for his modest services. Before the first year's stay had ended Colley was receiving the princely salary of ten shillings a week, and he considered himself the happiest of mortals.

To be sure, he burned with an ardent ambition to play the lovers to the heroines of the chaste Bracegirdle, but he was soon snubbed out of any such wild hopes. An inexperienced, unattractive looking actor with an insufficient voice, a " meagre person (tho' then not ill made) with a dismal pale complexion " was not a fit companion for one of the most charming of her sex. But there was no such word as discouragement in the egotistical lexicon of this curious "poor creature." Soon he is playing the *Chaplain* in *The Orphan* of Otway, and winning the honest praise of Goodman, now retired from the stage, who says with more vigor than elegance, " If he does not make a good actor I 'll be d——d." Then he gets married, on twenty pounds a year from his father and twenty shillings a week from the theatre ; looks upon his wife and himself as " the happiest young couple that ever took a leap in the dark," and completes this vision of bliss by wooing the poetic muse after that unblushingly absurd way of his.

Once the illness of a superior serves him a good turn. The *Double Dealer* is to be played before Queen Mary, and Mr. Congreve, its author, finding that Kynaston is too sick to take the part of *Lord Touchwood*, and much disturbed by the discovery, at last asks Cibber to try the character. The substitute is delighted, he plays with confidence and success, her Most Gracious Majesty is present and listens to the dulcet voice of Mrs. Barry reciting a prologue proclaiming that

> " .   .   .   never were in Rome nor Athens seen,
> So fair a Circle, or so bright a Queen,"

and after the performance the grateful Congreve thanks Cibber warmly for his impersonation and induces the management to increase the new *Touchwood's* wages by five shillings. This, Cibber very frankly admits, only served to heighten his own vanity, but could not recommend him to any new trials of his capacity. " Not a step farther could I get, 'till the company was again divided ; when the desertion of the best actors left a clear stage, for younger champions to mount, and show their best pretensions to favor."

The rupture to which Cibber alludes occurred in 1695, when Rich, the manager of Drury Lane, attempted to reduce the salary of his players, and ordered several of Betterton and Mrs. Barry's favorite parts to be given to Powell and Mrs. Bracegirdle respectively. The secession of Betterton and his sympathizers left the old company in a much weakened condition, and Mr. Rich was glad to keep Colley at the Theatre Royal at a salary now fixed at thirty shillings a week. In the meanwhile, the new theatre of the deserters, in Lincoln's Inn Fields, opens with a great flourish ; the town crowds to see Betterton, as of old, but neglects Drury Lane, as well it might, and Cibber mourns at the decadence of the once favorite house. It is an ill wind that blows him good, however, even though he feels like shutting his eyes when his colleagues slaughter Shakespeare or otherwise provoke uncomplimentary comparisons with the work of their rivals.

On a certain Saturday morning the players at the old house got information that *Hamlet* was to be revived at Lincoln's Inn Fields on the following Tuesday, for the first time at the new establishment. In order to steal a march upon the enemy it was determined to present *Hamlet* at Drury Lane on Monday, one day ahead of the other people, and this piece of enterprise was received with unnecessary consternation by the latter, considering that they had among them the greatest *Hamlet* of the age. As Cibber very shrewdly observes, they paid too much regard to the matter, "for they shortened their first orders, and resolv'd that *Hamlet* should to *Hamlet* be opposed, on the same day; whereas had they given notice in their bills, that the same play would have been acted by them the day after, the town would have been in no doubt, which house they should have reserved themselves for; ours must certainly have been empty and theirs, with more honor, been crowded." But managers, ancient or modern, with all their nerve, find it hard to play this sort of an "off"-game; and so *Hamlet* was irrevocably fixed upon for Monday, at the new house. The announcement fell like a bomb into the camp of the Rich forces and in this predicament Powell, who was vain enough to look upon himself as the rival, even the equal, of Betterton, suggested that the company should drop Shakespeare for Monday, and replace him with the *Old Batchelor*. With magnificent audacity he promised to play the title part, one of Betterton's famous characters, and to mimic the veteran therein. This scheme meeting with great approval—"as whatever can be supposed to ridicule merit, generally gives joy to those that want it "—the bills were changed, and it was given out that the part of the *Old Batchelor* would be performed " in Imitation of the Original."

Powell and his companions were so busy in thinking about their individual impersonations that it was not until the last moment that they rectified a strange oversight. The part of *Alderman Fondlewife* in which the natural Dogget (who had gone over to the enemy at Lincoln's Inn Fields and who was later to be associated with Cibber as manager) formerly created so delightful an impression, was unassigned, and nobody had courage enough to invite odious comparisons by playing it. Nobody? No, that were too sweeping a term, when Cibber was in the company, and so he gladly volunteered to take up what no one else dared to touch. "If the fool has a mind to blow himself up, at once," politely exclaimed Powell, "let us ev'n give him a clear stage for it."

The young man *was* given a clear stage, in a way that was hardly intended, for to judge from his own narrative he proved quite as strong an attraction as the over-bearing Powell, whose mimicking of Betterton possessed only a passing interest and diminished rather than increased the artistic reputation of the imitator. Colley had but a few hours in which to study the part, but as he had often witnessed Dogget's performance of it, possibly with the view of trying it himself at some future date, he had no trouble in committing the lines to memory. This was but half the battle, however, and it is clear that the youthful aspirant, who knew full well that the audience would care nothing for an original interpretation of his own, diplomatically determined to closely imitate the redoubtable Dogget. But let us tell the result in his own words, wherein seeming modesty and natural vanity find such funny combination.

" At my first appearance, one might have imagined, by the various murmurs of the audience, that they were in doubt whether Dogget himself were not return'd, or that they could not conceive what strange face it could be, that so nearly resembled him ; for I had laid the tint of forty years, more than my real age, upon my features, and, to the most minute placing of an hair, was dressed exactly like him. When I spoke, the surprise was still greater, as if I had not only borrowed his cloaths, but, his voice too. But tho' that was the least difficult part of him, to be imitated, they seem'd to allow I had so much of him, in every other requisite, that my applause was, perhaps, more than proportionable : for, whether I had done so much, where so little was expected, or that the generosity of my hearers were more than usually zealous, upon so unexpected an occasion or from whatever motive, such favor might be pour'd upon me I cannot say; but, in plain and honest truth, upon my going off from the first scene, a much better actor might have been proud of the applause that followed me; after one loud plaudit was ended, and sunk into a general whisper, that seem'd still to continue their private approbation, it reviv'd to a second, and again to a third, still louder than the former. If, to all this, I add that Dogget himself was in the pit, at the same time, it would be too rank affectation, if I should not confess, that, to see him there a witness to my reception, was, to me, as consummate a triumph as the heart of vanity could be indulg'd with. But whatever vanity I might set upon myself, from this unexpected success, I found that was no rule to other people's judgment of me. There were few or no parts, of the same kind, to be had; nor could they conceive from what I had done in this, what other sort of character I could be fit for. If I solicited for anything of a different nature, I was answered, *that was not in my way.* And what was in my way, it seems, was not, as yet, resolv'd upon. And though I reply'd, *that I thought anything, naturally written, ought to be in everyone's way that pretended to be an actor,* this was looked upon as a vain, impracticable conceit of my own. Yet it is a conceit, that, in forty years farther experience, I have not yet given up; I still think that a painter who can draw but one sort of objects, or an actor that shines but in one light, can neither of them boast of that ample genius which is necessary to form a thorough mastery of his art."

These were wise sentiments, but the new *Fondlewife* could not get his superiors at the theatre to believe either in them or in him. Nothing daunted, he turned playwright, wrote *Love's Last Shift*, which was acted with success in 1695, and essayed the part of *Sir Novelty*, a fop of the type then fashionable. Southern, the author of the once popular drama of *Oroonoko*, was pleased to commend Cibber's work, but, with the common distrust as to his powers as an actor, took the precaution to say to him : " Young man, I pronounce thy play a good one ; I will answer for its success, if thou does not spoil it by thy own action."

But the complaisant Colley records that he made such a good impression, both as actor and author "that the people seem'd at a loss which they should give the preference to." Some good-natured persons were kind enough to hint that he had never written the comedy, and Mr. Congreve, than whom there was no greater authority on such matters, said that it contained many things that were like wit, but, "in reality were not wit " *; while on the other hand, the Lord Chamberlain sagely gave out that it was the best first play that any author in his memory had produced. And so, between praise and censure, Cibber was getting himself

* Curiously enough, this criticism has been applied to Oscar Wilde's bright but frothy comedies.

talked about ; whereat his heart must have waxed exceeding joyful, even though his fellow actors still elbowed him out of "fat" parts. When Sir John Vanbrugh actually composed a play * as a sequel to *Love's Last Shift*, and cast Colley for the leading character, *Baron Foppington*, a sort of ennobled successor to the gay *Sir Novelty*, the actor "began, with others, to have a better opinion of himself."

Cibber was now developing into an experienced playwright, a profession wherein he was to meet with several dismal failures and as many brilliant successes. He was not always paid his salary of thirty shillings a week, and he says apologetically, "I think I may very well be excused in my presuming to write plays, which I was forced to do, for the support of my increasing family, my precarious income as an actor being then too scant to supply it with even the necessaries of life. It may be observable too, that my muse and my spouse were equally prolific ; that the one was seldom the mother of a child but in the same year the other made me the father of a play." One of the dramatic children of this father has come down to us in his still used adaptation of *Richard III.*

These were trying days for the buoyant Colley, but like a cork, every time he was shoved under water, he came bobbing up only the more serenely ; when greater men sank, never to rise again, he kept swimming on, for with all his frivolity and aping of the fashionable,

**The Relapse.*

he had before him continually one inspiring idea. He must succeed ; whether as dramatist, comedian, or poet, he perhaps cared not, but the name of Cibber was to be famous, if its bearer could exert any influence on the public mind. Everything conspired, apparently, to crush the young man ; he was ridiculed, gossiped about, and maligned, and his very energy at the theatre only set the actors against him. Of his manager, Rich, he had no very exalted idea. "Our good master," he dryly says, "was as sly a tyrant as ever was at the head of a theatre ; for he gave the actors more liberty, and fewer days' pay than any of his predecessors. He would laugh with them over a bottle, and bite them, in their bargains. He kept them poor that they might not be able to rebel ; and sometimes merry that they might not think of it." If the author of the *Apology* is to be relied upon, Mr. Rich had at least one quality very suggestive of certain modern managers who are nothing more or less than shrewd business men. He "had no conception himself of theatrical merit, either in authors or actors, [it is evident that he had snubbed Colley in both capacities,] yet his judgment was governed by a saving rule in both : he look'd into his receipts for the value of a play, and from common fame he judg'd of his actors." A convincing proof, if one were needed, that the manager who looks at theatrical art from a purely commercial basis is not of recent growth.

Until philanthropists with well-lined pocket-books

undertake the conduct of a theatre no one can wonder at the eye to windward which the less wealthy lessee keeps on his exchequer, and it is agreeable to know that while he may resemble the prudent Rich in this respect he does not, as a rule, imitate the latter in cheating the players out of their hard-earned wages.

As Cibber struggles cheerfully on, the Theatre Royal Company steadily gains ground, and begins to take precedence over the rival organization. " Betterton's people (however good in their kind) were most of them too far advanc'd in years to mend ; and tho' we, in Drury Lane, were too young to be excellent, we were not too old to be better. But what will not satiety depreciate. For though I must own, and avow, that in our highest prosperity, I always thought we were greatly their inferiors, yet by our good fortune of being seen in quite new lights, which several new-written plays had shewn us in, we now began to make a considerable stand against them." Who can doubt it, when in addition to Wilks and other favorites the charming Mistress Anne Oldfield, of whom anon, was now a member of the Drury Lane forces.

As time goes on, the new Queen's Theatre in the Haymarket is erected and opened, and the forces from Lincoln's Inn Fields take up their quarters there ; then Owen Swiney becomes Sir John Vanbrugh's successor in the management by promising to pay five pounds rental for "every acting day." Swiney was a great friend of his presumable rival, Mr. Rich, and there seems at first to have been a secret understanding between them by which the two houses were to be run under the same interest. Be that as it may, Wilks, Estcourt, Mrs. Oldfield, and other players soon deserted Drury Lane, to act at the new house, and before long, after a disagreement between Rich and Swiney that must have delighted Cibber, since he was the cause of it, the latter joined the seceders.

His triumph was fast approaching. The players at the Haymarket appear with varying success ; the patentee of Drury Lane tries his luck with singers and dancers ; then his house is closed, and finally, sometime after it had been reopened with William Collier, M. P., as manager, we find the players reunited at the Theatre Royal, and Messrs. Collier, Cibber, Wilks, and Dogget in command. The three last-named actors were the real managers and formed the celebrated " triumvirate," under which the theatre enjoyed such unusual prosperity.

Dogget, " who was naturally an œconomist," writes Cibber, " kept our expenses and account to the best of his power, within regulated bounds and moderation. Wilks, who had a stronger passion for glory than lucre, was a little apt to be lavish, in what was not always as necessary for the profit as the honor of the theatre. For example, at the beginning of almost every season, he would order two or three suits to be made, or refresh'd, for actors of moderate consequence, that his having constantly a new one for himself might seem less particular, tho' he had, as yet, no new part for it. This expeditious care of doing us good, without waiting for our consent to it, Dogget always looked upon with the eye of a man in pain. But I, who hated pain (tho' I as little liked the favor as Dogget himself), rather chose to laugh at the circumstance, than complain of what I knew was not to be cured but by a remedy worse than the evil. Upon these occasions, therefore, whenever I saw him and his followers so prettily dress'd out for an old play, I only commended his fancy; or at most but whisper'd him not to give himself so much trouble about others, upon whose performance it would be thrown away ; to which, with a smiling air of triumph over my want of penetration, he has replied : ' Why, now, that was what I really did it for ! to shew others that I love to take care of them, as well as of myself.' "

Cibber confesses that of the two fellow-managers he was rather inclined to Dogget's way of thinking, but he was too tactful to let Wilks know this, and reading between the lines of his autobiography we can easily see how often his worldly-wise suggestions and concessions must have warded off conflicts between the lessee of artistic taste and the one who had a more prosaic and business-like view of his profession. While Wilks kept dreaming of gorgeous costumes and accessories, Dogget was seeing to the payment of bills and putting the house on a financial basis unheard of in those days when the very name of actor conjured up a disordered vision of unsatisfied accounts, impecuniosity and bailiffs.

"In the twenty years while we were our own directors," Cibber goes on to say, with pardonable complacency, "we never had a creditor that had occasion to come twice for his bill; every *Monday* morning discharged us of all demands, before we took a shilling for our own use. And from this time, we neither asked any actor, nor were desired by them, to sign any written agreement (to the best of my memory) whatsoever. The rate of their respective salaries were only enter'd in our daily pay-roll; which plain record every one look'd upon as good as City-Security."

The early history of the Triumvirate must have been a sort of honeymoon, when everybody was in good humor. The managers settled their weekly acounts with a satisfaction not always to be derived from such a process, the actors congratulated themselves on the novel sensation of being well-paid and well-fed, and the audience found nearly everything that the latter did a source of delight. But life in a theatre is much as it is on the large stage of the world, and there were clouds as well as sunshine. Sometimes the clouds were formed by the most petty causes, as in the storm stirred up by the arrival of two performers from Ireland. They were two un-celebrated actors from the Dublin Theatre, and as Wilks had been so kindly received on his visit to the Emerald Isle he determined to do what he could, in turn, for the indigent new-

comers. He introduced them to the stage of Drury
Lane, and by the way in which he took them under his
theatrical mantle gave great offence to the exacting
Dogget.

" While Wilks was only animated by a grateful hos-
pitality to his friends, Dogget was ruffl'd in a storm,
and looked upon this generosity as so much insult and
injustice upon himself, and the fraternity. During
this disorder I stood by, a seeming quiet passenger,
and, since talking to the winds, I knew, could be to no
great purpose (whatever weakness it might be call'd)
could not help smiling to observe with what officious
ease and delight Wilks was treating his friends at our
expense who were scarce acquainted with them. For
it seems, all this was to end in their having a benefit-play, in the height of the season, for the unprofit-
able service they had done us, without our consent,
or desire to employ them. Upon this Dogget bounc'd
and grew almost as untractable as Wilks himself.

" Here, again, I was forc'd to clap my patience to
the helm, to weather this difficult point between them.
Applying myself therefore to the person I imagin'd
was most likely to hear me, I desired Dogget to consider, that I must naturally be as much hurt by this
vain and over-bearing behaviour in Wilks as he could
be, and that tho' it was true these actors had no pretence to the favor design'd ; yet we could not say they
had done us any further harm, than letting the Town
see, the parts they had been shown in, had been better

done by those to whom they properly belonged." Thus the diplomatic Colley went on arguing, and as a result of his efforts to keep the peace in the theatrical family the benefit took place, but in his endeavor to make everything run along smoothly he went too far and by himself supplying a deficiency of ten pounds in the expected receipts put Wilks in an unreasonable rage. The irate actor vowed he would leave the management and go to Ireland, and that if he were gone Dogget and Cibber would not be able to keep the doors open a week, and that " by ——, he would not be a drudge for nothing."

" As I knew all this was but the foam of the high value he set upon himself, I thought it not amiss to seem a little silently concerned, for the helpless condition to which his resentment of the injury I have related was going to reduce us: for I knew I had a friend in his heart, that, if I gave him a little time to cool would soon bring him to reason : the sweet morsel of a thousand pounds a year was not to be met with at every table, and might tempt a nicer palate than his own to swallow it, when he was not out of humor." The morsel was so tempting, indeed, that Wilks soon got in the best of humor, but never offered to reimburse his companion for that much-objected-to ten pounds.

To detail the incidents and vicissitudes of the Triumvirate would be to fill a book ; they must be left within the borders of the fascinating *Apology*, nor is there need to go into an account of how Barton Booth, then a rising genius of the stage, was admitted to a share in the management, to the disgust of Dogget, who retired; or how, a year or two later, Sir Richard Steele was associated with the re-organized trio of Cibber, Wilks, and Booth.   Poor obstinate Dogget, he took life hard to the last.   He sued his old partners for money alleged to be due him as his share in the profits of the theatre, and got a verdict of six hundred pounds, with interest, but when his lawyers' bills were paid he "scarce got one year's purchase," chronicles Cibber, "of what we had offered him without law, which (as he surviv'd but seven years after it) would have been an annuity of five hundred pounds, and a *sine cure* for life."   When he went to the famous Button's coffee-house, where such men as Addison, Steele, and Pope were wont to meet and discuss the affairs of mankind, he had the mortification of finding the hated Wilks there, not to speak of the now detested Colley.   "For as Wilks and he were differently proud; the one rejoicing in a captious, over-bearing valiant pride; and the other in a stiff sullen purse-pride, it may be easily conceived, when two such tempers met, how agreeable the sight of one was to the other."

But Cibber was to succeed in thawing out the icy reserve with which his former partner now surrounded himself, and he did it, as might be expected, in a canny fashion.   One of the coffee-house wags, seizing the humor of the situation, wrote him declaring that Dogget had passed away to another world, where there were neither lawsuits nor unreasonable managers. Colley was too old a bird to be deceived by the trick, but seeing that he might himself make capital out of it, answered the letter as though he believed the sad news, and took occasion to deliver a fervent eulogy on the character of the supposed dead man.

Dogget was only human, and when he was shown what his former friend had so kindly written about him, his heart softened.   But let the diplomatist himself tell us the result :

"One day sitting over-against him, at the same coffee-house, where we often mixt at the same table, tho' we never exchanged a single syllable, he graciously extended his hand, for a pinch of my snuff. As this seem'd from him, a sort of breaking the ice of his temper, I took courage upon it, to break silence on my side, and ask'd him how he lik'd it. To which, with a slow hesitation, naturally assisted by the action of his taking the snuff, he reply'd—*Umh !   the best—Umh— I have tasted a great while.*"   And, after "a few days of these coy lady-like compliances on his side, he grew into a more conversable temper."

For all his managerial prosperity, his success as a playwright and his popularity as a comedian, departments wherein he was in his legitimate sphere, Colley Cibber probably cared less than for his appointment, in 1730, to the Poet Laureateship.   Yet among men with literary pretensions he was the least deserving of the laurel, for as has been well said, in the whole twenty-seven years that he boasted of the honor (he died in 1757) he never wrote a really good poem. He made it a point to laugh publicly at his own effusions, but he must have had a belief, in that curious old heart of his, that they were by no means as poor as some jealous fellow-poets would make out.

" His friends gave out," Dr. Johnson tells Boswell, " that he *intended* his birthday Odes should be bad ; but that was not the case, Sir ; for he kept them many months by him, and a few years before he died he showed me one of them with great solicitude to render it as perfect as might be, and I made some corrections to which he was not very willing to submit. I remember the following couplet in allusion to the King * and himself :

> ' Perch'd on the eagle's soaring wing,
> The lowly linnet loves to sing.'

" Sir, he had heard something of the fabulous tale of the wren sitting upon the eagle's wing, and he had applied it to a linnet."

But the Poet Laureate probably still considered himself a linnet, despite the objections of the ponderous philosopher, and went on singing as badly and happily as ever until death put an end to his career. He had gone through many experiences, some of them passing bitter (had not Pope ungenerously made him the hero

* George II.

of his *Dunciad?*) but he would write verses to the end.
They are long since forgotten, but that entrancing
Apology with its delightful pictures of his theatrical
contemporaries, is as fresh as ever. It will be read
when greater poets than he have sunk into oblivion,
and thus perpetuate the name of one of the most remarkable characters of a by-gone epoch.

9

CHAPTER VII.

NEW MASKS AND FACES.

> " ' Odious ! in woollen ! 't would a saint provoke,'
> (Were the last words that poor Narcissa spoke ;)
> ' No, let a charming chintz and Brussels lace
> Wrap my cold limbs and shade my lifeless face :
> One would not, sure, be frightful when one's dead,
> And Betty—give this cheek a little red.' "

THUS wrote the classic Pope in an imaginary description of the last moments of that most ravishing and graceful comedienne of her day, Mistress Anne Oldfield, whose greatness consisted in a thousand and one dainty attractions which still live in the writings of her contemporaries. That she is preserved to us even in this shadowy form is cause for gratitude, for until the indefatigable Edison shall have improved his kinetoscope, so that the achievements of a player, either in gesture, voice, or look, may be stereotyped for all time, the lover of the drama can only familiarize himself with dead-and-gone heroes and heroines of the stage by reading the testimony of their admirers.

If such testimony is to count for anything, " Nance " Oldfield was one of the most *naïve* and fascinating women who ever trod the boards of an English theatre.

And yet, strange to say, this daughter of Comedy, who was to win such unforgettable distinction in impersonating ladies of quality, was apprenticed in early life to a seamstress, and had for her humble relative a Mrs. Voss, hostess of the Mitre Tavern, in St. James Market, London. Nance, as a young girl, made her headquarters at this public house, and it was here that the dashing Farquhar accidently heard her reading a play as she stood behind the bar. He was so much impressed "with the proper emphasis and agreeable turn that she gave to each character, that he swore the girl was cut out for the stage." As the child had a wild desire to become an actress, her mother, " the next time she saw Captain Vanbrugh (afterward Sir John) who had a great respect for the family, acquainted him with Captain Farquhar's opinion, on which he desired to know whether her heart was most tragedy or comedy. Miss being called in, informed him that her principal inclination was to the latter, having at that time gone through all Beaumont and Fletcher's comedies ; and the play she was reading when Captain Farquhar had dined there having been *The Scornful Lady*."

As a result of this confession of youthful ambition Captain Vanbrugh soon introduced Nance to the patentee of Drury Lane, Mr. Rich, who took her into his house at the sumptuous salary of fifteen shillings a a week. " However, her agreeable figure and sweetness of voice soon gave her the preference in the opinion of the whole town, to all the young actresses of that time, and the Duke of Bedford, in particular, being pleased to speak to Mr. Rich in her favor, he instantly raised her to twenty shillings per week. After which her fame and salary gradually increased, till at length they both obtained that height which her merit entitled her to."

When perhaps not more than sixteen years old, in 1700, the young aspirant drew attention to herself by playing *Alinda* in *The Pilgrim*, a re-arrangement by Vanbrugh of one of Beaumont and Fletcher's plays, but she had still several seasons to wait before she should burst upon the town in all her glory by impersonating the charming *Lady Betty Modish* in Cibber's comedy of *The Careless Husband*. But let Cibber himself tell us the story of her beginning and ultimate success.

"In the year 1699," he relates, "Mrs. Oldfield was first taken into the house, where she remained about a twelvemonth almost a mute, and unheeded, till Sir John Vanbrugh, who first recommended her, gave her the part of *Alinda* in *The Pilgrim*, revised. This gentle character, happily, became that want of confidence which is inseparable from young beginners, who, without it, seldom arrive at any excellence: Notwithstanding, I own I was then so far deceived in my opinion of her that I thought she had little more than her person, that appear'd necessary to the forming of a good actress : for she set out with so extraordinary diffidence, that it kept her too despondingly down, to a formal, plain (not to say) flat manner of speaking. Nor could the silver tone of her voice, 'till after some time, incline my ear to any hope in her favor. But public approbation is the warm weather of a theatrical plant, which will soon bring it forward to whatever perfection nature has design'd it. However Mrs. Oldfield (perhaps for want of fresh parts) seem'd to come but slowly forward, 'till the year 1703.

"Our company, that summer, acted at Bath during the residence of Queen Anne at that place. At that time it happen'd that Mrs. Verbruggen, by reason of her last sickness (of which she some few months after dy'd) was left in London; and though most of her parts were, of course, to be dispos'd of, yet so earnest was the female scramble for them, that only one of them fell to the share of Mrs. Oldfield, that of *Leonora* in *Sir Courtly Nice;* a character of good plain sense, but not over elegantly written. It was in this part that Mrs. Oldfield surprised me into an opinion of her having all the innate powers of a good actress, though they were yet but in the bloom of what they promised. Before she had acted this part I had so cold an expectation of her abilities, that she could scarce prevail with me to rehearse with her the scenes she was chiefly concerned in, with *Sir Courtly*, which I then acted. However, we ran them over, with mutual inadvertency, of one another. I seem'd careless, as concluding that any assistance I could give her would be to little or no purpose; and she mutter'd out her words in a sort of misty manner, at my low opinion of her. But when the play came to be acted, she had a just occasion to triumph over the errors of my judgment, by the (almost) amazement that her unexpected performance awak'd me to ; so forward and so sudden a step into nature I had never seen ; and what made her performance more valuable, that I knew it all proceeded from her understanding, untaught and unassisted by any more experienced actor."

It is curious that in the early part of her career Mrs. Oldfield suffered from the same fate that beset the incredulous Cibber—several competent judges refused to believe in those remarkable powers which later were to set all London agog, especially when she should appear in parts of the genteel comedy type. Even in 1712-13 Swift contemptuously writes to his beloved Stella : "I was this morning at ten at the rehearsal of Mr. Addison's play called *Cato*, which is to be acted on Friday. There was not above half a score of us to see it. We stood on the stage, and it was foolish enough to see the actors prompted every moment, and the poet directing them ; *and the drab that acts Cato's daughter* out in the midst of a passionate part, and then calling out ' What 's next ? ' "

But the " drab " that acted *Cato's* daughter had become as famous as ever was that bitter, bishopric-hunting Dean. Once that Cibber became converted to her praises he was quick to utilize her shining talents to his own advantage. Her success as *Leonora* decided him in the belief that she would soon be the " foremost ornament of our theatre," and he adds :

" Upon this unexpected sally, then, of the power and disposition of so unforeseen an actress, it was that I again took up the two first acts of the *Careless Husband*, which I had written the summer before, and had thrown aside in despair of having justice done to the character of *Lady Betty Modish*, by any one woman then among us ; Mrs. Verbruggen being now in a very declining state of health, and Mrs. Bracegirdle out of my reach, and engag'd in another company : But, as I have said, Mrs. Oldfield having thrown out such new proffers of a genius, I was no longer at a loss for support ; my doubts were dispell'd, and I had now a new call to finish it. Accordingly, the *Careless Husband* took its fate upon the stage the winter following in 1704. Whatever favorable reception this comedy has met with from the Publick it would be unjust in me not to place a large share of it to the account of Mrs. Oldfield ; not only from the uncommon excellence of her action, but even from her personal manner of conversing. There are many sentiments in the character of *Lady Betty Modish* that I may almost say were originally her own, or only dress'd with a little more care, than when they negligently fell from her lively humor. Had her birth * placed her in a higher rank of life, she had cer-

---

* It is said that Mrs. Oldfield's father, Captain Oldfield, was by birth a gentleman.

tainly appear'd in reality, what in this play she only excellently acted, an agreeably gay woman of quality, a little too conscious of her natural attractions.''

" I have often seen her," writes on the admiring Colley, " in private societies where women of the best rank might have borrowed some part of her behaviour, without the least diminution of their sense or dignity.   And this very morning, where I am now writing at the Bath, November 11, 1738, the same words were said of her by a Lady of Condition, whose better judgment of her personal merit in that light has embolden'd me to repeat them."

The Oldfield's morals were of a somewhat flexible character, to put it mildly, yet the fashionable people of her time looked with leniency upon her little irregularities, and made more of her than if she had been the most exemplary of actresses. She had many masculine admirers, and when Arthur Maynwaring, a wealthy, influential bachelor, connected with Government, crossed her smooth and easy-going path, she succumbed to what she may have considered the exigencies of the occasion, took charge of his household, and loved him devotedly until his death, in 1712, left her without a protector.

But General Charles Churchill, the son of an elder brother of the Duke of Marlborough, came to the rescue, and helped to dispel the sorrow into which she had been plunged by the decease of the handsome Maynwaring.

> "None led through youth a gayer life than he,
> Cheerful in converse, smart in repartee,"

so it may be imagined that he proved a gay companion for the yielding Nance. By him she had one son who married Lady Mary Walpole, a natural child of the great Sir Robert Walpole, and she was also the mother of a son who had been publicly acknowledged by his father, Mr. Maynwaring. Little eccentricities of conduct like this were tenderly treated.

Chetwood, in his *General History of the Stage*, kindly observes that " her amours seemed to lose that glare which appears round the persons of the failing Fair ; neither was it ever known that she troubled the repose of any lady's lawful claim ; and was far more constant than millions in the conjugal noose."

The same writer, who had himself seen Oldfield in the meridian of her fame, remembered that " in her full round of glory in comedy she used to slight tragedy. She would often say *I hate to have a page dragging my tail about. Why do they not give Porter these parts ? She can put on a better Tragedy face than I can.* When *Mithridates* was revised, it was with much difficulty she was prevailed upon to take the part, but she perform'd it to the utmost length of perfection, and, after that, seem'd much better reconcil'd to Tragedy."

Indeed, while the actress was much more *en rapporte* with comedy *à la mode* she could play tragic parts on occasion, just as Chetwood pointed out. " What a majestical dignity in *Cleopatra !* " he exclaims fer-

vently, recalling her achievements. "Such a finish'd
figure on the stage was never yet seen. In *Calista*, the
Fair Penitent, she was inimitable in the third act, with
Horatio, when she tears the letter, with

'   .   .   . To atoms ! thus !
Thus let me tear the vile detested falsehood,
The wicked lying evidence of shame ! '

her excellent clear voice of passion, her piercing flaming
eye, with manner and action suiting, us'd to make me
shrink with awe, and seem'd to put her monitor *Horatio*
into a mouse-hole. I almost gave him up for a troublesome puppy ; and though Mr. Booth play'd the part of
Lothario I could hardly lug him up to the importance
of triumphing over such a finish'd piece of perfection,
that seemed to be too much dignified to lose her Virtue."

The power of Mrs. Oldfield's acting seems to have
come from a subtle charm difficult to suggest because
of its delicacy and elusive-like quality, just as the most
fluent dramatic critic finds it hard to photograph the
witchery and piquancy of Ellen Terry through the
prosaic medium of pen, ink, and paper. "She was
tallish in stature," as Cibber pictures his frail friend,
"beautiful in action and aspect, and she always looked
like one of those principal figures in the finest paint-
ings that first seize and longest delight the eye of the
spectator. Her countenance was benevolent like her
heart, yet it could express contemptuous indignity so
well that once, when a malignant beau rose in the pit

to hiss her, she made him instantly hide his head and vanish by a pausing look, and her utterance of the words, ' poor creature.' "

Her benevolence of heart, to which Cibber thus alludes in passing, had practical exemplification in her assisting, with a pension of fifty pounds a year, that curious literary individual, Richard Savage. She was charitable in other directions, too, and she added to this virtue a great good-sense and amiability in matters connected with her art. It appears that " to the last year of her life " (again I must quote from the indispensable *Apology*) " she never undertook any part she liked without being importunately desirous of having all the helps in it that another could possibly give her. By knowing so much herself, she found how much more there was of nature yet needful to be known.* Yet it was a hard matter to give her any hint that she was not able to take or improve. With all this merit she was tractable and less presuming in her station than several that had not half her pretensions to be troublesome. But she lost nothing by her easy conduct ; she had everything she ask'd, which she took care should be always reasonable, because she hated as much to be grudg'd as deny'd a civility. Upon her extraordinary action in the *Provoked Husband*, the managers made her a present of fifty guineas more than her agreement, which never was more than

* This quotation deserves to be posted in the greenroom of every theatre.

a verbal one ; for they knew she was above deserting them to engage upon any other stage, and she was conscious they would never think it their interest to give her cause of complaint.''

What a shining example is Mistress Oldfield for many an actress who, without one tenth of her ability, turns the managerial hair almost white by her exactions and assumption, and thinks the breaking of the most ironclad contract quite in order—if the violation thereof is done by herself.

With all her amiability the genial Nance had a mind of her own, and even in her lovers she showed herself a woman of decision. She might sacrifice her honor and risk her reputation for Mr. Maynwaring or Charles Churchill, but she also could be as icy to an admirer as was the chaste Bracegirdle. That trait was displayed very clearly in the case of Sir Roger Mostings, a baronet who was madly enamoured of the actress, despite the indifference with which his attentions were invariably treated. After the unsuccessful Jacobite uprising of 1715, Sir Roger, who then commanded a troop in the Life Guards, spoke so freely in behalf of the noblemen imprisoned for complicity in the rebellion, that he was banished from Court and ordered to retire at once to his estates. When the news of his disgrace came, his greatest concern was at the prospect of leaving the irresistible Oldfield. She might snub him as much as she dared, yet it was a pleasure for him to see her, notwithstanding, and now that even this enjoyment was

MR. AND MRS. SPRANGER BARRY.

IN A SCENE FROM ROWE'S TRAGEDY OF "TAMERLANE."—"NOW, NOW, THOU TRAITRESS !"—FROM A DRAWING BY ROBERTS.

denied him he shed bitter tears, soldier as he was. Heroic measures were necessary unless he were to lose the dear charmer forever, and so away he went to the obdurate lady, hoping to soften her heart, by a proposal of marriage. They should wed at once, and the happy pair could pass their honeymoon on the estates to which an unkind Government had ordered the too talkative baronet. But this dream of happiness was not to be ; Oldfield contemptuously refused the opportunity of prefixing Lady to her name, and the disconsolate Sir Roger had to retire into the country, hopeless and alone.

When Mistress Oldfield died in 1730, her fame was considered great enough to justify her burial in Westminster Abbey, and the ceremonies attending her funeral were marked by a pomp that might have sufficed for the putting away of royalty itself. Yet in France, at this very time, actors were treated by the Church as social lepers, and when their poor lives were finished, and their last parts played, no consecrated ground might hold their clay ; thieves, liars, and murderers were not grudged a final lodging within the sacred confines, but the unfortunate Thespian, however estimable might have been his private character, was only deemed fit for the cold grave of an unbaptized vagabond.

How different was the picture in England, where we have already seen the noble Betterton interred with every circumstance of funereal glory. As the remains of that "incomparable sweet girl" (for incomparable, sweet, and girlish Oldfield continued to the end, despite her forty-seven years), were reverently borne to the Abbey, through the very street in which she had once worked as a poor seamstress, more than one eyewitness must have felt that, unlike the prophets, actresses were not without honor in their own country, and that transcendent genius, like charity, would cover a multitude of sins—even though the sinner belong to the sometime despised player's craft. But no one could despise the lovable Nance ; sooner would her contemporaries have railed at the rare sunshine for which they often sighed, than have cast a stone at this fair, fragile woman who had done so much to bring laughter into their foggy, humdrum existence.

And so let us bid farewell to the comedienne in the same Christian frame of mind. We never had the inestimable privilege of seeing her, yet we can read of the charmer in the graphic pages of Cibber, and even in this reflected fashion are glad to keep her image before us. Her amours may be forgiven, at least on this side the grave ; the two men for whom she sacrificed so much have been relegated to the limbo of oblivion, and for the name of Oldfield there will always be a pleasant thought, a grateful word.

As that selfsame Savage, to whom she had been so kind, wrote of her :

> " So bright she shone, in ev'ry different part,
> She gain'd despotic empire o'er the heart ;

Knew how each various motion to control,
Soothe ev'ry passion, and subdue the soul :
As she or gay, or sorrowful appears,
She charms our mirth, or triumphs in our tears.
When *Cleopatra's* form she chose to wear,
We saw the Monarch's mien, the beauty's air ;
Charm'd with the sight, her cause we all approve
    And like her lover, give up all for love :
Antony's fate, instead of *Cæsar's* choose,
And wish for her we had a world to lose.

" But now the gay delightful scene is o'er,
And that sweet form must glad our world no more ;
Relentless Death has stop'd the tuneful tongue,
And clos'd those eyes, for all, but Death, too strong :
Blasted that face where ev'ry beauty bloom'd,
And to eternal rest the graceful mover doom'd."

One of the best known of Oldfield's associates was
the Robert Wilks of whom we have heard not a little
from Colley Cibber—the selfsame Wilks who took
more interest in the artistic part of the management at
Drury Lane than he did in the very practical details
so dear to the business-like Dogget. He may have
had a weakness, just as the *Apology* shows, for deck-
ing himself in fine clothes, but it is to be remembered
that he likewise took care that his fellow-actors should
be similarly adorned. Indeed, he was one of the most
charitable actors of his time ; he it was who stirred
himself to help the two children of the unfortunate
Farquhar after the melancholy death of the soldier-
playwright ; he materially aided the erratic Richard
Savage,* who lacked the faculty of aiding himself, and

* When Savage was so destitute that starvation stared him
in the face a subscription was started in his behalf. He re-

he was kindly in a thousand and one ways that bespoke the possession of a warm, sympathetic heart.
He was "a man," says Dr. Johnson, "who, whatever
were his abilities or skill as an actor, deserved at least
to be remembered for his virtues, which are not often
to be found in the World, and perhaps less often in his
profession than in others"—which shows that while
the learned lexicographer had a very correct idea as
to this actor's character, he put an unfair stigma upon
a fraternity noted for the generosity of its members.

Wilks came of an old Worcestershire family ; he was
born, however, near Dublin, where his father was one
of the pursuivants of the Lord Lieutenant of Ireland.
The son received what was then considered a genteel
education ; he wrote a fine hand, and when he reached
the age of eighteen got a clerkship in the Secretary of
State's office. But the drudgery and commonplace of
the work hardly proved an ideal occupation for the
young man, and his genius was soon to show itself in
a far different direction. It so happened that he lodged
near Mr. Richards, an actor well-known to Dublin
audiences, and with whom he formed a great intimacy.
Wilks, no doubt, looked upon his friend as something
wonderful and quite apart from the generality of mankind, and was only too glad to hold Richards's play-
book, to see if the latter were letter-perfect in his lines.

ceived the money, set out on a journey for Wales, and after
getting as far as Bristol spent all of his new-found gold, ending
his remarkable career by dying in the jail of that place.

" Mr. Wilks used to read the introductive speeches,"
says Chetwood, " with such proper emphasis, cadence,
and all the various passions, that the encomiums given
by Mr. Richards began to fire his mind for the drama.
It was with very little persuasion he ventured to act
privately the *Colonel* in the *Spanish Fryar*, at Mr.
Ashbury's,* the ensuing Christmas ; where he received
such approbation from that great master as confirm'd
his intention. The first part he played in the theatre
was *Othello*, with the utmost applause ; and, as he told
me, pleased all but himself. He went on with great
success for two years when his friend Mr. Richards
advised him to try his fortune in England, and gave
him letters of recommendation to Mr. Betterton, who
receiv'd him very kindly, and entered him at fifteen
shillings a week."

At the very outset of his career in London Wilks unconsciously paid Betterton one of the most flattering
of compliments, and it is probable that the dear old
man regarded him with all the more favor in consequence. " His first appearance on the English stage
was in the part of the young Prince in the *Maid's
Tragedy*, a very insignificant character, requiring little
more than an amiable figure. Mr. Betterton performed
Melantius ; but when that veteran actor came to address him on the battlements, to excuse himself for the
death of the *King* in the play, Mr. Wilks affirmed to

* Joseph Ashbury was Master of the Revels in Ireland, and
an eminent actor and teacher as well.

10

me that the dignity of Mr. Betterton struck him with such an awe, that he had much ado to utter the little he had to say. Mr. Betterton, observing his confusion, said to him, *Young man, this fear does not ill become you ; a horse that sets out at the strength of his speed will soon be jaded.*"

The young man recovers from this fortunate fright, rises rapidly in the estimation of the public, has his salary raised, and is professionally fathered by Betterton. Then he marries, applies for an increase of compensation, which is denied him, and thereupon contracts with Mr. Ashbury to play in Dublin for sixty pounds a year and a clear benefit, "which in those times was much more than any other ever had." When he takes his leave of "old Thomas" the great actor expresses much regret at his coming departure and says: "I fancy that gentleman (pointing to the manager *), if he has not too much obstinacy to own it, will be the first that repents your parting ; for, if I foresee aright, you will be greatly wanted here."

This is balm to the wounded soul of Wilks, and he goes to Ireland with the praise of the immortal Betterton ringing pleasantly through his head ; soon the genteel Mountford dies and Drury Lane is bereft of one of its strongest and most graceful pillars. The deserter is thereupon sent to with proposals to return at a salary of four pounds a week (the equivalent to the stipend of the English Roscius), and the temptation is

* Mr. Rich.

so great that a favorable answer is returned to the directorate of the Theatre Royal. But Ashbury has no wish to let his new acquisition slip so easily through his fingers; he obtains an order from the Duke of Ormond, Lord Lieutenant of Ireland, to prevent the departure of Mr. Wilks, and the latter, having timely warning of so bold a stratagem on the part of a too admiring manager, secretly boards a vessel at Hoath and is soon landed, safe and sound, on English soil. Back again at Drury Lane, he becomes a greater favorite than ever; a few years later he is one of the famous Triumvirate of Drury Lane and contributing to that golden era when "the stage was in full perfection"; while "greenrooms were free from indecencies of every kind, and might justly be compared to the most elegant drawing-rooms of the prime quality." This was the epoch when "no fops or coxcombs ever shew'd their monkey tricks there; but if they chanced to thrust in, were aw'd into respect; even persons of the first rank and taste, of both sexes, would often mix with the performers, without any stain to their honour or understanding; and, indeed, Mr. Wilks was so genteelly elegant in his fancy of dress for the stage, that he was often followed in his fashion, tho', in the street, his plainness of habit was remarkable." *

This remarkable actor, who was

"   .   .   .   born with ev'ry art to please !
Politeness, grace, gentility and ease,"

* Chetwood.

had a happy faculty of dressing himself to the best advantage, and this quality, combined with the fact that he was an admirable comedian in a certain range of debonair parts, made him a model for the elegant beaux of his day. "Whatever he did on the stage," said an admiring writer, "let it be ever so trifling— whether it consisted in putting on his gloves, or taking out his watch, lolling on his cane, or taking snuff— every movement was marked by such an ease of breeding and manner, everything told so strongly the involuntary motion of a gentleman, that it was impossible to consider the character he represented in any other light than that of reality ; but what was still more surprising, that person who could thus delight an audience from the gayety and sprightliness of his manner, I met the next day in the street, hobbling to a hackney-coach, so enfeebled by age * and infirmities that I could scarcely believe him to be the same man."

As Steele nicely puts it, Wilks had "a singular talent in representing the graces of nature ; Cibber the deformity in the affectation of them," and he draws this fine contrast between the respective methods of the two actors :

"Were I a writer of plays I should never employ either of them in parts which had not their bent this way. This is seen in the inimitable strain and run of good humor which is kept up in the character of

---

* Wilks died in 1732, two or three years after this criticism was penned.

Wildair, and in the nice and delicate abuse of understanding in that of *Sir Novelty*. Cibber in another light hits exquisitely the flat civility of an affected gentleman usher, and Wilks the easy flatness of a gentleman. . . . To beseech gracefully, to approach respectfully, to pity, to mourn, to love, are the places wherein Wilks may be said to shine with the utmost beauty. To rally pleasantly, to scorn artfully, to flatter, to ridicule and neglect are what Cibber would perform with no less excellence."

Of that third member of the Triumvirate, Thomas Dogget, we have already heard something from Cibber himself. He has been pictured as the most original and the strictest observer of nature of his time, who was ridiculous, without impropriety, and had a different look for every different kind of humor. "Though he was an excellent mimic, he imitated nothing but nature." He was a queer man, this Dogget, with a wonderful eye for the main chance and an essentially practical way of viewing men and things. Once when his landlady's maid went into his room and cut her throat with one of the player's razors, he exhibited great emotion on being told of the sad occurrence, but as he exclaimed "Zounds! I hope it was not with my best razor," it was naturally inferred that his grief would not prove incurable.

In his will Dogget bequeathed a sum of money the interest whereof was to be devoted to the purchase of a coat and silver badge to be rowed for every year by

Thames watermen, from London Bridge to Chelsea. This gave rise to the following lines, written by a facetious poet some years after the death of the testator :

> " Tom Dogget, the geatest sly drole in his parts,
> In acting was certain a master of arts.
> A monument left—no herald is fuller,
> His praise is sung yearly by many a sculler.
> Ten thousand years hence, if the world lasts so long,
> Tom Dogget must still be the theme of their song."

A greater actor than Dogget was Barton Booth, one of the most scholarly of tragedians, the creator of the title part in Addison's *Cato*, and the dear friend of Lord Bolingbroke, who was wont to send his chariot to the theatre every evening to convey the great man to the country. Pope has immortalized him in the lines :

> " Booth enters : hark ! the universal peal !
> ' But has he spoken ? ' Not a syllable.
> ' What shook the stage and made the people stare ? '
> Cato's long wig, flower'd gown, and lacquer'd chair."

Booth was a gentleman by birth, a relation of the Earl of Warrington, and a prospective candidate for Holy Orders. When seventeen years old he ran away from home, and before very long, in 1698, had made his *début* on the Dublin stage as the dusky *Oroonoko*. The event was a triumph for the young actor, but, curiously enough, came very near being a dismal failure, because of an odd accident that befell him. The evening was very warm, and in the last scene of the play, as he waited to go on, he unthinkingly wiped his darkened face, so that the lamp-black on it became streaked, and, as he afterward expressed it, gave him the appearance of a chimney-sweeper. Of course there was much laughter from the audience at sight of the strangely marked *Oroonoko*, but the next night when the performance was repeated, an actress fitted a crape mask to his face. As ill-luck would have it, this contrivance slipped off in the very first scene, and "Zounds!" subsequently related the tragedian, "I looked like a magpie! When I came off they lamp-blacked me for the rest of the night, so that I was flayed before it could be got off again."

Booth remained in Ireland nearly two years, and then began his long career of triumphs in London. In Dublin he had been an ardent lover of the flowing bowl, but the sad straits into which Powell had fallen as the result of drink made so distressful an impression on him that he completely reformed in this direction, and as he was naturally a student, possessed a melodious voice, great personal beauty, and an intuitive dramatic spirit, he quickly developed into an artist who in some respects was looked upon, and justly, as Betterton's successor.

He seems to have had much of the latter's amiability of character, or, to quote a quaint passage from Chet-wood, "he had a vast fund of understanding as well as good nature, and a persuasive elocution even in common discourse, that would even compel you to believe him against your judgment of things.'' It appears, further, that '' in his younger days he admired none of the Heathen Deities so much as *Jolly Bacchus;* to him he was very devout; yet, if he drank ever so deep, it never marr'd his study or his stomach. But, immediately after his marriage with Miss Santlow,* whose wise conduct, beauty, and winning behaviour so wrought upon him that home and her company were his chief happiness, he entirely contemn'd the folly of drinking out of season, and from one extreme fell, I think, into the other too suddenly ; for his appetite for food had no abatement. I have often know Mrs. Booth, out of extreme tenderness to him, order the table to be removed, for fear of overcharging his stomach.'' Thus may we leave him to the care of the watchful Santlow.

* Miss Santlow, his second wife, was an attractive actress, once a ballet dancer.

CHAPTER VIII.

LOOKING IN AT THE OPERA.

ONE of the most disturbing yet popular factors in the theatrical life of Queen Anne's reign was the introduction, on an ambitious scale, of Italian opera. It proved disturbing because it filled with fear the jealous hearts of legitimate actors and managers, who saw in this thoroughly un-English and unusual form of amusement a dangerous rival ; it was popular since it gave Londoners something melodious and quite different from the dramatic fare they were generally regaled with. Theatre-goers, even the best of them, like novelty, and so when this new-fangled operatic entertainment was brought into conservative Britain from across the sea it became quite the vogue, much to the sorrow of so critical an authority as Addison. It was a sorrow, too, which he expressed in season and out, and so we are not surprised when he announces, in the *Spectator*, his design "to deliver down to posterity a faithful account of the Italian opera, and of the gradual progress which it has made upon the English stage," for "there is no question," he thinks, "but our great-grandchildren will be very curious to know the reason why their forefathers used to sit together like an audience of foreigners in their own country, and to hear whole plays acted before them, in a tongue which they did not understand."

Short-sighted Addison ! The great-grandchildren had no such curiosity. They sat together themselves "like an audience of foreigners," and their own descendants do the same thing now. But to read on further from the *Spectator :*

"*Arsinoe* was the first opera that gave us a taste of Italian music. The great success this opera met with produced some attempts of forming pieces upon Italian plans, which should give a more natural and reasonable entertainment than what can be met with in the elaborate trifles of that nation. This alarmed the poetasters and fiddlers of the town, who were used to deal in a more ordinary kind of ware ; and therefore laid down an established rule, which is received as such to this day, 'That nothing is capable of being well set to music, that is not nonsense.' This maxim was no sooner received, but we immediately fell to translating the Italian operas, and as there was no great danger of hurting the sense of those extraordinary pieces, our authors would often make words of their own which were entirely foreign to the meaning of the passages they pretended to translate ; their chief care being to make the numbers of the English verse answer to those of the Italian, that both of them might go to the same tune."

"The next step to our refinement," it is pointed out, "was the introducing of Italian actors into our opera, who sung their parts in their own language, at the same tune that our countrymen performed theirs in our native tongue. The King or hero of the play generally spoke in Italian, and his slaves answered him in English. The lover frequently made his court, and gained the heart of his princess, in a language she did not understand. One would have thought it very difficult to have carried on dialogues after this manner without an interpreter between the persons that conversed together, but this was the state of the English stage for about three years."

And yet the very posterity for whose benefit Addison was writing, is so hardened to the anomalies and inconsistencies of Italian opera, that a little defect like this could not possibly shock it. Nay, within the past two or three years I have myself witnessed a performance where the tenor sang in French, the soprano in German, the baritone in Italian, and the other participants showed more or less of a *penchant* for the English mode of expression. Yet the production gave unlimited enjoyment, as well it might, for in opera the music's the thing, so far as the general public is concerned, and a polyglot incident of this kind passes almost unnoticed. What matters the language, if the voice be melodious. The tenor may warble in Chinese if he so please, and depict the most profound woe in the liveliest of florid arias ; but so long as his notes have power to charm the ear there will be no complaint. Wagner strove to inject a certain amount of realism and dramatic unity into his works, and Verdi, who in most of his own operas was a flagrant offender against probability, has tried the same thing in *Otello*, yet for all that our venerable friends, *Trovatore* and the perennial *Bohemian Girl*,— who has outgrown her girlhood these many seasons,— still exert the old influence on the music-lover.

To return to Addison. "At length," he relates, "the audience grew tired of understanding half the opera ; and therefore, to ease themselves entirely of the fatigue of thinking, have so ordered it at present, that the whole opera is performed in an unknown tongue. We no longer understand the language of our own stage ; insomuch that I have often been afraid, when I have seen our Italian performers chattering in the vehemence of action, that they have been calling us names, and abusing us among themselves ; but I hope, since we do put such entire confidence in them, they will not talk against us before our faces, though they may do it with the same safety as if it were behind our backs. In the meantime I cannot forbear thinking how naturally an historian who writes two or three hundred years hence, and does not know the taste of his wise fore-fathers will make the following reflection : ' In the beginning of the eighteenth century, the Italian tongue was so well understood in England, that operas were acted on the public stage in that language.' "

The *Arsinoe* referred to in this essay was given in

its Anglicized form in 1705, and the advertisement of the performance in the *Daily Courant* sets forth that there will be presented at the Theatre Royal, Drury Lane, " a new Opera, never perform'd before, call'd Arsinoe, Queen of Cyprus, After the Italian manner, all Sung, being set to Musick by Mr. Clayton. With several Entertainments of Dancing by Monsieur l'Abbée, Monsieur du Ruel, Monsieur Cherrier, Mrs. Elford, Mrs. du Ruel, Mrs. Moss, and others. And the famous Signora Francisca Margaretta de l'Epine will, before the Beginning and after the Ending of the Opera, perform several entertainments of singing in Italian and English." It was further announced that no person should " be admittted into the Boxes or Pitt but by the Subscribers Tickets, to be delivered at Mrs. White's Chocolate House."

During the season *Arsinoe* had twenty-four performances, although it was a trashy sort of compilation, and it was followed, the succeeding year, by *Camilla*. This proved to be a much more meritorious work, and was an adaptation from the Italian of Stampiglio by Cibber's old friend, Owen Swiney. The bright particular star of the performance happened to be the famous Mrs. Tofts, an English *prima donna*, who had a handsome presence, a fine voice, and accomplished methods. Cibber says that " whatever defects the fashionably skilful might find in her manner, she had, in the general sense of her spectators, charms that few of the most learned singers ever arrived at. The beauty of her fine proportioned figure, and exquisitely sweet silver tone of her voice, with that peculiar rapid swiftness of her throat, were perfections not to be imitated by art or labor."

Mrs. Tofts retired from the stage as early as 1709, having amassed a modest fortune by her singing, and at the very height of her beauty and popularity married a scholarly and wealthy gentleman, Joseph Smith, who was afterwards appointed English consul to Venice. Her reason gave way about this time, and although she recovered for a season, the trouble finally returned and she died many years later, old, forgotten, and demented. Steele thus dwells upon her infirmity in the *Tatler*:*

"The great revolutions of this nature bring to my mind the distresses of the unfortunate *Camilla*, who has had the ill-luck to break before her voice, and to disappear at a time when her beauty was in the height of its bloom. This lady entered so thoroughly into the great characters she acted, that when she had finished her part she could not think of retrenching her equipage, but would appear in her own lodgings with the same magnificence that she did upon the stage. This greatness of soul had reduced that unhappy princess to an involuntary retirement, where she now passes her time among the woods and forests, thinking on the crowns and sceptres she has lost, and often humming over in her solitude,

> ' I was born of royal race,
>   Yet must wander in disgrace,'† etc.

* May 26, 1709.   † A quotation from *Camilla*.

But for fear of being overheard, and her quality known, she usually sings it in Italian,

> ' Nacqui al regno, nac qui al trono
>   E per sono
>   I ventura pastorella.' "

It was of this unfortunate songstress that a poet of her day wrote * :

> " Music has learn'd the discords of the State,
>   And concerts jar with Whig and Tory hate.
>   Here Somerset and Devonshire attend
>   The British Tofts, and every note commend ;
>   To native merit just, and pleas'd to see
>   We 've Roman arts, from Roman bondage free."

The more sweetly sang such charmers as Tofts or handsome De l'Épine the more anxious and indignant waxed certain watch-dogs of the English drama, whose vivid imaginations pictured the total extinction of the latter through the introduction of the hated opera. Dennis, in an *Essay on the Operas after the Italian Manner* (1706) complained that " tho' the Reformation and Liberty and the Drama were established among us together, and have flourished among us together, and have still been like to have fall'n together, notwithstanding all this, at this present juncture, when Liberty and the Reformation are in the utmost danger, we are going very bravely to oppress the Drama, in order to establish the luxurious diversions of those very nations, from whose attempts and designs, both Liberty and the Reformation are in the utmost danger."

* Hughes, author of *The Siege of Damascus.*

But despite the warnings of the worthy Dennis, opera, "after the Italian manner" continued in favor, to the great danger, in his own mind, of Drama, Liberty, and the Reformation. The works of this kind, where the English and Italian elements had incongruous and inartistic combination, came to an end with *Pyrrhus and Demetrius*, a translation of the *Pirro e Demetrio* of Adriano Morselli. Steele writes entertainingly of it in the *Tatler* *:

" Letters from the Haymarket inform us that on Saturday night last the opera of *Pyrrhus and Demetrius* was performed with great applause. This intelligence is not very acceptable to us friends of the theatre ; for the stage being an entertainment of the reason and all our faculties, this way of being pleased with the suspense of them for three hours together, and being given up to the shallow satisfaction of the ears and eyes only, seems to arise rather from the degeneracy of our understanding than an improvement of our diversions. That the understanding has no part in the pleasure is evident from what these letters very positively assert ; to wit, that a great part of the performance was done in Italian : and a great critic fell into fits in the gallery at seeing not only time and place, but language and nations, confused in most incorrigible manner. His spleen is so extremely moved on this occasion, that he is going to publish another treatise against the introduction of operas, which, he thinks,

* No. 4.

has already inclined us to thoughts of peace, and, if, tolerated, must infallibly dispirit us from carrying on the war. He has communicated his scheme to the whole room and declared in what manner things of this kind were first introduced. He has on this occasion considered the nature of sounds in general, and made a very elaborate digression upon the London cries, wherein he was shown, from reason and philosophy, why oysters are cried, card-matches sung, and turnips and all other vegetables neither cried, sung nor said, but sold with an accent and tone neither natural to man nor beast.''

At the time that Sir Richard wrote this he was an arch-enemy to the style of production which he thus satirized, but he had the good grace, in a subsequent number of the *Tatler* * to praise one of the principals in the cast, the favorite Nicolini. '' For my own part,'' he admits, '' I was fully satisfied with the sight of an actor, who, by the grace and propriety of his action and gesture does honor to the human figure. Every-one will imagine I mean Signor Nicolini, who sets off the character he bears in an opera by his action, as much as he does the words of it by his voice. Every limb and every finger contributes to the part he acts, inasmuch that a deaf man may go along with him in the sense of it. There is scarce a beautiful posture in an old statue which he does not plant himself in, as

* No. 113.

the different circumstances of the .story give occasion for it."

This opera singer, who was known in private life as the Cavaliere Nicolino Grimaldi, enjoyed great public favor, in the days when the *Tatler* was at the height of its prosperity. He came from Naples, where he had decided musical prestige, arriving in England in 1708, appearing first in this very *Pyrrhus and Demetrius*, and returning to his native Italy in 1712.

Of course Addison has something to say about him, as for instance, in the fifth issue of the *Spectator*, a portion of which may be quoted here as showing up the all-absorbing question of opera in a humorous light :

" An opera may be allowed to be extravagantly lavish in its decorations, as its only design is to gratify the senses, and keep up an indolent attention in the audience. Common sense, however, requires that there should be nothing in the scenes and machines which may appear childish and absurd. How would the wits of King Charles's time have laughed to see Nicolini exposed to a tempest in robes of ermine, and sailing in an open boat upon a sea of pasteboard? What a field of raillery would they have been led into, had they been entertained with painted dragons spitting wildfire, enchanted chariots drawn by Flanders mares, and real cascades in artificial landscapes? A little skill in criticism would inform us, that shadows and realities ought not to be mixed together in the same piece ; and that the scenes which are designed as the representations of nature should be filled with resemblances, and not with the things themselves. If one would represent a wide champaign country filled with herds and flocks, it would be ridiculous to draw the country only upon the scenes, and to crowd several parts of the stage with sheep and oxen. This is joining together inconsistencies, and making the decorations partly real, and partly imaginary. I would recommend what I have here said to the directors, as well as the admirers, of our modern opera.

"As I was walking in the street about a fortnight ago, I saw an ordinary fellow carrying a cage full of little birds upon his shoulder; and as I was wondering with myself what use he would put them to, he was met very luckily by an acquaintance, who had the same curiosity. Upon his asking him what he had upon his shoulders, he told him that he had been buying Sparrows for the opera. Sparrows for the opera, says his friend, licking his lips. What! are they to be roasted? No, no, says the other, they are to enter towards the end of the first act, and to fly about the stage.

"This strange dialogue awakened my curiosity so far, that I immediately bought the opera, by which means I perceived the sparrows were to act the part of singing-birds in a delightful grove; though, upon a nearer inquiry, I found the Sparrows put the same trick upon the audience, that *Sir Martin Mar-all* *

* In Dryden's comedy of that name.

practised upon his mistress ; for though they flew in sight, the music preceded from a concert of flageolets and bird calls, which were planted behind the scenes. At the same time I made this discovery : I found, by the discourse of the actors, that there were great designs on foot for the improvement of the opera ; that it had been proposed to break down a part of the wall, and to surprise the audience with a party of a hundred-horse, and that there was actually a project of bringing the New River into the house, to be employed in *Jets d'eau* and water-works. This project, as I have since heard, is postponed till the summer season ; when it is thought that the coolness which proceeds from the fountains and cascades will be more acceptable and re-freshing to people of quality.

.   .   .   .

" But to return to the sparrows : there have been so many flights of them let loose in the opera that it is feared the house will never get rid of them ; and that in other plays they make their entrance in very wrong and improper scenes, so as to be seen flying in a lady's bed-chamber, or perching upon a king's throne. I am credibly informed that there was once a design of cast-ing into an opera the story of Whittington and his cat ; and that in order to do it, there had been got together a great quantity of mice ; but Mr. Rich, the proprietor of the playhouse, very prudently considered that it would be impossible for the cat to kill them all, and that consequently the princes of the stage might be as much infested with mice, as the prince of the island was before the cat's arrival upon it; for which reason he would not permit it to be acted in his house.

.   .   .   .

" Before I dismiss this paper, I must inform my reader, that there is a treaty on foot between London and Wise * (who will be appointed gardeners of the playhouse) to furnish the opera of *Rinaldo and Armida* with an orange-grove ; and that the next time it is acted, the singing birds will be personated by tom-tits : the undertakers being resolved to spare neither pains nor money for the gratification of the audience."

So much for Addison's banter. Laugh as he might at the inconsistencies of opera, (the laugh was all the more bitter because his own opera of *Rosamund* had failed,) the people went on patronizing the importation and getting wellnigh hysterical on occasion, over the attractions of the foreign Nicolini or the home-born Tofts. Another singer who inspired enthusiasm was Madame de l'Epine, a dangerous rival to the latter, and the happy possessor of a lovely voice. She came over to England in company with a German musician, Herr Greber, whereby she derived her rather undignified nickname, " Greber's Peg." The De l'Epine's personal appearance was not as beautiful as her powers of expression, and so when she retired from the stage in 1718 and married Dr. Pepusch, the musician,

* The Queen's gardeners.

he dubbed her " Hecate," a title which hardly proved more complimentary.

This *prima donna*, as well as Nicolini, and Valentini, a singer of considerable note, appeared in *Almahide*, which is only remembered now because it was the first opera to be given in London entirely in Italian. It soon gave way to Francesco Mancini's *Hydaspes*, a much written about opera which became quite the fashion, notwithstanding that its merits, musical or otherwise, were hardly prominent. Its chief claim on the interest of posterity lies in its much satirized scene where a supposedly dreadful combat takes place between *Hydaspes* and a lion. Even the amount of poetic license allowed to so flexible a thing as an Italian libretto has limits, and in this case the bounds of probability were so grossly exceeded that the wits of the town soon had everybody laughing at an encounter where the hero had the pleasant duty of throwing down an inoffensive man attired in a lion's skin, and then posing before the audience as a mighty Nimrod.

As the story of the opera goes, *Hydaspes* and his brother, *Artaxerxes*, the King of Persia, are both in love with the beautiful *Princess Berenice*. The King coming to the convenient conclusion that the best way to dispose of a dangerous rival is to have him nicely and very thoroughly devoured by a lion (one who has n't dined for a day or two preferred,) orders *Hydaspes* to be thrown into the public arena, where the hungry animal will do the rest. So when the third act arrives, we see the unfortunate but always virtuous young man brought on the stage closely guarded by soldiers, while the Persians fill the royal amphitheatre, waiting eagerly for the coming sport.

Of course *Berenice* loves this noble specimen of prospective mince-meat, and, quite naturally, she is on hand to have a front-row view of the little divertisement so thoughtfully prepared by the fraternal *Artaxerxes*.

"For thee, my life, I die," wails the hero (in Italian) as he cordially greets his beloved.

"Oh, my soul ! a long farewell !" continues *Berenice* with customary Italian-opera cheerfulness.

"Oh, Berenice ! my love !" answers her admirer.

"Hydaspes !" she lisps, and thereupon both exclaim placidly : "Oh ! farewell !"

This eminently proper dialogue is evidently too much for the impatient populace, for the stage directions now read :

"*Berenice* places herself on the steps of the amphitheatre, with *Arbaces* and the soldiers : *Hydaspes* remaining alone in the arena ; after which a lion comes out of his den, which, not yet seeing *Hydaspes*, stalks about looking at the spectators."

This is an accommodating sort of lion ; he kindly resolves to give the hero time for a farewell sentiment, and so we find *Hydaspes* crying out :

> "Why dost thou, horrid monster pause ?
> Come on ; now sate thy ravenous jaws ;
> This naked bosom tear ;

> But thou within shalt find a heart
> Guarded by flames will make thee start,
> And turn thy rage to fear."

Then *Berenice* comes forward, says something about
"Ah, miserable me ! I die ! "and straightway goes off
into a dead faint, in true feminine fashion. However,
things soon take a cheerful turn for everybody excepting *Artaxerxes* and the lion. "*Hydaspes*, grasping
the lion's neck with his arms, strangles him, when
falling at last on the ground, he sets his foot on his
neck in sign of victory"—which, though a trifle obscure in expression, means that as an animal throttler
Berenice's cher ami is a decided success.

Hydaspes now feels so valiant that he asks :

> " Is there another monster yet
> Remains for me t' encounter ?
> No force that 's new
> This fear can e'er subdue ! "

But we may leave the resuscitation of *Berenice* to the
imagination. The whole affair was, no doubt, su-
premely idiotic, for, to quote George Hogarth,* "the
exhibition of Nicolini, alternately vaporing and ges-
ticulating to a poor biped in a lion's skin, then breath-
ing a love-tale in the pseudo-monster's ear, and at last
fairly throttling him on the stage, must have been ludicrous in the extreme."

The humor of the situation was sportively dwelt upon
in the *Spectator* (number 13), where Addison writes :

* *Memoirs of the Musical Drama.*

"There is nothing that of late years has afforded matter of greater amusement to the town than Signior Nicolini's combat with a lion in the Haymarket, which has been very often exhibited to the general satisfaction of most of the nobility and gentry in the kingdom of Great Britain. Upon the first rumor of this intended combat, it was confidently affirmed, and is still believed, by many in both galleries, that there would be a tame lion sent from the Tower every opera night, in order to be killed by *Hydaspes;* this report, though altogether groundless, so universally prevailed in the upper regions of the playhouse, that some of the most refined politicians in those parts of the audience, gave it out in whispers that the lion was a cousin-german of the tiger who made his appearance in King William's days, and that the stage would be supplied with lions at the public expense, during the whole session. Many likewise were the conjectures of the treatment which this lion was to meet with from the hands of Signior Nicolini; some supposed that he was to subdue him in recitative, as Orpheus used to serve the wild beasts in his time, and afterwards to knock him on the head; some fancied that the lion would not pretend to lay his paws upon the hero, by reason of the received opinion, that a lion will not hurt a virgin. Several, who pretended to have seen the opera in Italy, had informed their friends, that the lion was to act a part in High Dutch, and roar twice or thrice to a thoroughbass before he fell at the feet of *Hydaspes.*"

So Addison sets himself the task of finding out the identity of the ferocious monster. There were three lions in all, he learns. The first was a candle-snuffer, "who being a fellow of a testy, choleric temperament, overdid his part and would not suffer himself to be killed so easily as he ought to have done." Next came a tailor by trade, "who belonged to the playhouse and had the character of a mild and peaceable man'in his profession. If the former was too furious, this was too sheepish for his part ; insomuch that after a short modest walk upon the stage, he would fall at the first touch of *Hydaspes*, without grappling with him, and giving him an opportunity of showing his variety of Italian trips. It is said, indeed, that he once gave him a rip in his flesh color doublet ; but this was only to make work for himself in his private character of a tailor."

The third lion was much more acceptable to all concerned. He was "a country gentleman, who does it for his diversion, but desires his name may be concealed. He says, very handsomely, in his own excuse, that he does not act for gain ; that he indulges an innocent pleasure in it ; and that it is better to pass away an evening in this manner, than in gaming and drinking ; but at the same time says, with a very agreeable raillery upon himself, that if his name should be known the ill-natured world might call him, ' the ass in the lion's skin.' "

Operatic art in England was given a remarkable impetus by the arrival of Handel during the latter part of

1710. Though but a young man he had already become celebrated as a composer, and no sooner was he in London than Aaron Hill, who then managed the Haymarket Theatre, asked him to write an opera for production at that house. The arrangements were perfected, the music was composed within a fortnight and the librettist, the poet Rossi, had a hard time to finish his own work so as to keep pace with the rapid Handel. The opera was entitled *Rinaldo* and when produced met with the greatest success. Subsequently another of his compositions, *Il Pastor Fido*, was brought out, and in 1713 his *Theseus* was presented. In the *Daily Courant* of January 24th it is announced by the management of the Haymarket that:

"This present Saturday the 24th of January, the Opera of Theseus composed by Mr. Handel will be represented in its Perfection, that is to say with all the Scenes, Decorations, Flights and Machines. The Performers are much concerned that they did not give the Nobility and Gentry all the Satisfaction they could have wished, when they represented it on Wednesday last, having been hindered by some unforseen Accidents, at that time insurmountable."

But what were the successes of the inane *Hydaspes* or the classic, dignified *Rinaldo* as compared to that of the *Beggars' Opera*, a work illustrating the now recognized managerial axiom that it is useless to prophecy as to the fate of a production. In one of those inimitable conversations photographed for us by the obliging

Boswell, Sir Joshua Reynolds says :   "The *Beggars'
Opera* affords a proof how strangely people will differ
in opinion about a literary performance.   Burke thinks
it has no merit "—to which the sage Johnson replies :
" It was refused by one of the houses ; but I should
have thought it would succeed, not from any great excellence in the writing but from the novelty and the
general spirit and gaiety of the piece, which keeps the
audience always attentive, and dismisses them in good
humor."

But the circumstances attending the introduction of
the piece were discouraging up to the moment of its
performance.   It was written by the poet Gay, who
provided for it a story of low-life that seemed anything
but attractive on a first perusal of the libretto, and the
music was nothing more or less than an adaptation, by
Dr. Pepusch, of a number of national ditties.   When
Gay went to his patron, the Duke of Queensbury, to
get an opinion of the affair, the noble critic remarked :
" This is a very odd thing, Gay ; it is either a very
good thing or a bad thing."   So experienced a manager as Cibber utterly refused to produce it, and when
Rich * consented to put it on at his house in Lincoln's
Inn Fields (1727) it was by no means in an enthusiastic frame of mind that he yielded.   To add to the trials
of the author, Quin refused to take the part of *Macheath,*

* John Rich opened the theatre in Lincoln's Inn Fields in
December, 1714, under letters-patent originally granted by Charles II., and restored by George I.

because he had so poor an opinion of the opera, and it was assigned to Thomas Walker, one of the most entertaining, jovial, and hard-drinking actors of his time. The leading feminine role of *Polly* was given to a Miss Fenton * who was handsome, to be sure, but whose chief claim to Mr. Rich's regard seems to have been her offer to accept the modest salary of fifteen shillings a week. In fact, all the preparations were made on the most economical basis, as though no extravagance could be justified in connection with pre-doomed failure.

The looked-for disaster never came. On the contrary, the *Beggars' Opera* passed into theatrical history as one of the greatest of successes ; the town went wild over it, and Rich made a fortune out of the enterprise. To be sure, the Archbishop of Canterbury and many other pious persons objected to the work on the ground that its story, dealing, as it did, with highwaymen and other lawless characters, was calculated to foster immorality. This far-fetched argument troubled the audiences not one bit ; they found in the piece a light, agreeable entertainment just to their liking, and always went away from the performance in that good humor to which Dr. Johnson referred many years later. Whether they would have extracted as much enjoyment from *Polly*, the second part which Gay wrote for

* Lavinia Fenton became famous in a day by her appearance as *Polly*. She was a witty, charming woman who had a remarkable career, which included her marriage to the Duke of Bolton.

the *Beggars' Opera*, is doubtful, but there was never a chance for comparison, as the Lord Chamberlain refused to license the sequel.

Everything was in readiness for the introduction of *Polly* when the decision was announced. Rich and Gay were deeply disappointed and mortified at so unexpected a blow. Some uncharitable enemies of Cibber charged that the refusal of a license was due to his jealousy of Gay and his own ambition to bring out a piece on the order of the *Beggars' Opera*, and so justice demands that we give Colley a hearing on the subject.

"After the vast success of that new species of dramatic poetry," he says, "the year following I was so stupid as to attempt something of the same kind, upon a quite different foundation, that of recommending virtue, and innocence ; which I ignorantly thought might not have a less pretence to favor, than setting greatness and authority in a contemptible, and the most vulgar vice and wickedness, in an amiable light. But behold how fondly I was mistaken ! *Love in a Riddle* (for so my new-fangled performance was called) was as vilely damn'd and hooted at as so vain a presumption, in the idle cause of virtue, could deserve."

Cibber then goes on to say how it came about that he was falsely accused of being privy to the suppression of *Polly*, how many of his friends got out of humor with him in consequence, and how *Love in a Riddle* suffered such dire failure because of the popular belief in the unjust rumor. He brought out his opera without considering that "from the security of a full pit dunces might be criticks, cowards valiant, and prentices gentlemen."

"Whether any such were concerned in the murder of my play, I am not certain ; for I never endeavor'd to discover any one of its assassins ; I cannot afford them a milder name, from their unmanly manner of destroying it. Had it been heard, they might have left me nothing to say to them. 'T is true, it faintly held up its wounded head a second day, and would have spoke for mercy, but was not suffered. Not even the presence of a Royal Heir-apparent could protect it. But then I was reduced to be serious with them ; their clamor, then, became an insolence, which I thought it my duty, by the sacrifice of any interest of my own, to put an end to. I therefore quitted the actor for the author, and stepping forward to the pit, told them, *That since I found they were not inclin'd that this play should go forward, I gave them my word that after this night it should never be acted again : but that, in the meantime I hop'd they would consider in whose presence they were, and for that reason, at least, would suspend what further marks of their displeasure they might imagine I had deserved.* At this there was a dead silence ; and, after some little pause, a few civiliz'd hands signify'd their approbation. When the play went on I observ'd about a dozen persons, of no extraordinary appearance, sullenly walk'd out of the pit. After which, every scene of it, while uninterrupted,

met with more applause than my best hopes had expected. But it came too late : Peace to its *Manes!* I
had given my word it should fall, and I kept it by
giving out another play for the next day, though I
knew the boxes were all let for the same again."

" Peace to its *Manes* " indeed. It was doubtless
poor stuff, this *Love in a Riddle*, but good or bad, the
public had resolved to have none of it, and there was
an end to the matter. But the *Beggar's Opera* continued popular for many a day, and we can imagine the
prosperous, illiterate John Rich, whom the success of the
piece lifted from comparative poverty to affluence, telling his friends how he had been one of the first to discover its merits. Even managers are forgetful, and
Rich was not less so than others of the same ilk.
He was the son of Christopher Rich, and for many
years enjoyed great celebrity as an effective pantomim-
ist ; indeed he seems to have been the first manager to
put pantomine on a popular and respectable footing on
the English stage. His *Harlequins* proved so attractive that he often drew the attention of play-goers from
the legitimate drama, and, in his own curious way he
even proved a rival of Garrick, who wrote of him :

" When Lun* appeared, with matchless art and whim,
    He gave the power of speech to every limb ;
    Tho' mask'd and mute convey'd his quick intent,
    And told in frolic gestures what he meant :
    But now the motley coat and sword of wood
    Require a tongue to make them understood."
*Rich used to appear in pantomime under the name of Mr. Lun.

His pantomime was, indeed, faultless, but not so his grammar or his general education. One of his peculiarities was to call everybody "Mister," and this habit once brought forth an unkind jest from the coarsest and most unkind of men, the mimic Foote. The latter on being addressed several times as "Mister," took Rich to task for his bad manners in not adding " Foote." " Don't be angry," said the manager, " for I sometimes forget my own name." " That 's extraordinary," replied Foote, " for though I knew you could not write it, I did not suppose you could forget it."

12

CHAPTER IX.

AN ACTOR OF THE OLD SCHOOL.

WE often hear the elderly play-goer speak lovingly of the "actors of the old school," deploring the fact that they are passing away, and sighing because their successors have not inherited all their excellences. "There's poor So and So," he says sadly, "he's almost the last one left ; how I wish some of the younger generation of players would take pattern by him." And then he adds, mournfully : "The palmy days of the drama are done for."

Dear old croaker ! Don't you know that it has been the fashion for the past two centuries to talk about those "palmy days," and to look upon the "old school" as something never to return. Nay, those among us who are now young will grow eloquent, thirty years hence, over favorites of to-day, and complain that the theatre is no longer what it was. It will always be thus, venerable sir, and so take heart of grace, for the "old school," like the poor, is sure to be ever with us. If you are skeptical, read of Quin, who was spoken of, in the autumn of his life, as one of the last of the "old school," and who was, no doubt,

JAMES QUIN.

FROM THE PAINTING BY HUDSON.

regarded by some of his contemporaries as a melancholy survivor of all that was best in the drama. He has been dead for more than a century, but many who came after him have had the same sort of honor paid them by admirers who could see no health in any but the theatrical heroes of their youth.

Like some other by-gone celebrities, Quin would probably be regarded as a very bad actor, could he be resuscitated for the amusement of a modern audience. The *fin de siècle* critics would write him down as a " ranter," and probably dispose of his performance much after their fashion of dealing with the average second-rate Shakesperian spouter. Yet for all that he was one of the great players of his time, even though Churchill did say of him :

> " In fancied scenes, as in life's real plan,
> He could not for a moment sink the man.
> In whatever cast his character was laid,
> Self still, like oil, upon the surface played.
> Nature, in spite of all his skill, crept in ;
> Horatio, Dorax, Falstaff—still 't was Quin."

James Quin was born in 1693, and his father is said to have been an English gentleman who settled in Ireland several years after this event. When the youth had arrived at what was supposed to be the age of discretion he was sent off to London to study for the bar, but the leading of a gay life and the reading of Shakespeare proved much more to James's liking than the perusual of musty law books. His father dying about this time, and the parental legacy not being very large, the presumable law student made up his mind to go on the stage, a conclusion to which he was doubtless influenced by the intimacy he had formed with Booth, Wilks, and other well-known actors. But in the meantime he had contracted another intimacy by no means so creditable ; a woollen draper's wife was the heroine of it, and a subsequent encounter with the indignant husband brought about such a scandal that young Quin was glad to take temporary refuge in Ireland, where he appears to have made his first essay on the boards.

However, the woollen draper accommodatingly died ; the *affaire d'amour* was hushed up, and the aspirant returned to London, to appear at Drury Lane in 1715. For some time he seems to have remained " the mere scene drudge, the faggot of the drama," assuming secondary parts, and making little headway except in obtaining a deal of valuable experience. It was not until 1720, we are told, that he was able to properly display his talents, and this was after he had left Drury Lane to join Rich's forces.

"Upon the revival of the *Merry Wives of Windsor* at Lincoln's Inn Fields, of which the late Mr. Rich was the manager, there was no one in the whole company who would undertake the part of *Falstaff ;* Rich was, therefore, inclined to give up all thought of representing it, when Quin, happening to come in his way, said, if he pleased he would attempt it. ' Hem ! ' said

Rich, taking a pinch of snuff, ' You attempt *Falstaff!* Why (hem !)—You might as well think of acting *Cato* after Booth. The character of *Falstaff*, young man, is quite another character from what you think ' (taking another pinch of snuff) ; ' it is not a snivelling part, that —that—in short, that any one can do. There is not a man among you that has any idea of the part but myself. It is quite out of your walk. No, never think of *Falstaff*—never think of *Falstaff*—it is quite—quite out of your walk, indeed, young man.' '' *

Quin had a firm friend in Lacy Ryan, that delightful exponent of tragic lovers or fine gentlemen in comedy, and through Ryan's influence Rich was persuaded to give the bold young fellow a trial. '' The first night of his appearance in this character he surprised and astonished the audience ; no actor before ever entered into the spirit of the author, and it seemed as if Shakespeare had by intuition drawn the knight so long before for Quin only to represent. The just applause he met with upon this occasion is incredible ; continued clappings and peals of laughter, in some measure interrupted the representation, though it was impossible that any regularity whatever could have more increased the mirth or excited the approbation of the audience.''

This was the beginning of a success that, with one or two interruptions, was to last until the powers of the younger and more natural Garrick would put a

* *The Life of Mr. James Quin, Comedian.*

heavy extinguisher on the histrionic fire of the sententious James. An earlier interruption which threatened to extinguish that fire before it had been wellnigh kindled, was the unfortunate affair which involved Quin in involuntary manslaughter.

He and another actor, William Bowen, got into an altercation one April afternoon (1718) at the Fleece Tavern, in Cornhill, after wine had been flowing pretty freely and the conversation had drifted from good-natured banter into a somewhat less pleasant channel. Mr. Bowen taunted Quin with having acted *Tamerlane* in a slipshod manner, and the latter replied that Bowen " had no great occasion to value himself · for his performance, in that Mr. Johnson, who had acted it but seldom, acted the part of *Jacomo* in *The Libertine* as well as he [Bowen] who had acted it often." * Then the talk grew warmer, Quin told a story that reflected on his friend's honor, and finally Bowen rose up angrily, paid his reckoning and left the tavern, with the remark that he would not stay in such company any longer.

Quin, as he afterward testified in his own defence, was sent for, a quarter of an hour later, by Bowen, who insisted, strangely enough, upon drinking a pint of wine with him. So after some discussion, the two actors finally ended by going to the Pope's Head Tavern, where, being shown a room, they called for something to drink. The wine was brought, and each

* From a record of Quin's trial.

of them had taken a glass, when suddenly Bowen rose and barricaded the door with two chairs, at the same time telling his companion that "he had injured him past verbal reparation, and nothing but fighting should make him amends." Thereupon, as Quin himself related, "he argued with him, endeavoring to dissuade him, but Mr. Bowen bid him not trifle with him. That he then desired Mr. Bowen again to defer his resentment and sleep upon it, and if he could not come into temper by the next day, he would meet him and ask his pardon in the same company that he had injured him in ; but Mr. Bowen bid him again not to trifle with him, for that he [Quin] had injured him in his reputation, which he was resolved never to survive and would now do himself justice, and drawing his sword in a violent passion, swore if he did not draw he would run him through, upon which he [Quin] was obliged to draw in his own defence." In the struggle Bowen * was mortally wounded and as the whole evidence went to show that his death was due to his own rashness Quin got off with a conviction for manslaughter, which practically amounted to an acquittal.

Several seasons later (1721) the actor was to figure in another exciting episode, although one of a far different character. "A certain noble earl, who was said (and with some degree of certainty, as he drank usque-baugh constantly at his waking) to have been in a state

---

* Bowen was evidently half crazy at the time from his numerous libations.

of intoxication for six years, was behind the scenes (at Lincoln's Inn Fields) at the close of a comedy, and, seeing one of his companions on the other side among the performers, crossed the stage and was accordingly hissed by the audience. Mr. Rich was on the side the noble earl came over to, and on hearing the uproar in the house at such an irregularity, the manager said, ' I hope your lordship will not take it ill if I give orders to the stage door keeper not to admit you any more.' On his saying that, his lordship saluted Mr. Rich with a slap on the face, which he immediately returned, and, his lordship's face being round and fat, made his cheek ring with the force of it. Upon this spirited return my lord's drunken companions collected themselves directly, and Mr. Rich was to be put to death ; but Quin, Ryan, Walker, etc. stood forth in the defence of the manager, and a grand scuffle ensued, by which the gentlemen were all drove out at the stage door into the street. They then sallied into the boxes, with their swords drawn, and broke the scenes, cut the hangings, which were gilt leather, finely painted, and continued the riot until Mr. Quin came round with a constable and watchmen, and charged them every one into custody. They were carried before Justice Hungerford, who then lived in the neighborhood, and all bound over to answer the consequences ; but they were soon persuaded by their wiser friends to make up this matter, and the manager got ample redress. The King, being informed of the whole affair, was highly offended, and ordered a guard to attend that theatre as well as the other."

From his memorable appearance as *Falstaff* Quin's success seemed assured, and the death of such favorites as Wilks, Mistress Oldfield, and Booth all tended to his own advantage, as giving him so much the wider field for his achievements. But now he had left Rich's company, where the prospects for his own advancement were not very encouraging, and returned to his first love, Drury Lane. Here it was that he was called upon to essay Booth's old role of *Cato*, which was looked upon as peculiarly the property of the latter, and the new impersonator of the character had the tact to announce in the play-bill that " the part of *Cato* would be only attempted by Mr. Quin." This at once put the town in an amiable frame of mind towards one who thus publicly intimated that he had no hope of supplanting memories of Booth in the same play, and only desired to modestly follow, as best he might, in such illustrious footsteps. The first night of the performance saw a large and favorably disposed audience assembled at the theatre, and when Quin spoke the lines :

"Thanks to the Gods !—my boy has done his duty,"

the spectators were so carried away with the effectiveness of his acting that they cried out " Booth outdone ! Booth outdone ! "

At this period of prosperity Quin was in receipt of a

very large salary, having been engaged on such advantageous terms, it was reported, "as no hired actor has had before." His manager was a Mr. Fleetwood, who had come into possession of Drury Lane under rather curious circumstances, which resulted from the selling of their interest in the old house by Booth and Cibber. The new managers (including Highmore) were not to the liking of the company, and so the players quietly took themselves off (1733) to the Little Theatre in the Haymarket and there set up an establishment on their own account. This was a serious blow to Highmore and his colleagues ; like *Othello* they found their occupation gone, and they tried to invoke the majesty of the law to force the mutineers back, on the presumption that the revolt, being without authority of patent or license, was manifestly illegal. An accommodating magistrate granted a warrant for the arrest of one of the malcontents, who was seized while he was on the stage, and taken to Bridewell, but investigation showed that his incarceration was itself illegal. This put a damper on the proceedings determined upon by the proprietors of Drury Lane, who were left in the ridiculous position of monarchs without subjects to reign over,* and so they were very glad to dispose of five sixths of their shares to Mr. Fleetwood.

Fleetwood was a gentleman of fortune, and when

* It should be noted, however, that Highmore tried to keep his house open by engaging Macklin and other players, but the plan was not crowned with success.

the pantomimic Rich (who was now manager of the Covent Garden Theatre, whither the Lincoln's Inn Fields company had moved a short time before) came to him with a proposal to unite in the purchase of Drury Lane, he thought it a very good idea. It so happened, however, that Mr. Fleetwood contributed the money and Mr. Rich simply furnished the experience, and so, when a disagreement arose between the two, the former retained possession of the theatre and his ex-partner had to take himself off with nothing to show for his scheme but the one thing he did not need—a little more of the self-same experience.

The new manager of Drury Lane now proposed to the revolters that they should enlist under his own standard and they, nothing loth, put up the shutters of their house in the Haymarket and ensconced themselves once more under the protecting roof of the Theatre Royal. Each actor who had a say in the management was to receive two hundred pounds a year and that perquisite then so dear to the heart of a professional—a " clear benefit." Quin's salary was made even higher, in recognition of the commanding position which he now had on the stage.

One of the company happened to be that very good-for-nothing gentleman, Mr. Theophilus Cibber, who, had he not been the son of so influential a man as the energetic Colley, would, in all probability, never have been heard of by London play-goers. He was by no means a bad actor, for he made a capital *Pistol* and could put much sparkle and humor into parts of the coxcomb order, yet, as Davies records, he generally mixed so much of falsity and grimace in his work that he often displeased the judicious spectator. He was constantly in trouble of some kind, treated his wife—a far finer artist than he—in a low-spirited manner, and ended his variegated career by getting drowned while crossing over to Ireland. Dibdin refers to Theophilus as one "who was forward in all manner of scrapes, who has been considered by Goldsmith and others to have fortunately escaped hanging by being drowned, who, in short, was a constant imposition in everything he said or did, all which is attributed by an author to his having been born on the day of the most memorable storm ever known in this kingdom, which happened November 26, 1703." *

This grim caricature of a distinguished father (for there was much about him that suggested a distorted image of the worthy Colley) soon displayed the inherent impishness of his nature by disloyalty to his new manager. Mr. Fleetwood had an attack of gout, as seemed to befit a gentleman of his means, and Theophilus made use of the circumstance to go about telling everybody, in the most confidential manner, that the manager was heavily in debt, that the actors' wages were in arrears, and that affairs at the theatre were in the most deplorable state imaginable. This treachery was too much for Quin, who, whatever may have been his faults,

* The English long after spoke of it as the "great Storm."

was straightforward and honest, and as he did not hesitate to express his opinion of it very forcibly, he and Mr. Cibber soon had a falling out.

From that time Theophilus had nothing good to say of Quin, and the ill-feeling that ever after existed between them came to a head, years later, when the latter was about to retire to Bath to spend the residue of his days in the society of fashionable people, eat well-cooked dinners, and give free exercise to

> " That tongue, which set the table in a roar,
> And charm'd the public ear."

The affair happened in the Bedford coffee-house, which the great actor was wont to frequent, and is thus related by the author of the before quoted *Life of Mr. James Quin, Comedian.** Cibber, whose impertinence constantly kept pace with his vanity, having taken something amiss that Quin said concerning his acting, came one night strutting into the coffee-house, and having walked up to the fireplace he said "He was come to call that *capon-loined rascal*† to an account for taking liberties with his character." Somebody told him that he had been passed by Quin, who was sitting at the other end of the room, by a window. "Ay, so I have sure enough," says he, "but I see he is busy talking to Rich, and I won't disturb them now : I 'll take another opportunity." "But," continued his informant, finding the backwardness of Cibber, and willing to have

* This book was originally published in 1766.

† A delicate allusion to Quin's love for the pleasures of the table.

some sport, " he sets off for Bath to-morrow, and may
not, perhaps, be in town again this twelvemonth."
" Is that the case," said Cibber (somewhat nettled at
finding his courage was suspected), " then I e'en chas-
tise him now."

Upon this he goes up to Quin and calls out aloud :
" You—Mr. Quin, I think you call yourself, I insist
upon satisfaction for the affront you gave me yesterday
—dem-me."   " If you have a mind to be flogged " (replied Quin) " I 'll do it for you with all my heart, d—mn
me !"   " Draw, Sir !" resumed Cibber, " or I 'll be
through you this instant."

" This " (said Quin) " is an improper place to rehearse
Lord Foppington in ; but if you 'll go under the Piazza,
I may, perhaps, make you put up your sword faster
than you drew it."   Cibber now went out ; Quin followed, when they immediately drew.   Cibber parried,
and retreated as far as the garden rails, when Quin,
tired with trifling so long, made a lunge and stumbled
over a stone.   This is too golden an opportunity for
the valiant Theophilus to lose, so he accordingly makes
a bold thrust at the prostrate actor, slightly injuring
him in the forehead, and runs off " full speed towards
the church, as if for sanctuary."

It seems to have been the fate of Quin, with all his
good traits, to go through life with an excitement of
some sort always on hand.   On one occasion he waxed
very angry over a paragraph written by Aaron Hill in
The Prompter (1735) and had a rough and tumble fight

with the author as a result. The offending article spoke of the actor as " Mr. All-weight" and informed him that " to be always *deliberate* and solemn is an error, as certainly, though not as unpardonably, as never to be so. To pause where no pauses are necessary, is the way to destroy their effect when the sense stands in need of their assistance. And, though dignity is finely maintained by the weight of majestic composure, yet are there scenes in your parts where the voice should be sharp and impatient, the look disordered and agonized, the action precipitate and turbulent ; for the sake of such difference as we see in some smooth canal, where the stream is scarce visible compared with the other end of the same canal, rushing rapidly down a cascade, and breaking beauties which owe their attraction to violence." Mr. Hill's critique was evidently a just one, yet what actor, be he ever so great, cares to have his faults publicly analyzed. He may talk very beautifully about his desire to court criticism, but even one dissenting word in a long pæan of praise will grate on him as harshly as does one false note on the sensitive ear of a musician.

But to return to the artistic career of the " deliberate " player who was chided in the above sketch. In the season of 1738-39 he scores a fine success in *Mustapha*, a play wherein the parts of *Solyman, the Magnificent,* and *Rustan*, his vizier, are supposed to refer indirectly to King George II. and Sir Robert Walpole. On the night of its first performance the opponents of the Court party are out in force, and there, in one of the boxes, is the distinguished Pope, who goes behind the scenes and warmly compliments Quin on his impersonation of *Solyman*. The actor is delighted, of course, and when a servant brings the poet his scarlet coat Mr. Quin, all smiles and politeness, rushes forward and adjusts it with his own hands.

The next season sees him giving a personal explanation to his audience, all because a certain play called *The Fatal Retirement* has proved a fiasco. Quin had refused to act in it, and the author, a Mr. Brown, makes up his mind that this circumstance had much to do with the failure of the piece. So the friends of the angered Brown fly to his rescue and make things unpleasant for James every time he appears on the stage after the single performance of the quickly retired *Retirement*. Quin, not to be browbeaten, comes forward one night and tells the house "that at the request of the author he had read his piece before it was acted, and given him his very sincere opinion of it ; that it was the very worst play he had ever read in his life, and for that reason he had refused to act in it." This quickly disposed of Mr. Brown and his admirers.

The next year Quin is basking in the bright sunshine of royalty, for he acts in the gardens of Cliefden before Frederick, Prince of Wales, Prince George (afterward George III.), and others of the heir-apparent's household. Milward, Mills, and more players were there, not forgetting the hoydenish Kitty Clive, who "pleas'd by hiding all attempts to please," and Davies says of the affair : "The accommodation for the company, I was told, was but scanty and ill-managed, and the players were not treated as persons ought to be who are employed by a prince. Quin, I believe, was admitted among those of the higher order, and Mrs. Clive might be safely trusted to take care of herself anywhere." The favored Quin was held in high esteem by Frederick, whose children he instructed in elocution and even in the art of amateur acting, and it is related that when, in after years, he was told what a good impression George III. made in delivering his first speech from the throne, the old man cried out proudly : " Ay ; I taught the boy to speak ! "

In the summer of 1741, Quin paid a professional visit to Dublin (where he had played two years before), in company with Ryan, Mrs. Clive, and Mademoiselle Chateauneuf, a *danseuse* of great European reputation. This was a delightful combination for the appreciative Irish, who were quick to recognize the value of the dramatic feast spread out for their approval, even though the receipts at the theatre were often so meagre that the prudent Quin would never allow the curtain to be raised until his salary had been brought to him behind the scenes. He played the classic *Cato* to the delight of a crowded audience, and afterward figured as *Othello*—a very ponderous sort of Moor he must have been—and went through a round of his other favorite parts, including the senile *Lear*. In the latter performance he was assisted by the bouncing Clive as *Cordelia*, and a pretty bad example of the good daughter she probably made.

"Mrs. Clive was the best player I ever saw" was the comment of Dr. Johnson, which was "praise indeed" from a Sir Hubert who affected to despise the stage, and there is no doubt that in her own line of bustling chambermaids and irrepressible hoydens she must have been a delight even to the most critical. She "had a facetious turn of humor," says Chetwood, "and infinite spirits, with a voice and manner in singing songs of pleasantry peculiar to herself." When only twelve years old, Kitty Raftor (her father was an Irish gentleman named Raftor who followed the fortunes of James II., accompanied him to France, and served for a time as an army officer under the standard of Louis XIV.), had such a love for the theatre that she used to tag after Mr. Wilks in the street, to use her own expression, and gape at him as a wonder. Later on Chetwood brought her to the attention of Colley Cibber, who took her into his company on a salary of twenty shillings a week, and from that moment her future was assured. Even when the London public would have none of Cibber's *Love in a Riddle* her presence in the cast commanded attention, and Chetwood relates that as she came on in the part of *Phillida* the tumult in the house temporarily subsided. "A person in the stage box, next to my post, called out to his companion in the following elegant style:

' Zounds, Tom ! take care, or this charming little devil will save all.' "

This " charming little devil," who, by the way, once referred to Garrick as " that artful devil," must have been a remarkable compound of ugliness and fascination, vulgarity and *naïveté*, bad temper and shrewd common-sense. In her last years she retired to a villa at Strawberry Hill, where she had for an admiring neighbor the gossipy Horace Walpole, and it was in these quiet days that Frederick Reynolds met her at a card party and found out that the inroads of time had exerted no effect on her well-known petulence. " Quadrille was proposed, and all immediately took their stations. . . . I soon observed Mrs. Clive's countenance alternately redden and turn pale, while her antagonist vainly attempted the suppression of a satisfaction that momentarily betrayed itself in the curling corners of her ugly mouth, and in the twinkling of her piggish eyes. At last her Manille went, and with it the remnants of her temper. Her face was of an universal crimson, and tears of rage seemed ready to start into her eyes. At that very moment, as Satan would have it, her opponent, a dowager whose hoary head and eyebrows were as white as those of an Albiness, triumphantly and briskly demanded payment for the two black aces. ' Two black aces ! ' answered the enraged loser, in a voice rendered almost unintelligible by passion, ' here, take the money, though instead, I wish I could give you *two black eyes, you old white cat.* ' "

Quin remained in Ireland until February, 1741–42, and when he got back to London he was pained to learn that the young Garrick, then in the very beginning of his career, had caught the fancy of the fickle public. " Garrick is a new religion, and Whitefield is followed for a time," he growled, " but they will all come to church again." And to this the younger rival answered by writing :

> "Pope Quin, who damns all churches but his own,
>   Complains that heresy corrupts the town :
>   That Whitefield *Garrick* has misled the age.
>   'Schism,' he cries, ' has turned the nation's brain,
>   But eyes will open, and to church again !'
>   Thou great Infallible, forbear to roar,
>   Thy bulls and errors are rever'd no more ;
>   When doctrines meet with general approbation,
>   It is not heresy, but reformation."

From this time on Quin made ineffectual attempts to keep himself upon the pedestal which he had so long occupied, but Garrick was the coming man, and nothing that the veteran could do proved great enough to bring back the undivided allegiance of the town. In the season of 1746-7 he acted at Covent Garden, where Garrick also appeared, and it is recorded that his *Richard III.* " could scarcely draw together a decent appearance of company in the boxes, and he was with some difficulty tolerated in the part, when Garrick acted the same character to crowded houses, and with very great applause."

Poor Quin. He had fallen on strange days, and

his temper, never a model one, suffered not a little from his reverses. He soon had a falling out with Rich, the manager, and went off in a huff to Bath, (1748,) where he rusticated until the beginning of the next season. Then he sent the following brief note to Rich, intending it, probably, in the double light of an apology and a gentle reminder:

"I am at Bath. QUIN." To this the manager laconically replied:

"Stay there and be damned. RICH."

Subsequently, however, he returned to London, and continued on the stage with varying fortune until May, 1751. A few weeks earlier he had been given a benefit, just three days before the death of his most influential patron, the Prince of Wales. By command of the latter the play selected was *Othello*, with Quin as *Iago*, Spranger Barry in the title part, and Mrs. Cibber as *Desdemona*. And yet, melancholy to say, the theatre was far from well-filled. Quin emerged several times afterward from his pleasant exile at Bath to play in London, the last occasion being in 1753, when he revived his famous impersonation of *Falstaff* at a benefit for his friend Ryan. It is cheerful to think that on this "positively last appearance" the old actor had a right worthy reception; indeed, his success was so great that Ryan asked him to repeat the performance the following year. He declined, however, for he had recently lost two of his front teeth, and he explained his refusal in this terse letter:

"My dear friend—There is no person on earth, whom I would sooner serve than Ryan—but, by——, I will whistle *Falstaff* for no man."

Once that he had settled down comfortably at Bath, to enjoy the tittle-tattle of the visitors, and his wine, whist, and venison, all of which he could command through his income from a respectable annuity, Quin forgot his troubles and became one of the wits of the place. He loved to talk of the good things of the table, and he even invented what he styled his " Siamese " soup*; indeed, he prated so incessantly about his gourmandizing that he probably got a worse reputation in that respect than he deserved. How widespread was the popular belief on the subject is shown by Smollett's saying in *Humphrey Clinker* that " Quin is a real voluptuary in the articles of eating and drinking ; and so confirmed an epicure in the common acceptation of the term, that he cannot put up with ordinary fare." And Garrick in a prologue to *Florizel and Perdita*, spoken at Drury Lane in 1756, had a thought for Quin's weakness when he said :

* It is told that Quin was so much bothered by importunate friends to divulge the recipe of this soup that, in revenge, he invited a number of them to dinner, promising to tell them of the ingredients before they departed. When it came time to leave the guests were horrified to discover that the liquid they had so much enjoyed, on the supposition that they were tasting the genuine " Siamese " decoction, had been seasoned with a pair of old shoes, chopped into mincemeat.

" But should you call for *Falstaff*, where to find him,
He's gone, nor left one cup of sack behind him.
Sunk in his elbow chair, no more he'll roam,
No more with merry wags to Eastcheap come ;
He's gone—to jest, and laugh, and give his sack at home."

The old fellow departed this life, with all its capons, turtle soup, and cheering liquors, early in the year 1766. A malignant fever carried him off ; but the ruling passion was strong even in his last moments, and the day before his taking away he drank a bottle of claret—the worst thing that he could have done under the circumstances—and expressed the hope that he should leave all the pleasures of life with becoming dignity. And so ended the career of one of the most striking personalities of the eighteenth century, in whom so many contradicting qualities struggled for mastery. As an actor stilted yet commanding and forceful, as a man bad tempered and sensual, but generous, honest, and witty—such was James Quin, on whose tomb might justly have been written : " After life's fitful fever he sleeps well."

CHAPTER X.

SINCE the golden days of the old Globe Theatre the character of *Shylock* had been a favorite one for the English actor to test his mettle with, yet it remained for an Irishman to play the money-lender as none other had been able to do before him, and as few, if any, have done since. This *Shylock*, of whom the critical Pope said

> " This is the Jew
> That Shakespeare drew,"

was none other than Charles Macklin, who, though he played many different parts, is now best known to fame in connection with the *Merchant of Venice*. He was one of the most disagreeable personalities, as he was also one of the grandest actors, who ever trod the boards of an English theatre ; boorish, quarrelsome, and coarse, with an unpleasant face, (whose lines were once irreverently spoken of as " cordage,") yet for all this a rough diamond of the first water, who sparkled ever so brilliantly on the stage, however unpolished he might seem amid less congenial surroundings.

MACKLIN AND DUNSTALL.

A SCENE FROM COLLEY CIBBER'S "THE PROVOKED HUSBAND." FROM THE DRAWING BY DODD.

Macklin's span of life almost exactly covered the eighteenth century, his birth occurring, presumably, about 1699 and his death in 1797. His first king was William III., his last was George III. ; when he was an ugly, unattractive little brat Marlborough dominated the military stage, and Betterton still figured on the mimic boards, the lovely Bracegirdle charmed all London, and Garrick was yet unborn ; when he died Napoleon Bonaparte had appeared on the horizon of history, Garrick had been gathered to his fathers these eighteen years, and the boy Edmund Kean had already begun, in poverty and drudgery, that phenomenal career whose blaze of glory would be quenched in tears and fire-water. The father of the future *Jew* was a Presbyterian farmer of Ulster, William McLaughlin by name, and his mother happened to be a devout Roman Catholic, so that the contradictions and contrasts in the disposition of young Charles seem to have had a certain excuse in the want of religious harmony existing in the paternal household. In the course of several years McLaughlin, who, despite his Presbyterianism had been a firm adherent of the cause of James II., died of a broken heart, "a victim to misapplied loyalty and mistaken generosity," and the widow dried her eyes in time to marry the landlord of a Dublin inn. Her first husband was the descendant of an Irish King, but Celtic sovereigns could be had at a discount in the Emerald Isle, and well-to-do tavern keepers were not fit subjects for the turning up of one's pretty nose.

Charles was now packed off to a boarding-school near Dublin, kept by a Scotch pedagogue, and here he proved a troublesome sort of pupil, getting a sound whipping pretty much every day, and developing what his biographer, Kirkman, calls a talent of mimicry "which he exercised to the continual annoyance of the pedant, by counterfeiting alternately the voices of him and his wife Harriet, and calling aloud upon either, in the voice of the other so exactly, as to baffle all their vigilance in guarding against his pranks."

During these wild school-days young McLaughlin took part in a performance of *The Orphan*, gotten up by a lady of the neighborhood, and being cast for the fair *Monimia*, acquitted himself with glory, imbibing, at the same time, that taste for the drama which was soon to have such influence on his career. "To those who recollect the figure and the cast of countenance of the veteran," writes William Cooke, another biographer of Macklin, "it must be difficult to reconcile the possibility of his performing this part at any time of life with the smallest degree of propriety ; however, if we are to take his own word for it (which is all the authority that can be adduced) he not only *looked* the *gentle Monimia*, but performed it with every degree of applause and encouragement. The play was repeated three times with great applause before several of the surrounding gentry and tenants, and every time he felt himself acquire additional reputation."

Soon after this juvenile triumph the aspiring *Monimia*,

now in very masculine mood, ran away from home
with a few pounds of his mother's money in his pockets
and escaped over to London in company with two
equally fly-away youths, one of whom eventually ended
his career on the scaffold. After arriving at the metropolis, McLaughlin (for he had not then changed his name
to Macklin) lived in great luxury for several weeks, patronizing all the theatrical performances and otherwise
enjoying himself, and then, when his funds had disappeared, found employment in a public-house which a
lot of mountebanks used as a rendezvous. Here, "by
dint of genius and a high flow of spirits," he "became
the delight of all who frequented the house. He sung
for them, he danced, he mimicked, he spouted, and he
played the droll, insomuch that his fame spread abroad,
and the house was every night filled with respectable
opulent dealers. Clubs and meetings were instituted
for the purpose of enjoying the entertainment he afforded. In short, he became a most pleasing and popular character in that circle, and more than trebled the
income of the house by his talents." *

The rosy widow who kept the inn thought so much
of Master McLaughlin that she proposed to marry him,
and it is even said that they went through the form of
a wedding, but be that as it may, he was soon induced
to return to Dublin and accept the modest position of
"badgeman" or porter at Trinity College. A badgeman was subject to the call of the students, upon

* Kirkman.

whom he was expected to wait, and whenever it was
his turn to serve, and he heard the cry of "Boy" he
would reply "What number?" to learn what room
he should go to for his orders. Long after these unpleasant experiences of servitude Macklin happened to
be playing at the Dublin Theatre when a party of bois-
terous young fellows created a disturbance in the house.
The actor came forward and soundly scolded them for
their impertinence, much to the chagrin of the black-
guards, and one of them, intending to be very insult-
ing, brutally cried out "Boy!" This ungenerous
reference to his old college days disconcerted Macklin
for a second, but when he replied, the very next
moment, "What number?" the house fairly shook
with the applause that rewarded his ready wit and
presence of mind.

For a youth like Macklin the life of a badgeman
proved even more than usually repulsive, and it was
not long before he shook the dust of Trinity from his
feet, and turned strolling actor, finally bringing up as
a member of an itinerant company recently established
in a small theatre at Bristol. With this place as a base
of operation he travelled through Welsh and English
towns and villages, being all things by turns, from
stage manager or preserver of the peace to playwright
and actor, and gaining in this curious school of dramatic adversity no end of valuable experience. "Sometimes he was an architect, and knocked up the stage
and seats in a barn ; sometimes he wrote an opening

prologue, or a parting epilogue, for the company : at others he wrote a song, complimentary and adulatory to the village they happened to play in, which he always adapted to some sprightly popular air, and sung himself ; and he often was champion, and stood forward to repress the persons who were accustomed to intrude upon and be rude to the actors.''

Those were days when a player's path was seldom strewn with roses, but for all that his very trials and tribulations helped to bring out any talent that might be in him. What would not a few Thespians of modern times say to roughing it after such a fashion, accustomed, as they too often are, to presenting but one character night after night, perhaps for three or four seasons at a stretch, and thinking themselves in poor luck when called to take part in an occasional rehearsal. How would they like the sensation, quite a familiar one to Macklin, of playing in one evening *Antonio* and *Belvidera* in *Venice Preserved*, *Harlequin* in the incidental entertainment, singing three humorous songs between the acts and furnishing, in addition to all this, a lively Irish jig. But this was the sort of discipline the stroller was subjected to until he drifted back to London, and appeared at Lincoln's Inn Fields in 1725 as *Alcander* in the *Œdipus* of Dryden and Lee.

But it was to be some years, however, before Macklin could score any real success on the metropolitan stage, for his cultivation of dramatic methods more natural than those of his contemporaries was by no means appreciated on his first emerging from the provinces. "I spoke so *familiar*, sir," he related years afterwards, "and so little in the *hoily-toily* tone of the tragedy of that day, that the manager* told me I had better go to grass for another year or two." To grass he did go for a year or two, playing once more in oft-visited neighborhoods, making Herculean efforts to get rid of his Irish brogue, and succeeding, changing his name to Mecklin or Macklin, as a concession to English prejudice, changing his religion too, and boasting that he was as staunch a Protestant as the Archbishop of Canterbury. It was during this transition period, also, that the adopter of a new accent, name, and creed, further altered his condition by taking to himself a wife who was afterwards to win distinction in her husband's profession.†

When the Drury Lane actors revolted from the management of Highmore and set up for themselves in the Haymarket, Macklin and his wife were engaged to appear at the former house, and it was here that the man

---

* Rich.

† One authority says that before her marriage Mrs. Macklin was a Mrs. Ann Grace, the widow of a Dublin hosier, while according to another oracle she was originally a Miss Grace Purvor, with whose charms His Grace of Argyle had been deeply smitten. She eventually achieved a great reputation in "old woman's" parts of the comic order, and Chetwood writes of her: "She never sets up for a heroine, or attempts to appear in an improper light; she knows the power of her own talents, and always shines with unborrow'd light, without the danger of being eclipsed."

who had been invited to " go to grass " began to build
the foundations of a great reputation by essaying, with
considerable approbation, a number of the elder Cibber's parts. On the return of the original company,
under the standard of Fleetwood, Macklin left Drury
Lane, and played for a time in the Haymarket. He
soon re-appeared at the old stand, however, and quickly
became the confidant and adviser of the new manager,
as well as his companion at White's gambling establishment. Fleetwood lost large sums of money through
too frequent visits to this delectable resort, and having
recourse to borrowing once induced Macklin to go his
bond to the tune of three thousand pounds. The actor contrived to have the poet Whitehead take his place
as the bondsman, and when Fleetwood, head over ears
in debt, fled from the kingdom to escape his creditors,
the obliging versifier, being utterly unable to pay the
amount for which he was now responsible, had to languish in jail for a lengthy period.

The excuse of Macklin, that " every man will save
himself from ruin if he can " will not heighten our idea
of his personal character, nor does a tragic occurrence
of the year 1735 put his fierce temper before us in any
but a wretched light. This occurrence was nothing less
than the killing of Thomas Hallam, a fellow-member
of the Drury Lane company, as the result of a childish
quarrel over the ownership of a wig. Perhaps the story
will be best told by giving the testimony of Thomas
Arne, who happened to be a witness when Macklin had

to stand trial for his life at the Old Bailey.   Arne deposed * :

"I have the honor to be the numberer of the boxes of Drury Lane play-house, under Mr. Fleetwood.   On Saturday night [May 10th] I delivered my accounts in at the property office ; and then, at eight, I came into the scene room, where the players warm themselves, and sat in a chair at the side of the fire.   Fronting the fire there is a long seat, where five or six may sit.   The play [*Trick for Trick*] was almost done, and they were making preparations for the entertainment, when the prisoner came into the same room and sat down next to me, and high words arose between him and the deceased about a stock wig for a disguise in the entertainment.   The prisoner had played in the wig the night before, and now, the deceased had got it.   ' D—n you for a rogue,' says the prisoner ; ' what business have you with my wig ? '   ' I am no more a rogue than yourself,' says the deceased.   ' It 's a stock wig, and I have as much right to it as you have.'   Some of the players coming in, they desired the deceased to fetch the wig, and give it to the prisoner, which he did and then said to him, ' Here is your wig.   I have got one I like better.'   The prisoner sitting by me, took the wig, and began to comb it out, and all seemed to be quiet for about half a quarter of an hour ; but the prisoner began to grumble again, and said to the deceased,

* This testimony is quoted by Edward A. Parry in his interesting memoirs of Macklin.

'G—d d—n you for a blackguard, scrub, rascal, how durst you have the impudence to take this wig?'

"The deceased answered, 'I am no more a rascal than yourself.' Upon which the prisoner started up from his chair, and with a stick in his hand, made a lunge at the deceased, and thrust the stick into his left eye, and, pulling it back again, looked pale, turned on his heel, and, in a passion, threw the stick into the fire. 'G—d d—n it!' says he; and, turning about again on his heel, he sat down. The deceased clapped his hand to his eye, and said it was gone through his head. He was going to sink, but they set him in a chair. The prisoner came to him, and leaning upon his left arm, put his hand to his eye. 'Lord!' cried the deceased, 'it is out!' 'No,' says the prisoner, 'I feel the ball roll under my hand.' Young Mr. Cibber came in, and immediately sent for Mr. Coldham, the surgeon."

The unfortunate Hallam died within a few hours, and the only punishment that seems to have been meted out to Macklin was an empty verdict of manslaughter. Viewing the latter simply as an actor, we are glad to see him soon back again at Drury Lane, popular as ever, but judging him quite apart from his profession one cannot but regret that he suffered so little for his brutal lack of self-control.

During these early days in London a great rivalry sprang up between Quin and Macklin, and for many years these two giants of the stage—one so tenacious of the old, artificial methods, and the other struggling

for a freer, truer standard of acting—were at metaphori-
cal daggers drawn.   In old age they became reconciled,
yet they probably never forgot the most absurd of all
their quarrels, which occurred a year or two after the
death of Hallam.   One night when Macklin came off
the stage from playing *Jerry Blackacre* in the *Plain
Dealer*, Quin, who was doing *Captain Manly*, reproached
him for trying to dominate the scene and obtaining the
attention of the audience at the expense of the other
performers.   "Well, sir," said Macklin in narrating
the affair half a century later, "I told him that I did
not mean to disturb *him* by my acting, *but to show off a
little myself*.   Well, sir, in the other scenes I did the
same, and made the audience laugh incontinently, and
he scolded me again, sir.   I made the same apology,
but the surly fellow would not be appeased.   Again,
sir, however, I did the same ; and when I returned to
the greenroom he abused me like a pickpocket, and
said I must leave off my *damned* tricks.   I told him I
could not play otherwise.   He said I could, and I
should.   Upon which, sir, egad ! I said to him flatly,
'you lie !'   He was chewing an apple at this moment ;
and spitting the contents into his hand, he threw them
into my face.

"It is a fact, sir !   Well, sir, I went up to him directly (for I was a great *boxing cull* in those days) and
pushed him down into a chair and pummelled his face
damnably.   He strove to resist but he was no match
for me ; and I made his face swell so with the blows,

that he could hardly speak. When he attempted to go on with his part, sir, he mumbled so, that the audience began to hiss. Upon which he went forward and told them, sir, that something very unpleasant had happened, and that he was really very ill. But, sir, the moment I went to strike him, there were many noblemen in the greenroom, full dressed, with their swords and large wigs (for the greenroom was a sort of stateroom then, sir). Well, they were all alarmed, and jumped upon the benches, waiting in silent amazement, till the affair was over."

To curtail Macklin's description of the episode it may be added that at the end of the performance Quin demanded the doubtful sort of "satisfaction" that is supposed to come from the code of honor, but through the entreaties of Fleetwood, who had no desire to lose so valuable an actor as the fuming challenger, the matter was settled peaceably by an apology from Macklin. The latter could afford to offer one with good grace, for he had inflicted a glorious thumping on his hated rival. It was that rival who once said of Macklin, when it was remarked that the Irishman had strong *lines* in his face, "Lines, sir! I see nothing in the fellow's face but a damned deal of *cordage*."

But let us leave all this interesting pettiness and come down to the year 1741, when Macklin, who by this time had blossomed out into an unquestioned popular favorite, would put forth a *Shylock* radically different from the comic *Jew* of the red wig type to which theatre-goers had been accustomed. He had long debated, no doubt, on the dramatic possibilities and seriousness of the role, and the absurdity of regarding it as material for merry-making, and finally he induced Fleetwood to revive the real *Merchant of Venice*, which had long been superseded by Lord Lansdowne's adaptation known as *The Jew of Venice*. In the latter, an unnecessary version of a noble original, the inimitable Dogget had once upon a time represented *Shylock* from a low-comedy standpoint, to the great amusement and edification of the groundlings, and in later years the frolicksome Clive played *Portia* after the manner of a stage chambermaid, and took such liberties with the character that she even mimicked well-known lawyers in the trial scene. Strange to say, it was this rompish actress who did *Portia* on the memorable night when Macklin revolutionized the public conception of the usurious *Jew*.

While the rehearsals were in progress it began to be whispered around that Macklin intended to spring a very dangerous innovation on the management of Drury Lane; the amiable Quin (who was cast for *Antonio*, predicted that the new *Shylock* would be hissed off the stage, and Fleetwood, becoming alarmed, tried to abandon the production altogether. But Macklin never faltered in his purpose, and held the manager to his promise, so on the evening of St. Valentine's Day the frequenters of Drury Lane had the pleasure of assisting at one of the most historical of all the important performances in the eighteenth century. Let us quote the actor himself as to the outcome of his risky experiment.

"The long-expected night at last arrived, and the house was crowded from top to bottom with the first company in town. The two front rows of the pit as usual were full of critics, who, Sir, I eyed through the slit of curtain, and was glad to see them, as I wished in such a cause to be tried by a special jury. When I made my appearance in the greenroom, dressed for the part, with my red hat on my head, my piqued beard, loose black gown, etc., and with a confidence which I never before assumed, the performers all stared at one another, and evidently with a stare of disappointment. Well, sir, hitherto all was right till the last bell rung ; then, I confess, my heart began to beat a little. However, I mustered up all the courage I could, and, recommending my cause to Providence, threw myself boldly on the stage, and was received by one of the loudest thunders of applause I ever before experienced.

"The opening scenes being rather tame and level, I could not expect much applause, but I found myself well listened to. I could hear distinctly in the pit the words ' Very well—very well indeed ! This man seems to know what he is about,' etc., etc. These encomiums warmed me, but did not overset me. I knew where I should have the pull, which was in the third act, and reserved myself accordingly. At this period I threw out all my fire, and, as the contrasted passions of joy for the *Merchant's* losses, and grief for the elopement of *Jessica*, open a fine field for an actor's powers, I had the good fortune to please beyond my warmest expectations. The whole house was in an uproar of applause, and I was obliged to pause between the speeches to give it vent, so as to be heard.

" When I went behind the scenes after this act, the manager met me and complimented me very highly on my performance, and significantly added : ' Macklin, you *was* right at last.' My brethren in the greenroom joined in this eulogium, but with different views. He was thinking of the increase of his treasury ; they, only for saving appearances, wishing at the same time that I had broke my neck in the attempt. The trial scene wound up the fulness of my reputation. Here I was well listened to ; and here I made such a silent yet forcible impression on my audience, that I retired from this great attempt most perfectly satisfied. On my return to the greenroom after the play was over it was crowded with nobility and critics, who all complimented me in the warmest and most unbounded manner, and the situation I felt myself in, I must confess, was one of the most flattering and intoxicating of my whole life. No money, no title could purchase what I felt. And let no man tell me after this what Fame will not inspire a man to do, and how far the attainment of it will not remunerate his greatest labors. By G—d, sir, though I was not worth fifty pounds in the world at that time, yet, let me tell you, I was Charles the Great for that night."

Thus, at one bound, Macklin reached a commanding position on the stage, added to his repertoire a character which he would exploit successfully, at intervals, for the next half century, and showed the conservative British public that "the *Jew* that Shakespeare drew" should be played as a malevolent, passionate creature, and not as a semi-buffoon from whom the unthinking might extract many a hearty guffaw.

The *Merchant of Venice* drew crowded houses for twenty-one nights, while noblemen, critics, and the general theatre-goers vied with one another in praising the iconoclastic Macklin, who must have felt by this time that nothing succeeded so well as success. The dramatic force and almost ferocious attributes of his *Shylock* soon enlisted the royal attention of his very German Majesty George II., who went to see the performance, and was made so nervous by its realism that he hardly slept the whole of that night. " In the morning," according to the actor Bernard, " the Premier, Sir Robert Walpole, waited on the King, to express his fears that the Commons would oppose a certain measure then in contemplation. ' I wish, your Majesty,' said Sir Robert, ' it was possible to find a recipe for frightening a House of Commons.' ' What do you think,' replied the King, ' of sending them to the theatre to see that Irishman play *Shylock?* ' "

The enthusiasm over the *Merchant of Venice* might have been turned to good account by Fleetwood, but that worthy, having apparently made up his mind to ruin himself and his theatre as fast as circumstances would allow, went on gambling and borrowing to make good his losses, getting into debt right and left, leaving his actors' wages unpaid, and generally behaving in a way to scandalize all decent men who had any dealings with him. Affairs finally got so bad that Garrick, by this time a very important member of the company, proposed that the players should leave Fleetwood and his house in a body, it being hoped that the Lord Chamberlain, otherwise the Duke of Grafton, would grant them permission to start a separate theatrical establishment of their own. After some objection from Macklin, the plan was adopted, and a petition setting forth the grievances and desires of the actors brought to the attention of the Duke. The latter, however, had no very high opinion of the "profession," and when he heard that Garrick received a salary of five hundred pounds a year his Grace was horrified at the fellow's presumption in wanting an increase. Oliver Twist asking for more gruel must have been modesty itself compared to so audacious a suggestion. Grafton doubtless thought that the compensation of Garrick's was just five hundred pounds of honest money wasted, and, indeed, he said to him : " And this you think too little, whilst I have a son, who is heir to my title and estate, venturing his life daily for his King and country at much less than half that sum.''

Thus it came to pass that the happy possessor of so precious a son refused to grant the petition, and it was not long before all the players had returned to the fold of the erratic Fleetwood, barring the obstinate Macklin. The great *Shylock* had been loth to enter into the revolt, but once that he did he resolved to hold out for good and all, with the result that he became *persona non grata* to the triumphant manager. Garrick, in negotiating for the return of the company, secured for himself the much-longed-for raise in his own salary, but no one else seemingly benefited in any way by the cessation of hostilities, and the unfortunate Macklin found himself very much in the cold. In the meantime a strong party was raised up in favor of the exile, whose banishment, it was considered, and probably with reason, might be directly traced to the desire of Garrick to take care of himself and allow his Satanic Majesty to look after the '' hindmost '' of the party. When little Davy made his reappearance at Drury Lane the excitement was intense ; he was greeted with hisses, groans, cat-calls, and showers of peas, eggs, and apples, but he held his own and in a few days the too-zealous friends of Macklin had to own that they could accomplish nothing for their favorite.

By no means downcast, the masterful subject of all this misplaced agitation organized a company of his own, comprising, for the most part, the veriest novices in dramatic art, and after putting them through a deal of training he managed to secure the Haymarket Theatre, which he opened in February, 1744. This piece of enterprise, which soon died a natural death, exerted an important influence on Macklin's life, in that it gave him the idea, which he afterward followed out so successfully, of coaching young aspirants. John O'Keefe gives an entertaining account of how the veteran, a number of years later, instructed two of his pupils, Miss Ambrose and Mr. Glenville. Macklin was then living in Dublin, and O'Keefe relates:

"In Macklin's garden there were three long parallel walks, and his method of exercising their voices was thus: his two young pupils with back-boards (such as they use in boarding-schools) walked firmly, slow and well up and down the two side-walks; Macklin himself paraded the centre walk. At the end of every twelve paces he made them stop; and turning gracefully, the young actor called out across the walk, 'How do you do, Miss Ambrose?' She answered, 'Very well, I thank you, Mr. Glenville!' They then took a few more paces and the next question was, 'Do you not think it a very fine day, Mr. Glenville?' 'A very fine day, indeed, Miss Ambrose!' was the answer. Their walk continued and then, 'How do you do, Mr. Glenville?' 'Pretty well, I thank you, Miss Ambrose!' And this exercise continued for an hour or so (Macklin still keeping in the centre walk) in the full hearing of their religious next-door neighbors. Such was Mack-

lin's method of training the management of the voice;
if too high, too low, a wrong accent, or a faulty inflec-
tion, he immediately noticed it, and made them repeat
the words twenty times till all was right."

In December, 1744, when Drury Lane had fallen into
new hands and Fleetwood had taken himself out of
England to escape his many creditors, Macklin re-appeared there, to the great satisfaction of the town.
Soon he tries his hand at play-writing. Then he is
acting under the management of Garrick and James
Lacy, and we hear grotesque stories of his living in
Bow Street lodgings, in company with the former and
delightful Peg Woffington, all three sharing in a common purse and behaving generally in a curiously
unconventional fashion. Next he visits Ireland, soon
quarrels with Thomas Sheridan, the manager of the
Smock Alley Theatre in Dublin, returns to England,
and joins the Covent Garden forces under Rich. Now
he has congenial work in bringing before the public
his talented daughter Mary, an actress who could play
anything from *Ophelia* to a young man's part, and
whose singing and dancing were always the object
of much admiration. Her father spent a great deal
of money on her preliminary education, having her
instructed in many polite accomplishments that were
regarded quite *de rigeur* in those days, but when she
came to die, in 1781, it was found that she had willed
her modest fortune away from the old man.

The year 1754 witnessed the putting into effect by

Macklin of one of the wildest and most impossible of schemes imaginable—nothing less indeed, than setting himself up in Hart street, Covent Garden, as a tavern-keeper. Here he expected to make a fortune by attracting to the place a host of brilliant men, who, after dining at his ordinary, would listen to a lecture by the ex-actor. This remarkable enterprise, to which he gave the imposing name of "The British Inquisition," came to an ignominious end, as might have been expected, with the bankruptcy of the projector.

But the scope of this unpretentious volume will not admit of a complete narrative of Macklin's life, however interesting are its varied and oft-times stirring incidents. That "sour-face dog," as Fielding once called him, lived to drag out a painful old age, rendered pathetic by his constant struggles to keep on the boards in spite of failing memory, and thus escape the misery of actual want.* We may pass over this time of mental decay, and content ourselves, by way of conclusion, with William Cooke's description of the old warrior's last appearance on an earthly stage. It was in May, 1789, when he was cast for the perennial *Shylock.*

"When Macklin had dressed himself for the part, which he did with his usual accuracy, he went into the greenroom, but with such a ' lack-lustre looking eye '

---

* It is cheerful to note, however, that the last four years of Macklin's life were made comparatively comfortable by the receipt of an annuity. It was purchased for him after the publication of his two plays, the *Man of the World* and *Love à la Mode,* had yielded £1500.

as plainly indicated his inability to perform, and coming up to the late Mrs. Pope, said, ' My dear, are you
to play to-night ? '   ' Good God ! to be sure I am, sir.
Why, don't you see I am dressed for *Portia ?* '   ' Ah !
very true ; I had forgot.   But, who is to play *Shylock ?*
The imbecile tone of his voice, and the inanity of the
look, with which the last question was asked, caused a
melancholy sensation in all who heard it.   At last Mrs.
Pope, rousing herself, said ' Why, you, to be sure ; are
you not dressed for the part ? '   He then seemed to recollect himself and, putting his hand to his head, exclaimed ' God help me !   My memory, I am afraid, has
left me.'   He, however, after this went on the stage,
delivered two or three speeches of *Shylock* in a manner
that evidently proved he did not understand what he
was repeating.   After a while he recovered himself a
little, and seemed to make an effort to rouse himself,
but in vain ; nature could assist him no further ; and,
after pausing some time as if considering what to do,
he then came forward and informed the audience,
' That he now found he was unable to proceed in the
part, and hoped they would accept Mr. Ryder* as his
substitute, who was already prepared to finish it.'   The
audience accepted his apology with a mixed applause
of indulgence and commiseration, and he retired from
the stage forever.''

* His understudy.

CHAPTER XI.

"A VERY GOOD MIMIC."

"ALL the run is now after Garrick, a wine merchant, who is turned player, at Goodman's Fields. He plays all parts and is a very good mimic. His acting I have seen and may say to you, who will not say it again here, I see nothing wonderful in it ; but it is heresy to say so."

Thus wrote, in 1742, the observant but cynical Horace Walpole, who could never see much to wonder at in anything, and who, doubtless, thought he was dealing liberally by Mr. Garrick in allowing him to be a "very good mimic." For an ex-wine-merchant this was generous praise.

The mimic who had excited the momentary attention of this most entertaining of gossips had come up to London from Litchfield in company with his tutor, gruff young Samuel Johnson, in the year 1736, with the intention of completing his studies under a Rev. Mr. Colson and ultimately practising at the bar. His arrival was preceded by several letters to the clergyman from an influential functionary of Litchfield, Gilbert Walmsley, who wrote : "My neighbor, Captain Gar-

DAVID GARRICK.

AFTER A PAINTING BY SIR JOSHUA REYNOLDS.   FROM AN ENGRAVING BY
W. H. WORTHINGTON.

rick * (who is an honest valuable man) has a son who is a very sensible young fellow, and a good scholar, and whom the Captain hopes, in some two or three years, he shall be able to send to the Temple, and breed to the Bar. But, at present, his pocket will not hold out for sending him to the University. I have proposed you taking him, if you think well of it, and your boarding him, and instructing him in mathematics, and philosophy, and humane learning. He is now nineteen, of sober and good dispositions, and is as ingenious and promising a young man as ever I knew. in my life." And in a subsequent letter Walmsley announces that Davy " and another neighbor of mine, one Mr. Johnson, set out this morning for London together ; Davy to be with you early the next week ; and Mr. Johnson to try his fate with a tragedy, and to see to get himself employed in some translation, either from the Latin or the French. Johnson is a very good scholar and poet, and I have great hopes will turn out a fine tragedy writer."

How differently things were to turn out. Garrick would be the one to " try his fate " with tragedy—and comedy as well, and the learned Johnson, though he

---

. * Captain Garrick, who held a commission in the King's army, was the grandson of a French Protestant of that name who settled in England after the revocation of the Edict of Nantes. The Captain married the daughter of a Litchfield vicar, and David was born in 1716 in the Angel Inn at Hereford, where the father of the future Roscius was then stationed as a recruiting officer.

might try his hand at play-writing, would live to culti-
vate a strongly expressed if hardly sincere aversion for
everything connected with the stage.   Young Garrick,
to be sure, had already imbibed a love for the theatre ;
he had been in London before, had there seen Macklin
and the stilted Quin, and his heart could never be in
the dry-as-dust volumes that he was required to pore
over as preparation for the prosaic law.   Soon an uncle,
(to see whom he had once made a trip to Lisbon,) conveniently died and left him a thousand pounds, then
came the taking off of his father, the Captain, and
Garrick, soon emerging from under the paternal wing
of the Rev. Mr. Colson, abandoned the classic atmosphere of philosophy and legal lore for the less exalted
air of the wine cellar.   In other words David and his
brother Peter went into business as wine-merchants,
and Foote, the mimic and comedian, would relate in
after years how the future actor thought he really was
a wine-merchant because he kept three quarts of vine-
gar in the cellar.

But whatever the Garrick vaults contained, it is certain that one of the partners took no interest in them,
fortunately for posterity, for the very man who was to
become so avaricious as to chide that Irish sorceress,
Peg Woffington, for wasting his tea, refused to settle
down into the humdrum existence of a liquor-flavored
life in Durham Yard.   While the plodding Peter attended to the affairs of the firm David's mind was far
away, wondering what the Drury Lane company would

play next, or dreaming, perhaps, that he were himself the hero of this very house, as, indeed, it shortly came to pass. But irregular ways and the building of air castles, did not harmonize very successfully with the selling of stimulants, so the partnership was soon dissolved, and David now joyfully turned his attention towards that consuming ambition to shine on the stage —an ambition which had possessed him ever since his school-boy days, when he electrified the good people of Litchfield by superintending a performance of *The Recruiting Officer* and playing *Sergeant Kite* with wonderful grace and vivacity. The last obstacle in his way, the natural objections of a mother who shared in the customary prejudices of her time, had been removed by the recent death of that amiable lady, and as Thomas Davies says in his memoirs of Garrick : " Mr. Garrick now found himself free from all restraint, and in a situation to indulge himself in his darling passion for acting, from which nothing but his tenderness for so dear a relation as a mother had hitherto restrained him."

It may be doing Garrick an injustice to say so, but it is quite possible that even this obstacle would not have interfered very materially with the plans of a youth who, with all his charm, grace of manner, genius and lovableness had a peculiar streak of selfishness and shrewdness in his curiously complex character. To be sure, Dibdin declared him to be " an actor, a complete actor and nothing but an actor," whether on or off the stage, alone or in company, " or about whatever study,

15

occupation or pursuit," but David was never so much
the actor as to forget his own interests, and while he
had the divine afflatus he also showed the instincts and
cold-blooded virtues of a man of the world. Macklin,
who knew him well, perhaps spoke half truly, if bit-
terly, when he said of the great player that " to friendship with man, or love and friendship with woman, he
never was disposed, for love of himself always forbid
it."

Soon after Garrick's retirement from the unclassic
precincts of hogsheads and wine casks we hear of him
fraternizing with the best known of the London actors,
cultivating the managers and others most likely to be
of service to him, studying and reciting passages from
popular plays and even posing, occasionally, as a dramatic critic for the public prints. In the latter capacity, we are told, he generally indulged in "judicious
observations and shrewd remarks, unmixed with that
gross illiberality which often disgraces the instructions
of modern stage critics." The next and by far the more
important step was his appearance at Ipswich, in the
summer of 1741, in a company under the direction of
Messrs. Giffard and Dunstall. He was not quite sure
of himself as yet, and did not wish to have the name of
Garrick associated with failure, so he chose " Mr. Lyddal" for a *nom de théâtre*. It was as Lyddal, therefore,
that he made his *début* in the character of *Aboan*, in
the still popular drama of *Oroonoko*, delighting the
audiences of commonplace Ipswich (who in after years

claimed that they had discovered the new Roscius) with this and other impersonations.

Even at this early stage of his career one detects the remarkable versatility of the man, for during his stay here he not only played the sorely tried *Aboan*,* the dashing *Sir Harry Wildair*, and other contrasting roles, but he actually scored a success as *Harlequin*. Garrick had from the first a genius for depicting a variety of emotions from the most tragic to the broadly farcical, so that whether he lent sublimity to *King Lear*, put new life into some genteel comedy role, or appeared in a character of the roughly humorous order, where his wonderful mimetic talents came into full play, he nearly always seemed peculiarly fitted by voice, gesture, look, and acting for whatever character he happened to be portraying at the time. In after years he would, on rare and ever-to-be remembered occasions, indulge his friends with what he called his *rounds.* "This he did by standing behind a chair, and conveying into his face every kind of passion, blending one into the other, and as it were shadowing them with a prodigious number of gradations. At one moment you laughed, at another you cried; now he terrified you, and presently you conceived yourself something horrible, he seemed so terrified at you. Afterward he drew his features into the appearance of

---

* Garrick chose this character for his *début* so that he might appear with a blackened face, and thus escape identification if he made a fiasco.

such dignified wisdom that Minerva might have been proud of the portrait ; and then—degrading, yet admirable transition—he became a driveller. In short, his face was what he obliged you to fancy it—age, youth, plenty, poverty, everything it assumed." *

While Garrick continued to give his Ipswichian admirers a series of performances the like of which it had never before been their pleasure to enjoy, that fertile brain of his was planning how he should make his initial metropolitan appearance in the autumn, when Messrs. Giffard and Dunstall were to bring their company for the winter season to the theatre in Goodman's Fields.† He finally decided to begin his venture with *Richard III.*, for, as he explained with a canniness worthy of a frugal Scotchman, "if I should come forth in a hero, or any part which is generally acted by a tall fellow, I shall not be offered a larger salary than forty shillings per week." Indeed, he could not have come to a better determination whether from an artistic or— what seemed equally important to the actor—a financial point of view. Then, as now, the fortunes of *Glocester* were a source of interest both to the groundlings and the critical, and there was the further advantage, as Garrick himself plainly said, of appearing in a

---

* Dibdin.

† This theatre was founded in 1729 by a certain Thomas Odell, much to the scandal of many pious citizens in the vicinity. It was subsequently shut up, owing to the objections of the neighbors, but reopened in 1732 under Giffard's management.

part where tallness of stature or heroic figure would
not be expected. For this young giant of the stage
was only a giant in ability ; he was a little fellow as
physical measurement went and in that way at least
justified the contemptuous remark of old Cibber that he
was " the completest little doll of a figure—the prettiest
little creature." Then Cibber had no wish to see any
good in Garrick, whom he foolishly looked upon as a
rival to his worthless son, Theophilus, and even the
sting of the description could never blind one to the
distinction and personal advantages of this " little doll."
He had, in the first place, the most expressive features
—something that once prompted the free-tongued
Clive * to cry " Damn him, he could act a *gridiron*"

* Clive, a thorough artist herself, appreciated Garrick's
dramatic worth even better than most of her contemporaries.
" In the height of the public admiration for you," she writes
him, " when you were never mentioned but as Garrick the
charming man, the fine fellow, the delightful creature, both by
men and ladies, when they were admiring everything you did,
and everything you scribbled, at this very time, I, *the Pivy*,
was a living witness that they did not know, nor could they be
sensible of half your perfections. I have seen you with your
Magic hammer in your hand endeavoring to beat your ideas
into the heads of creatures who had none of their own. I have
seen you with lamb-like patience, endeavoring to make them
comprehend you, and I have seen you when that could not be
done—I have seen your lamb turned into a lion ; by this your
great labor and pains the public was entertained ; they thought
they all acted very fine ; they did not see you pull the wires."
Discerning Clive, you would have made a charming writer had
fate not decreed that you should become famous by reciting
the words of others rather than your own. With a lusty eloquence like yours, perhaps it was better for your reputation.

—and, as Fitzgerald had so graphically written, he was "neatly and elegantly made ; handsome, with a French grace, yet combined with perfect manliness. His frame had a surprising flexibility, and even elasticity, which put all his limbs under the most perfect control ; there was an elegant freedom in every motion, regulated by the nicest propriety. His features were wonderfully marked ; the eyebrows well-arched, ascending and descending with rapid play ; the mouth expressive and bold ; and the wonderful eyes, bright, intelligent, and darting fire."

The new *Richard* appeared in October, 1741, at the Goodman's Fields theatre before a curious but not over-large audience.* The naturalness of his performance at first startled, not to say shocked, the more critical among the spectators, who had been used to a bombastic *Glocester*, with plenty of theatrical clap-trap but as the play progressed and they discovered the true effectiveness of the impersonation their half-formed censure turned into the most cordial sort of applause. So successful, indeed, proved the experiment of dressing *Richard* in this new guise, and so pleased were the discriminating theatre-goers, that the play was repeated six times. The receipts were not magnificent, the take for the seven nights amounting only to £216 or £217 ; but as Garrick began to be talked about, discussed, praised, or objected to, the

---

* He was billed as "A Gentleman (who never appeared on any stage)."

GOODMAN'S FIELDS.

October 19th, 1741.

At the late Theatre in Goodman's Fields, this Day will be performed,

A Concert of Vocal and Instrumental Music,

DIVIDED INTO TWO PARTS.

TICKETS AT THREE, TWO, AND ONE SHILLING.

Places for the Boxes to be taken at the Fleece Tavern, near the Theatre.

N. B. Between the Two Parts of the Concert will be presented an Historical Play, called the

LIFE AND DEATH OF

King Richard the Third.

CONTAINING THE DISTRESSES OF K. HENRY VI.

The artful acquisition of the Crown by King Richard,

The Murder of Young King Edward V. and his Brother in the Tower,

THE LANDING OF THE EARL OF RICHMOND,

And the Death of King Richard in the memorable Battle of Bosworth Field, being the last that was fought between the Houses of York and Lancaster; with many other true Historical Passages.

The Part of King Richard by A GENTLEMAN,

(Who never appeared on any Stage).

King Henry, by Mr. GIFFARD,   Richmond, Mr. MARSHALL,

Prince Edward, by Miss HIPPISLEY.   Duke of York, Miss NAYLOR,

Duke of Buckingham, Mr. PATERSON,   Duke of Norfolk, Mr. BLAKES,   Lord Stanley, Mr. PAGETT,

Oxford, Mr. VAUGHAN,   Tressel, Mr. W. GIFFARD,   Catesby, Mr. MARR,   Ratcliff, Mr. CROFTS,

Blunt, Mr. NAYLOR,   Tyrrel, Mr. PUTTENHAM,   Lord Mayor, Mr. DUNSTALL.

The Queen, Mrs. STEEL,   Duchess of York, Mrs. YATES,

And the Part of Lady Anne, by Mrs. GIFFARD.

WITH

Entertainments of Dancing,

By Mons. FROMET   Madame DUVALT,   and the Two Masters and Miss GRANIER.

To which will be added a Ballad Opera, of One Act, called

The Virgin Unmask'd.

The Part of Lucy, by Miss HIPPISLEY.

Both of which will be performed Gratis, by Persons for their Diversion.

——————

The Concert will begin exactly at Six o'Clock.

AN HISTORIC PLAYBILL.

FACSIMILE OF THE PROGRAMME FOR GARRICK'S FIRST LONDON APPEARANCE.

houses soon visibly increased in size, especially when he displayed the many-sided qualities of his art by essaying a round of characters. One of the latter, wherein he particularly caught the fancy of the town, was that of *Bayes* in *The Rehearsal*, and his acting in this part had, according to a story made public many years later, a prologue of a rather serious nature—which might have put an untimely extinguisher on the new star. As *Bayes*, Garrick was to caricature some of his brother performers, and he proposed to Giffard that he should begin with that manager, and thus prevent the other players from grumbling because they were burlesqued. Giffard, as the anecdote runs, "supposing that Garrick would only just glance at him, to countenance the mimicry of the others, consented, but Garrick hit him off so truly, and made him so completely ridiculous, at rehearsal, that Giffard, in a rage, sent him a challenge, which Garrick accepting, they met the next morning, when the latter was wounded in the sword arm." So the production of *The Rehearsal* had to be postponed for a few nights, "on account," as officially announced, " of the sudden indisposition of a principal performer," and when *Bayes* finally came on the scene the caricature of Giffard had been discarded.

As Garrick went on adding new parts to his repertoire, the playhouse in Goodman's Fields was more and more patronized ; persons from all classes of life rushed to see the prodigy, and the carriages of the nobility gave a gala air to the vicinity of the theatre whenever a performance was in progress. Drury Lane and Covent Garden were practically deserted. In fine, Garrick became the fashion, as he deserved to be, (this is more than can be said for some players who are elevated to the dignity of a fad,) and even the zealous Cibber had to admit that there was some merit in this iconoclastic young man who had with one blow of that "magic hammer," immortalized by Clive, destroyed the idols of rant, bombast, and unnaturalness. "But," added Colley, "he is not superior to my son Theophilus." At another time, when the old man was deprecating the fuss made about Garrick, the once charming Bracegirdle, now on the verge of the grave, exclaimed : "Come, come, Cibber, tell me if there is not something like envy in your character of this young gentleman ; the actor who pleases everybody must be a man of merit." Colley straightened himself up, took a pinch of snuff to gain a little time, and finally said : "Why, faith, Bracy, I believe you are right ; the young fellow *is* clever."

Of all the laudation that Garrick ever received perhaps nothing sank more deeply or gratefully into his heart than the praise of Pope. The little, deformed poet was looked upon as the very quintessence of taste and a past grand master in matters of criticism, and so when he actually condescended to go one evening to see the modern *Richard* the excitement in the theatre waxed intense. "When I was told that Pope was in the house," Garrick himself once narrated, "I instantly felt a palpitation at my heart, a tumultuous, not a disagreeable emotion in my mind. I was then in the prime of youth, and in the zenith of my theatrical ambition. It gave me a particular pleasure that *Richard* was my character when Pope was to see and hear me. As I opened my part, I saw our little poetical hero dressed in black, seated in a side box near the stage, and viewing me with a serious and earnest attention. His look shot and thrilled like lightning through my frame, and I had some hesitation in proceeding from anxiety and from joy. As *Richard* gradually blazed forth, the house was in a roar of applause, and the conspiring hand of Pope shadowed me with laurels." Garrick had every reason to be delighted on that eventful night, and to cap the climax the famous poet turned admiringly to Lord Orrery and said, with the emphasis of the Delphic Oracle : "That young man never had his *equal* as an actor, and he will never have a *rival.*" * Was he a true prophet ?

During this period Garrick produced his own farce of *The Lying Valet*, acted the *Ghost* in *Hamlet*, *Fondlewife* in the *Old Bachelor*, and *Costar Pearmain* in the *Recruiting Officer*, besides appearing, on one evening, as *Master Johnny*, a fifteen-year old lad, in Cibber's farce of *The Schoolboy*, and as the aged *Lear.* This was versatility with a vengeance, but the player knew his own powers.

One of the most sincere admirers of his perform-

* This was strong praise from Pope, who so well remembered Betterton (whose portrait he had painted).

ances happened to be the Reverend Thomas Newton, afterwards more celebrated as Bishop Newton. This accomplished clergyman had been partially educated in Litchfield, a circumstance which made him peculiarly interested in his fellow-townsman's career, and now that he was an assistant at St. George's, Hanover Square, he had an occasional opportunity of visiting Goodman's Fields. He kept up a correspondence with Garrick, encouraging him with the warmest sort of encomiums, if any were needed, offering a suggestion here and there, and on at least one occasion criticising him very severely. For he writes in January, 1742 :

" I was almost angry with you, to see your name last week in the bills for *Costar Pearmain.* I am not fond of your acting such parts as *Fondlewife*, or even *Clodio*,* nor should be of the *Lying Valet*, if it was not of your own writing. You who are equal to the greatest parts, strangely demean yourself in acting anything that is low and little ; and not only I, but really all who admire you and wish you well, that is all who know you, are grieved and wonder at it. There are abundance of people who hit off low humor, and succeed in the coxcomb and the buffoon very well ; but there is scarce one in an age who is capable of acting the hero in Tragedy, and the fine gentleman in Comedy. All who have seen you say you have talents for all this ; and when you can reap this field of fame alone without a rival, why should you be content with only surpassing

* In *Love Makes a Man.*

Chapman,* or Macklin, or young Cibber? Though you perform these parts never so well, yet there is not half the merit in excelling in them as in the others. If I was an actor, surely I would rather endeavor to be a Betterton, than a Nokes, or a Dogget," et cetera, et cetera. The Rev. Mr. Newton spoke plainly, a fact possibly due to Garrick's failure to provide him with a box for a certain evening. Even a clerical critic may be human.

When the season in Goodman's Fields came to an end Garrick entered into an agreement with Fleetwood, of Drury Lane, where he acted three nights, and then visited Ireland, accompanied by Peg Woffington. The Englishman was received with the greatest enthusiasm by the Dublinites ; the theatre was crowded every night, despite the intense heat, and the combination of packed houses, stifling atmosphere, and hot weather resulted in an epidemic called the "Garrick fever" which carried off a number of his Irish admirers. But not even this melancholy incident could put a damper on the glory of the engagement, and David returned to England with a plethoric purse, an increased reputation, and an added good-humor. Soon he was playing at Drury Lane in Otway's *Orphan*, with the celebrated tragic actress Mrs. Pritchard (of whom Garrick remarked that she was apt to blubber her sorrows) as *Monimia*. This production was de-

* An excellent comedian whose *Touchstone* in *As You Like It* was considered a great impersonation.

signed as an offset to a successful revival of *Othello* at
Covent Garden, in which Quin acted the *Moor* and
Mrs. Cibber signalized her return to the stage by
playing *Desdemona.*

Mrs. Cibber, strangely enough, bore a remarkable
personal resemblance to Garrick, to whom she wrote
once upon a time, "I desire you always to be my
lover upon the stage, and my friend off of it." "When
very young," relates Davies, "her voice was so melodious that her friends entertained great hopes of her
becoming a very excellent singer ; and I believe she
acted, when she was about fourteen years of age, the
part of *Tom Thumb* in the opera of that name, which
was set to music by her brother the celebrated Dr.
Arne, and performed at the little theatre in the Haymarket. She certainly made some considerable progress in music, and was occasionally employed to sing
at concerts. When she was married to Theophilus
Cibber, his father, Colley Cibber, observed to his son,
that though his wife's voice was very pleasing, and
she had a good taste in music, yet as she could never
arrive at more than the rank of a second-rate singer,
her income would be extremely limited. The old man
added, that he had overheard her repeat a speech from
a tragedy, and he judged by her manner that her ear
was good. Upon this she became a pupil to her father-
in-law ; and he publicly declared that he took infinite
pleasure in the instruction of so promising a genius.
. . . . Her great excellence consisted in that sim-

plicity which needed no ornament ; in that sensibility which despised all art. There was in her person little or no elegance ; in her countenance a small share of beauty ; but nature had given her such symmetry of form and fine expression of feature, that she preserved all the appearance of youth long after she had reached to middle life. The harmony of her voice was as powerful as the animation of her look. In grief or tenderness her eyes looked as if they were in tears ; in rage and despair they seemed to dart flashes of fire. In spite of the unimportance of her figure, she maintained a dignity in her action and a grace in her step." *

But to return to the now all-important "Davy." The revival of *The Orphan* was soon followed by his performance of *Hamlet*, a character for which he had long been carefully preparing himself, and which he had already submitted to the approval of a Dublin audience. The new conception of the Dane was received by the London public with every token of admiration, and while at this golden dawn of his fame anything that the "little great man" did was sure of an enthusiastic reception, it is plain that his acting in this deepest of Shakesperian parts would have commanded respect and interest even under other circumstances. It is recorded that "the strong intelligence of his eye, the

* When Garrick heard of Mrs. Cibber's death he exclaimed : "Then Tragedy is dead on one side "—that is to say, among women players.

animated expression of his whole countenance, the flexibility of his voice, and his spirited action riveted the attention of an admiring audience." But whether this was the ideal *Hamlet*—"there's the rub"—is a question hard to settle, and, for the matter of that, mankind will have to assume a phenomenal harmony of opinion before the real character of the *Prince* becomes a subject for agreement.

Garrick probably played *Hamlet* with a fine and romantic spirit quite foreign to the traditional ideas of the part, and with certain Gallic touches that can now be found in M. Mounet-Sully's picturesque, though somewhat un-English characterization. Indeed, one critic had the temerity to write to Roscius complaining that in spite of the grace and justness of his delivery, upon the whole he "acted the part ill." This plain-spoken person went on to say that "Instead of that lovely unfortunate creature in whose happiness the reader so warmly interests himself, and whose misfortunes he looks upon as his own, you exhibited a hot, testy fellow, forever flying into a passion, even when there was no provocation in the world." Could it be that the subtleties of the melancholy hero were missed?

At least one man had no very flattering opinion of Garrick's *Hamlet*, and that was Dr. Johnson, whose views on things theatrical were, at the best, far from optimistic. "Who," asked the faithful Boswell, horrified at his patron's assertion that a ballad-singer is a higher man than an actor, "can repeat *Hamlet's*

soliloquy ' To be or not to be ' as Garrick does it ?"
—Johnson : " Anybody may. Jemmy there (a boy
about eight years old who was in the room) will do it
as well in a week.—" Boswell : " No, no, sir ; and as a
proof of the merit of great acting, and of the value
which mankind set upon it, Garrick has got £100,000 "
—Johnson : " Is getting £100,000 a proof of excellence ?
That has been done by a scoundrel commissary."

We may pass over several incidents in Garrick's
early career, such as the break and ultimate reconcilia-
tion with Fleetwood, of which poor Macklin became
the scapegoat. When Fleetwood's affairs assumed so
wretched a condition that he had to leave Drury Lane,
and the house came under new management, the prudent David concluded to tempt fortune once again
among the Irish, partly moved thereto because the
Jacobite uprising of '45 threatened to keep London in
an unsettled and unappreciative condition for some
time to come. When Thomas Sheridan, who was then
the reigning dramatic favorite in Dublin, heard of this
intention he wrote his English rival encouraging the
project, and suggesting a joint engagement, with an
equal division of the net profits. The upshot of it all
was that Garrick and Sheridan were soon playing on
the same boards, much to the delight of the Irish and
of the Dublin Castle set, headed by the famous Lord
Chesterfield. Being Lord-Lieutenant at that time,
Chesterfield diplomatically endeavored to be more
Celtic than the natives. He excited much comment,

accordingly, by his studious patronage of Sheridan and
his offensive neglect of his own compatriot, whereby he hoped to prove his newly cultivated loyalty
for the people and institutions of the Emerald Isle.
He had been at particular pains to encourage Mr.
Sheridan's scheme of founding an academy of oratory,
remarking impressively, " Never let the thought of
your oratorical institution go out of your mind," but
several years later, when the politest of mankind no
longer figured as Lord-Lieutenant, he contented himself with the unwilling gift of a guinea to so commendable an enterprise.

It was during this season that a new and brilliant
star, Spranger Barry,* appeared in the theatrical firma-
ment and made so fine an impression in Dublin as
Othello that James Lacy immediately engaged him for
the forces at Drury Lane. This fascinating young
Irishman, in some respects so like the dead and gone

* Barry married Mrs. Dancer, the widow of an actor. She
was the daughter of a Bath apothecary, and attained much distinction on the stage during the height of Spranger's popularity.
After the latter's death she became the wife of a Mr. Crawford,
who was enough of a brute to make her declining years anything
but happy. Mrs. Crawford must have been an actress of uneven
merit, strikingly effective in scenes of violent passion, but commonplace amid less imposing surroundings. Boaden said her
voice " had a transpiercing effect that seemed absolutely to
wither up the hearer—it was a flaming arrow—it was the lightning of passion. . . . It was an electric shock that drove the
blood back from the surface suddenly to the heart, and made
you cold and shuddering with terror in the midst of a crowded
theatre."

Mountford, had a wonderfully sweet voice, admirably adapted to melt an audience in the portrayal of an unfortunate hero or a pathetic lover, and he possessed, in addition to rare talents, a handsome, expressive face, a graceful figure, and a general charm of manner that made him irresistible in a certain line of romantic characters. His *Romeo* was considered the *beau-ideal* of elegance, grace, and youthful fire, and was even held, by candid critics, to be superior to Garrick's. "It was nicely and accurately decided," says Fitzgerald, " that Barry was superior in the garden scene of the second act, and Garrick in the scene with the *Friar;* Barry being superior in the other garden scenes, and Garrick in the portrait of the *Apothecary*. Barry was also preferred in the first part of the tomb, and Garrick in the dying part. Some said that Barry was an Arcadian, Garrick a fashionable lover. But the best test is, that after an interval Garrick, with that excellent good sense which distinguished every act of his, quietly dropped the part out of his repertoire."

But this is anticipating events with both Garrick and Barry. The former, who proved generous enough to warmly praise his rival, returned to England in May, 1746, to play at Covent Garden under the management of Rich. It was in November of this year that Richard Cumberland, then a pupil in Westminster School, saw Garrick in Rowe's *Fair Penitent*, and he has left us a graphic pen-picture of the performance, with a quotation from which the present chapter may close.

"Quin," he remembers, "presented himself upon the rising of the curtain in a green velvet coat embroidered down the seams, an enormous full-bottom periwig, rolled stockings, and high-heeled, square-toed shoes ; with very little variation of cadence, and in deep, full tones, accompanied by a sawing kind of motion which had more of the Senate than the stage in it, he rolled out his heroics with an air of dignified indifference that seemed to disdain the plaudits bestowed on him.   Mrs. Cibber, in a key high-pitched, but sweet withal, sung, or rather recitatived Rowe's harmonious strain, somewhat in the manner of the improvisatore's. . . .   Mrs. Pritchard was an actress of a different cast, had more nature, and of course more change of tone, and variety both of action and expression.   In my opinion the comparison was decidedly in her favor.

" But when, after long and eager expectation, I first beheld little Garrick, then young and light, and alive in every muscle and in every feature, come bounding on the stage, and pointing at the wittol *Altamont* (Ryan) and heavy-paced *Horatio* (Quin), Heavens, what a transition !   It seemed as if a whole century had been stepped over in the changing of a single scene —old things were done away, and a new order at once brought forward, light and luminous, and clearly destined to dispel the barbarisms and bigotry of a tasteless age, too long attached to the prejudices of custom, and superstitiously devoted to the illusions of imposing declamation."

CHAPTER XII.

GARRICK proved so great a magnet at Covent Garden that Lacy, of the now almost deserted Drury Lane, had the good sense to take the figurative bull by the horns, by trying to catch the hero for his own house. The result was a series of negotiations ending in the purchase, by the actor, of a half interest in the patent of the latter theatre, for the sum of £8000. Thus he became co-partner with Lacy in the enterprise, and the strangest part of the whole transaction was the indifference, nay, actual pleasure, with which Rich, of Covent Garden, regarded the loss of his most important performer. Davies explains this singular philosophy when he says : " It was imagined by those who knew his [Rich's] humor best, that he would have been better pleased to see his great comedians show away to empty benches, that he might have had an opportunity to mortify their pride, by bringing out a new pantomime, and drawing the town after his raree-show. Often he would take a peep at the house through the curtain, and as often, from disappointment and disgust, arising from the view of a full audience,

break out into the following expression : " What, are
you there? Well, much good may it do you ! ' "

Mr. Rich had so firm a belief in the efficacy of
pantomime and of his own talents therein, that he
looked upon the " legitimate " as something of an
impertinence, at least when he was obliged to give it
house-room. " Though he might have easily fixed
Mr. Garrick in his service long before he had bargained
for a share of Drury Lane patent, he gave himself no
concern, when he was told of a matter so fatal to his
own interest ; he rather seemed to consider it as a
release from a disagreeable engagement, and consoled
himself with mimicking the great actor. It was a
ridiculous sight to see the old man upon his knees repeating *Lear's* curse to his daughter, after Garrick's
manner, as he termed it ; while some of the players
who stood round him gave him loud applause ; and
others, though they were obliged to join in the general
approbation, heartily pitied his folly and despised his
ignorance." And so good-day to you, intelligent Mr.
Rich, and stifle any after regrets you may experience
with the comforting thought that your artistic perceptions are quite as deep as those of the average manager.

While Rich extracted entertainment from his carica-
ture of Garrick the latter quickly gathered a goodly
company about him, including the tragic Mistress
Pritchard and the engaging Mrs. Cibber, and re-opened
Drury Lane in September, 1747, with the *Merchant of
Venice*. Garrick himself spoke a prologue written by

his friend, Dr. Johnson, who, for all his much vaunted hatred of the stage, could, on occasion, stand sponsor for it very gracefully. In these verses, which were long cherished as among the classics of modern literature, the sage of Grub Street, briefly but cleverly described the transitions of the drama from the time

> " When Learning's triumph o'er her barbarous foes
> First rear'd the stage, immortal Shakespeare rose ;
> Each change of many-color'd life he drew,
> Exhausted worlds, and then imagin'd new ; "

until coming down to his own time the poet says, truly enough, if a bit pompously :

> " The stage but echoes back the public voice ;
> The drama's laws, the drama's patrons give ;
> For we that live to please, must please to live,"

and in conclusion he calls upon the crowded and brilliant audience to

> " . . . bid the reign commence
> Of rescu'd Nature and reviving Sense ;
> To chase the charms of sound, the pomp of show,
> For useful mirth, and salutary woe,
> Bid scenic virtue form the rising age,
> And truth diffuse her radiance from the stage."

There was one joyous woman there that happy night, probably as the *Portia*, who could " diffuse her radiance from the stage " as few actresses have done before or since, and whose plastic art seemed almost equally suited to " useful mirth " or " salutary woe." This was brilliant Peg Woffington, she of the lovely pensive face, squeaky voice, and imperious yet charming spirit, who could shine in anything from gloomy *Lady Macbeth* to the rakish *Sir Harry Wildair*, and whose attractions, if her contemporaries can be believed, suggest a glorified mixture of Bracegirdle, Oldfield, and Ellen Terry. This bright particular star in Garrick's constellation, who might have been a great tragedienne had she not proved so wonderful in comedy, was the daughter of an Irish laundress, and though she could act the woman of quality as if " to the manner born " a few of her Dublin admirers remembered how, as a girl, she sold salad and water-cresses on the streets. After the death of her father, a bricklayer, Peg's mother opened a huckster's shop on Ormond Quay, in the Irish capital, and the daughter, already pretty and attractive, fell in with a rope dancer named Madame Violante, to whom she was apprenticed, so to speak, as a promising pupil.

Soon Woffington is dancing in the Violante's booth, and playing in a juvenile performance of the *Beggar's Opera*, and when only seventeen she appears on the Dublin stage. She tries the gentle *Ophelia*, and actually succeeds in the role, playing a number of other parts and giving nothing more welcome than an essentially *piquante*, feminine impersonation of the masculine *Wildair*. It was in this character that she would subsequently eclipse even Garrick and be the innocent cause of a proposal of marriage from an infatuated young lady, who would mistake *Sir Harry* for a man. So at least goes the romance, and why care to doubt it?

Next she is the centre of attraction, if not of gravity, at Covent Garden, and the unemotional Walpole chronicles that "there is much in vogue a Mrs. Woffington, a bad actress, but she has life." Later she meets Garrick, plays with him, and as she is not so strong in moral as in artistic sense, thinks nothing of sharing the same home with him. A curious partnership it must have been and with far less about it of "loves young dream" than one might imagine at the first blush. Garrick, with his habitual closeness in money matters, allowing Peg to share the expenses of the joint household, chiding her for spending too much during the month that he footed the bills, and content that she should make as lavish an outlay as she wished for the next month ; Peg, charming and housewifely, happy in the thought that Garrick may marry her, yet not above a flirtation in another direction—this is the not very edifying or even romantic picture as it has come down to us. If the canvas be a trifle dimmed by age we need not complain ; there is enough of it left to show that the original colors were gairish rather than alluring.

The new managment, so auspiciously inaugurated with the assistance of two such curiously unlike persons as Johnson and Mistress Woffington, was soon in full swing. There were numerous revivals, one of them being *Henry V.*, in which Garrick generously allowed Spranger Barry to play the *King*, (it was wisely done, too, for Barry must have been an ideal *Hal*) and modestly assigned himself to the *Chorus*. In the ensuing season of 1748-9 Woffington, whose intimacy with the actor-manager had come to a more or less prosaic end, returned to Covent Garden and the easily consoled Garrick went on producing a variety of plays, among them *Much Ado About Nothing*, *Romeo and Juliet*, with Barry as the fervid *Montague*, and Dr. Johnson's tragedy of *Irene*.

In bringing out the last named piece, Garrick exercised the greatest care in casting the parts, the four principal ones being divided between himself, Barry, Mrs. Pritchard, and Mrs. Cibber, and he provided the richest sort of a stage setting, but nothing could save this ponderous, not to say stupid child of Johnson's moralizing muse. On the first performance several of the critics disapproved of the strangling of the fair *Irene* in full view of the house, and the accommodating Garrick, anxious to do anything that might make the tragedy a success, modified the scene as desired, yet it is painful to learn that "the approbation of *Irene* was not so general as might have been expected." In other words, to put it less politely, after an enforced run of nine nights the play was quietly consigned to the limbo of oblivion. It had a fine moral, but all the fine morals in the world will not constitute a theatrical hit.

If the serious Dr. Johnson could not please the town just then a far different person had the power to do so, and this was that delightful mimic and entertainer, but

MRS. WOFFINGTON.

FROM AN OLD PRINT.

none the less unscrupulous scalawag, Samuel Foote. Garrick, who spoke of him as "a man of wonderful abilities, and the most entertaining companion I have ever known," was afraid of this heartless portrayer of human frailties, and so were many other Londoners of mark, for Foote made all his reputation, good or bad, by caricaturing his contemporaries. And charming caricatures they proved, too, excepting to the unfortunate subjects of the sarcasm. Even Johnson admitted the talents of this prince of mimics, although when it came his turn to be parodied, he took good care that no jest or jibe, however amusing, should be pointed at his own expense. "The first time I was in company with Foote," the lexicographer tells Boswell, " was at Fitzherbert's. Having no good opinion of the fellow, I was resolved not to be pleased ; and it is very difficult to please a man against his will. I went on eating my dinner pretty sullenly, affecting not to mind him ; but the dog was so very comical, that I was obliged to lay down my knife and fork, throw myself back, and fairly laugh it out."

Wonderful indeed he must have been, this witty Foote, to make the great Johnson forget for the nonce the pleasures of Fitzherbert's dinner-table. "No, sir, he was irresistible," the Doctor continues. "He upon one occasion experienced, in an extraordinary degree, the efficacy of his powers of entertaining. Among the many and various modes which he tried of getting money, he became a partner with a small beer brewer, and he was to have a share of the profits for procuring customers amongst his numerous acquaintance. Fitzherbert was one who took his small beer; but it was so bad that the servants resolved not to drink it. They were at some loss how to notify their resolution, being afraid of offending their master, who they knew liked Foote much as a companion. At last they fixed upon a little black boy, who was rather a favorite, to be their deputy, and deliver their remonstrance; and having invested him with the whole authority of the kitchen, he was to inform Mr. Fitzherbert, in all their names, upon a certain day, that they would drink Foote's small beer no longer. On that day Foote happened to dine at Fitzherbert's, and this boy served at table; he was so delighted with Foote's stories, and merriment, and grimace, that when he went downstairs he told them: 'This is the finest man I have ever seen. I will not deliver your message. I will drink his small beer.'" Verily, the man whose brilliancy can give sparkle to bad beer must indeed be a bit of a genius.

When Johnson became the subject of Mr. Foote's wit, the talents of the offender were hardly so well appreciated. As Boswell tells us, when the Doctor was informed that he was to be mimicked for the public amusement he asked Thomas Davies, at whose house he was dining, "what was the common price of an oak stick," and being answered sixpence, "Why, then, sir," he replied, "give me leave to send your servant to purchase me a shilling one. " I 'll have a double quantity ; for I am told Foote means to *take me off*, as he calls it, and I am determined the fellow shall not do it with impunity." Foote heard of the intended purchase, took the hint, and wisely concluded not to introduce the bulky portrait of Johnson in his gallery of celebrities.

It was in January of the year 1749 that Foote was brought into particular prominence by an episode afterwards spoken of as " the affair of the Bottle Conjuror." He had been giving at the Haymarket a highly characteristic and popular entertainment known as an " *Auction of Pictures*," when there appeared in the papers one morning a remarkable advertisement. It set forth that

" At the New Theatre in the Haymarket, this present day, to be seen a person who performs the several most surprising things following, viz. : First, he takes a common walking-cane from any of the spectators, and thereon he plays the music of every instrument now in use, and likewise sings to surprising perfection. Secondly, he presents you with a common wine bottle, which any of the spectators may first examine ; this bottle is placed on a table in the middle of the stage, and he (without any equivocation) goes into it, in the sight of all the spectators, and sings in it ; during his stay in the bottle any person may handle it, and see plainly that it does not exceed a common tavern bottle. Those on the stage or in the boxes may come in masked habits (if agreeable to them) and the performer (if desired) will inform them *who they are.*"

This adventurous person also undertook to show the dead, give a full view of the " persons who have injured you, dead or alive " and otherwise make things interesting for the audience.

At half-past six in the evening, the time appointed for the appearance of the mysterious bottle conjuror, a crowd of curious people had assembled in the Haymarket theatre, and when seven o'clock came and he had not materialized some of the more impatient began indulging in cat-calls and other signals of displeasure. Thereupon, a man come on the stage who announced that the admission money paid by the would-be spectators was to be returned ; somebody else facetiously called out that " if they would come again the next night, at double prices, the conjuror would go into a pint bottle," and after this a candle was suddenly thrown upon the stage. A row immediately ensued ; the Duke of Cumberland in trying to escape from the scuffle lost his diamond hilted sword ; and the more rowdy element of the audience, now turned into an angry mob, tore up the boxes and benches, pulled down the curtain and scenery, and made a large bonfire of the *débris* opposite the entrance to the theatre.

The next morning the town was merrily gossiping over the great hoax, and not a few averred that the unconscionable Foote himself was at the bottom of the whole affair, " the most disgraceful attack that was ever made upon the commonsense of the metropolis." Foote, however, very stoutly denied any complicity in or knowledge of the bottle-conjuring episode, and it is quite possible that he spoke truly.

The frantic efforts of the great mimic to prove that he had nothing to do with the trick, must have keenly amused Garrick, who, while he treated Foote with the greatest outward consideration, secretly feared and disliked him. Davies has left it on record that Foote considered Garrick as a rival in theatrical fame, and yet, as the biographer truly adds, " no two men were more opposite in their pretensions to stage merit : in acting, Mr. Garrick was, doubtless, an unlimited genius ; Foote was restrained to certain characters of his own composition : though he had, for a few years, been hired at a handsome salary as an actor, all his efforts, both in tragedy and comedy, from *Othello*, his first attempt, down to *Ben the Sailor*, one of his last, were mean, disagreeable, and often distorted by grimace and buffoonry."

The actor was wont to praise the mimic in the most ostentatious, not to say fulsome manner—oh, thou canny David—but these insincere commendations were thrown away upon the dangerous " rival," who only went on abusing Garrick and borrowing his money all the more. Foote " constantly railed at Mr. Garrick in all companies ; his abilities as an actor he questioned, in contradiction to all the world ; his compositions as a writer, he treated with scorn ; virtues, as a member

of society, he had none ; he was covetous and tricking ;
in short, according to his opinion, he was everything
that was mean and unworthy of a gentleman.*   Neither
his family, his friends, nor acquaintance, *his father,
mother, body, soul, or muse,* were spared by this strange
wit, who ran a-tilt at everybody, and was at the same
time caressed and feared, admired and hated by all.

" In the meantime, these rival wits would often meet
at the houses of persons of fashion, who were glad to
have two such guests at their table, though they certainly should have entertained their friends separately ;
for Mr. Garrick was a *muta persona* in the presence of
Foote : he was all admiration when this great genius
entertained the company, and no man laughed more
heartily at his lively sallies than he did.   It must be
owned that he tried all methods to conciliate Foote's
mind ; so far at least, as to prevail upon him to forbear
his illiberal attacks upon him when absent ; and this
he ought to have done for his own sake, for Foote often
rendered his conversation disgusting by his nauseous
abuse of Mr. Garrick ; but the more sensibility the
latter discovered, the greater price the former put upon
his ceasing from hostilities."

* In Roger's *Table Talk* is found a curious distinction made
by Arthur Murphy, the actor, between Garrick's private
and professional life.   "Mr. Murphy, sir, you knew Mr. Garrick ? "   " Yes, sir, I did, and no man better."   " Well, sir,
what did you think of his acting ? "   After a pause :   " Well,
sir, off the stage he was a mean sneaking little fellow.   But on
the stage "—throwing up his hands and eyes—"oh, my Great
God ! "

Richard Cumberland, who saw much of both these remarkable men, indicates in his memoirs that Garrick was far from being a *muta persona*, as Davies classically puts it, in the presence of the much-to-be-feared caricaturist. "I made a visit with him [Garrick] by his own proposal to Foote at Parson's Green; I have heard it said he was reserved and uneasy in his company; I never saw him more at ease and in a happier flow of spirits than on that occasion. . . . We had taken him [Foote] by surprise and of course were with him some hours before dinner, to make sure of our own if he had missed of his. He seemed overjoyed to see us, engaged us to stay, walked with us in his garden and read to us some scenes roughly sketched for his *Maid of Bath*. His dinner was quite good enough and his wine superlative. Sir Robert Fletcher, who had served in the East Indies, dropt in before dinner and made the fourth of our party. When we had passed about two hours in perfect harmony and hilarity, Garrick called for his tea, and Sir Robert rose to depart: there was an unlucky screen in the room that hid the door, and behind which he hid himself for some purpose, whether natural or artificial I know not; but Foote, supposing him gone, instantly began to play off his ridicule at the expense of his departed guest. I must confess it was (in the cant phrase) a *way that he had*, and just now a very unlucky way, for Sir Robert, bolting from behind the screen, cried out—'I am not gone, Foote; spare me till I am out of hearing; and

now with your leave I will stay till these gentlemen
depart, and then you shall amuse me at their cost, as
you have amused them at mine.'

" A remonstrance of this sort was an electric shock
that could not be parried. No wit could furnish an
evasion, no explanation could suffice for an excuse.
The offended gentleman was to the full as angry as a
brave man ought to be with an unfortunate wit, who
possessed very little of that quality, which he abounded
in. This event, which deprived Foote of all presence
of mind, gave occasion to Garrick to display his genius
and good nature in their brightest lustre : I never
saw him in a more amiable light ; the infinite address
and ingenuity, that he exhibited, in softening the enraged guest, and reconciling him to pass over an affront
as gross as could well be put upon a man, were at
once the most comic and the most complete I ever witnessed. Why was not James Boswell present to have
recorded the dialogue and the action of the scene ? My
stupid head only carried away the effect of it. It was
as if Diomed (who being the son of Tydeus was, I con-
clude, a great hero in a small compass) had been shield-
ing Thersites from the wrath of Ajax ; and so wrathful
was our Ajax, that if I did not recollect there was a
certain actor at Delhi, who in the height of the
massacre charmed away the furious passions of
Nadir Shaw, and saved a remnant of the city, I
should say this was a victory without a parallel. I
hope Foote was very grateful, but when a man has

been completely humbled, he is not very fond of recollecting it."

To wander back to more important events in Garrick's career, let us mention the appearance on the scene of the graceful Violette, whom he was afterwards to marry. Eva Maria Violette, or to give her real name, Eva Maria Veigel, was a native of Vienna, where she had been educated as a *danseuse.* She appeared at the Austrian Court, where she danced for the edification of the Empress-Queen, Maria Theresa, and soon after set out for London to seek her fortunes. The cause of this sudden departure has been explained, and perhaps truly, by the statement that Maria Theresa, perceiving that her husband, the Emperor, regarded Mlle. Violette with marked attention, proposed this journey to England and forwarded powerful recommendations in her favor. It is at least certain that she found most influential backing when she arrived ; King George II. commanded the play on her first appearance at Drury Lane, in December, 1746, and she was warmly befriended by the family of the Earl of Burlington.* With such distinguished patronage, added to the fact that she was very attractive both as to her personality and her dancing, the Violette soon became quite the fashion ; she resided with the Countess of Burlington, who used to go with her to the theatre, playing the part of an amateur lady's maid, and Walpole, in a letter to Montague, chronicles that " the

* There was an unfounded story afloat to the effect that Lord Burlington was Mlle. Violette's father.

17

fame of the Violette increases daily. The sister Countesses of Burlington and Talbot exert all their stores of sullen partiality and competition for her. The former visits her, and is having her picture " ; and so on, in the true Walpolian vein of gossip.

Soon Garrick is paying his court to the favorite, who returns his attachment ; then he makes a formal and very stately proposal to Lady Burlington for the hand of the charmer, and has the good fortune to be accepted. Next he becomes an honored guest at Burlington House, and we hear of him dancing attendance upon his *fiancée* at fashionable entertainments. In describing one given at Richmond, Walpole writes : " There was an admirable scene, Lady Burlington brought the *Violette*, and the Richmond had asked Garrick, who stood *ogling* and *sighing* the whole time, while my lady kept a most *fierce look-out*. Sabbatini asked me, ' And who is that ? ' It was a distressing question ; after a little hesitation I replied : ' *Mais, c'est Mademoiselle Violette.*"

But while Walpole's snobbishness might be pained at seeing a mere dancer among such a brilliant array of titled personages, Garrick had no such feeling, naturally enough, and he proudly made her the possessor of his now great name, just one month later (June, 1749). It proved to be a very happy marriage, and none the less so to the business-like husband, because the wife brought with her a dot of £6000, the gift of the Burlington family.

It was about this time that Garrick began to experience with full force those troubles and petty annoyances which inevitably fall to the lot of any successful manager who has long to deal with a company of his own. A man in such a position is like the ruler over a lot of children in whom, perhaps, he only takes an interest in so far as they contribute to his own glory and fortune. The players, on their side, are sensitive to a remarkable degree ; they have their jealousies and ambitions under poor control, and to the not infrequent idea of their own importance they combine a secret feeling that their manager is trying to get from them a maximum of work at a minimum of salary. And so it happened that Spranger Barry, and Mrs. Cibber became peevish and discontented with Garrick, believed that they were shabbily treated (no doubt they thought so without good reason), and finally went bag and baggage over to the enemy, in the person of Mr. Rich, of Covent Garden. This proved rather an unpleasant revolt for Garrick, but he showed himself equal to the emergency. The play-goers were the gainers by the episode, for it gave them two productions of *Romeo and Juliet* over which they could talk for many a day, and perhaps say to their open-mouthed grandchildren : " Egad, boys, you should have seen Barry's *Romeo*—there was a lover for you ! " or " I think Mr. Garrick was the better hero of the two ! " or " Zounds, what a glorious *Juliet* did my friend Mrs. Cibber make."

It was in October, 1749, when the two rebellious subjects of Drury Lane began their campaign at Covent Garden with their much admired impersonations in Shakespeare's tragic love story, but Garrick met them on their own ground by appearing in the same play. At first both houses were crowded by persons who rejoiced in the sensation of comparing the rival productions, and coffee-house and drawing-room were filled with discussions as to the relative merits of Garrick and Barry as well as of the two *Juliets*, Mrs. Cibber and Miss Bellamy. One critic remarked epigrammatically that "at Covent Garden he saw *Juliet* and *Romeo* and at Drury Lane *Romeo* and *Juliet*," which sounds very clever, to be sure, but is probably a poor opinion, for if contemporary testimony on the subject is to go for anything, Barry, rather than Garrick, proved the ideal *Romeo*. We can imagine Spranger, passionate, handsome, full of grace and very, very human—just the lover a woman would admire—while with Garrick the picture is equally interesting but the colors are not so warm and sensuous, and face and figure lack the indefinable but none the less potent charm that made his rival so fascinating a *Montague*.

But the theatre-goer, past and present, has been known to have too much of a good thing, as instanced in the case of these phenomenally-cast *Romeo and Juliets*. The public began to clamor for something new, and heartily sympathized with the hero of the epigram which ran

> "Well, what's to-night," says angry Ned,
>   As up from bed he rouses :
> "Romeo again!" and shakes his head ;
> "Ah, plague on both your houses."

So the play was duly withdrawn, but not until the Drury Lane revival had brought into greater prominence than ever the charming, the capricious, and the depraved George Ann Bellamy, whose checkered career was filled with an unhallowed, unclean spirit of romance that made her one of the most notorious women of her day. She was the illegitimate daughter of Lord Tyrawley, who had her educated in a French convent ; later on she was abducted by the then Lord Byron, a great scoundrel where women were concerned ; appeared with success on the Dublin stage and was soon the heroine of a riot; had an almost historic quarrel with the Woffington, and went through a series of experiences, amorous and otherwise, that "excited the wonder, admiration, and pitying contempt of the town for thirty years." "To say that she was a siren who lured men to destruction, is to say little," observes Dr. Doran, "for she went down to him with each victim ; but she rose from the wreck more exquisitely seductive and terribly fascinating than ever, to find a new prey whom she might ensnare and betray."

The same writer tells us in that entertainingly picturesque fashion of his how the feminine love of finery prompted the unclassic tussle between this same dangerous siren and the no less formidable Peg. "The

charming George Ann Bellamy had procured from
Paris two gorgeous dresses wherein to enact *Statira* in
the *Rival Queens.** *Roxana* was played by Peg Woffington ; and she was so overcome by malice, hatred, and
all uncharitableness, when she saw herself eclipsed by
the dazzling glories of the resplendent Bellamy, that
Peg at length resolved to drive her off the stage, and
with upheld dagger had wellnigh stabbed her at the
side-scenes. *Alexander* and a posse of chiefs with
hard names were at hand, but the less brilliantly clad
Roxana rolled *Statira* and her spangled sack in the
dust, pommelling her the while with the handle of her
dagger, and screaming aloud :

> ' Nor he, nor heaven, shall shield thee from my justice ;
> Die, sorceress, die, and all my wrongs die with thee.' ' '

The once magnificent Bellamy with her Parisian
gowns, her beauty, her talents, and her profligacy, she
whom Dr. Johnson said " left nothing to be desired,"
ended her life, sadly but appropriately enough, in poverty and what was for her worse than disgrace—comparative oblivion. When she made her final bid for
popular favor in Dublin (November, 1760), as *Belvidera*
in *Venice Preserved*, the theatre was so crowded that
many persons were hustled and jostled into the building
without paying the doorkeeper, but what a terrible disappointment was in store for them. Tate Wilkinson

---

* It will be remembered that the same play was the scene of
a nearly tragic quarrel, of which Mrs. Barry was the not very
creditable heroine.

saw the pathetic performance and notes in his memoirs
how, on her speaking the first line behind the scenes

"Lead me, ye Virgins, lead me to that kind voice,"

it struck the ears of the audience as uncouth and un-
musical ; yet she was received as was prepared and
determined by all who were her or Mr. Mossop's *
friends, and the public at large with repeated plaudits
on her *entrée*. "But the roses were fled ; the young, the
once lovely Bellamy was turned haggard ! and her eyes
that used to charm all hearts, appeared sunk, large,
hollow, and ghostly. O Time ! Time ! thy glass should
be often consulted ! for before the short first scene had
elapsed disappointment, chagrin, and pity sat on every
eye and countenance. . . . She left Dublin without a single friend to regret her loss. What a change
from the days of her youth !" †

To bid a painful adieu to the prematurely broken
down Bellamy and come back to more pleasant scenes
of which Garrick was the hero, let it be noted that the
latter went on his prosperous way rejoicing, reviving
old plays, producing new ones, and adding at every
turn to his already extensive repertoire. If he was an
ambitious actor, he was none the less a shrewd, money-
getting manager, and he thought it a happy idea to

* Henry Mossop, who was then manager as well as actor.

† Bellamy's last appearance was at a benefit given for her as
late as 1785. Miss Farren spoke an address which concluded :

" But see, oppress'd with gratitude and tears,
To pay her duteous tribute, she appears."

vary the exhibition of the "legitimate" at Drury Lane by an occasional entertainment of entirely different character. This is how it came to pass that in November, 1755, there was produced after the most elaborate preparations, a spectacle called *The Chinese Festival,* in which rich costumes, fine scenic effects, music, dancing, and a variety of other features made up a performance of a kind that would be highly popular in these "degenerate" days. The affair might have been just as popular then had not an unfortunate international matter, which had no real bearing on this "Chinese" or any other "Festival," arisen at that time. This was the breaking out of hostilities between England and France, and the London public, in its frantic endeavors to be patriotic, lost all common sense—as the public will do at certain seasons—and took violent umbrage because Mr. Garrick's new venture enlisted the services of a number of French dancers.

For five nights the theatre was the scene of tumults, the occupants of the boxes sustaining Mr. Garrick, and thereby only infuriating the more the malcontents in the pit and galleries, who insisted on having the spectacle withdrawn from the boards altogether. As a climax to the disorder some gentlemen jumped from their boxes, into the pit, and entered, sword in hand, into a conflict with the ringleaders; blood was shed, women screamed and fainted, as was to be expected, and the now exasperated mob ended up by wrecking the inside of the theatre and doing as much incidental damage as possible. Garrick actually feared for his life, and the rioters repaired to his house, where they smashed the windows as a slight mark of their august disapproval. Though the excitement ceased when the obnoxious " Festival " was retired and the Frenchmen sent about their business, many a day elapsed before the episode was forgotten.

One of the few amusing things about the whole affair was the dragging out for the occasion of his very peculiar Majesty, King George II., whose presence at the theatre on one of these memorable nights would, it was believed, have a restraining effect on the audience. So the old King, who knew nothing about the drama and cared less, commanded a performance of *Richard III.*, witnessed it himself and laughed at the disorder among the spectators. When the play was over Garrick eagerly asked Mr. Fitzherbert, who had been in the Royal box, how His Majesty liked the *Richard.* " I can say nothing on that head," replied Fitzherbert, " but when an actor told *Richard* ' The Mayor of London comes to greet you ' the King roused himself; and when Taswell entered buffooning the character, the King exclaimed : ' *Duke of Grafton, I like that Lord Mayor* '; and when the scene was over, he said again, ' *Duke of Grafton, that is good Lord Mayor.* ' " And this was the extent of his criticism, excepting that when *Richard* was in Bosworth Field, shouting for a horse, George exclaimed : " *Duke of Grafton, will that Lord Mayor not come again ?* "

CHAPTER XIII

A GREAT LIGHT GOES OUT.

GARRICK watched every action of the rival company at Covent Garden with the keen eye of a hawk, and there was one pathetic incident at that house that must have had for him a painful interest. It was the final appearance on the stage, as it turned out, of his one-time companion, Peg Woffington. Her powers and beauty were on the wane, although she was still on the right side of forty, when she volunteered in May, 1757, to play her favorite *Rosalind*, for the benefit of some fellow-artists. Tate Wilkinson, then a young actor who had shown enough hardihood to burlesque the Woffington, watched the progress of the performance from the wings, and we will let him tell the brief but pitiful story of her farewell.

"She went through *Rosalind* for four acts without my perceiving that she was in the least disordered; but in the fifth act she complained of great indisposition. I offered her my arm, which she graciously accepted. I thought she looked softened in her manner, and had less of the *hauteur*. When she came off at the quick change of dress, she again complained of being ill, but got accoutred, and returned to finish the part, and pronounced the Epilogue speech, ' If it be true that, good wine needs no bush,' etc. But when arrived at ' If I were a woman I would kiss as many of you as had beards,' etc., her voice broke—she faltered—endeavored to go on, but could not proceed ; then in a voice of tremor exclaimed, ' O God ! O God !' and tottered to the stage door speechless, where she was caught. The audience, of course, applauded till she was out of sight, and then sunk into awful looks of astonishment, both young and old, before and behind the curtain, to see one of the most handsome women of the age, a favorite principal actress, and who had for several seasons given high entertainment, struck so suddenly by the hand of Death, in such a time and place, and in the prime of life.''

She had indeed been stricken by the hand of Death, and never more could tread the boards she loved so well, but the final blow did not come until three years later, when she quietly passed away at Teddington. Perhaps Garrick shed an un-theatrical tear when he heard the news, and then—forgot her for ever.

Roscius never lived in the past, however charming it might have been, and even had he been disposed to do so, the cares of management forced him to

    '' Act,—act in the living present,''

but whether with

    '' Heart within, and God o'erhead ''

it is hard to determine. At any rate, one of the living issues which soon gave him not a little anxiety was the transient popularity of Thomas Sheridan, who had left Dublin and joined forces with the hero of Drury Lane. "Sherry is dull, naturally dull, but it must have taken him a great deal of pains to become what we now see him" growled Dr. Johnson, and it is plain that the father of Richard Brinsley was a pretty poor sort of actor, but he had the theatrical bee in his bonnet, and studied hard to be a genius. He was "acting mad, haranguing mad, teaching mad, managing mad," according to a sour epigram of old Macklin, but with all his madness he contrived to play *King John* so effectively at Drury Lane that Garrick became consumed with jealousy. Even so friendly a critic as Davies frankly admits that the manager grew very envious of his histrionic inferior, "especially when he was informed by a very intimate acquaintance, that the King was uncommonly pleased with that actor's [Sheridan's] representation of the part." It is added that "this was a bitter cup; and to make the draught still more unpalatable, upon his asking whether His Majesty approved his playing the *Bastard*, he was told, without the least compliment paid to his action, it was imagined that the King thought the character was rather too bold in the drawing, and the coloring was overcharged and glaring. Mr. Garrick, who had been so accustomed to applause, and who of all men living most sensibly felt the neglect of it, was greatly struck with a preference given to another, and which left him out of all consideration ; and though the boxes were taken for *King John* several nights successively, he would never after permit the play to be acted." There is a wee bit of the snob in most of us, and although Garrick knew in his heart that the opinion of Dutchy George was not worth a bagatelle, the Royal preference for Sheridan soon put an end to the relations, personal and professional, between the two actors, one of whom "could not bear an equal, nor the other a superior."

'T was not long, however, before George II. had departed this life and could cause no more heartburnings by his august critiques of things theatrical, while Garrick suddenly found himself the hero of a very remarkable work which must have gratified his vanity as much as it chagrined many of his fellow-players. It was Charles Churchill's poem of *The Rosciad,** which made a great commotion at the time because of its satirical flings against a number of stage favorites. Churchill, himself a constant theatre-goer, had studied their characteristics, more particularly their failings, with a calm, judicious eye, free from emotions that might blind his judgment, and while his criticisms in the *Rosciad* were frequently true and to the point, the unfortunate subjects of them were none the less angry on this score. He spoke of Macklin as a man

<blockquote>
" . . . who largely deals in half-form'd sounds,
Who wantonly transgresses nature's bounds,
Whose acting 's hard, affected and constrain'd ; "
</blockquote>

* Published in March, 1761.

he pointed out that Quin (who was still living to grit his epicurean teeth at the satire)

"   .   .   .   could not for a moment sink the man,"

and gave vent to that now historic saying about Davies, who

" Mouths a sentence as curs mouth a bone."

Of the urbane and painstaking Havard,* Churchill averred that he loved, hated and raged, triumphed and complained, all in the same strains, and that

" His easy, vacant face proclaim'd a heart
Which could not feel emotions nor impart,"

while he defined Foote's powers very succinctly by saying that

" His strokes of humor and his bursts of sport,
Are all contain'd in this one word, distort.
Doth a man stutter, look asquint, or halt ?
Mimics draw humor out of nature's fault ;
With personal defects their mirth adorn,
And hang misfortunes out to public scorn."

* " Havard undertook the tragedy of *Charles I.* at the desire of the manager of the company of Lincoln's Inn Fields, to which he then belonged, in 1737. The manager had probably read of the salutary effects produced on the genius of Euripides by seclusion in his cave, and he was determined to give Havard the same advantage in a garret during the composition of his task. He invited him to his house, took him up to one of its airiest apartments, and there locked him up for so many hours every day, well knowing his desultory habits, nor released him, after he had once turned the *clavis tragica*, till the unfortunate bard had repeated through the key-hole a certain number of new speeches in the progressive tragedy."—THOMAS CAMP-BELL.

SAMUEL FOOTE.

AS "MRS. COLE" IN HIS OWN COMEDY OF "THE MINOR."—"MY THOUGHTS ARE FIXED UPON A BETTER PLACE." FROM A DRAWING BY DODD.

Yet with all this acidity the author of the *Rosciad* knew how to indulge in the most mellifluous of compliments, as when he referred to the " giggling, plotting chambermaids," the " hoydens and romps " of " *General Clive*," who

> " Original in spirit and in ease,
>   She pleas'd by hiding all attempts to please.
>   No comic actress ever yet could raise
>   On humor's base more merit or more praise."

As to Garrick, the idol of the poem and poet, no praise could be too strong, no metaphor too eloquent, and so we read that

> " If manly sense, if nature link'd with art ;
>   If thorough knowledge of the human heart ;
>   If powers of acting vast and unconfin'd ;
>   If fewer faults with greatest beauties joined ;
>   If strong expression, and great powers which lie
>   Within the magic circle of the eye ;
>   If feelings which few hearts like his can know,
>   And which no face so well as his can show ;
>   Deserve the preference : Garrick, take the chair,
>   Nor quit it, till thou place an equal there."

This was all very pretty, but the subject of the adulation was enough a man of the world to know that his own popularity was not likely to be increased by a pen which so severely scratched many of his contemporaries. It is possible that his reception of the *Rosciad* proved disappointing to the writer, or that he said something on the subject which gave offence to the latter, but whatever may have been the reason Churchill soon got out a new poem entitled *The Apology*.

Here the panegyrist turned cynic, and not only aimed many an arrow at the player's art in general, but hurled a particularly poisonous one at his late hero, speaking of him as a "vain tyrant," surrounded by

> " His puny greenroom wits, and venal bards,
> Who meanly tremble at a puppet's frown,
> And for a playhouse freedom, sell their own."

Garrick was, at the best, peculiarly sensitive to any unfavorable criticism, and grew very uncomfortable over the newly conferred titles of " tyrant " and " puppet." But he could take a hand himself in poetical warfare of this kind, and being, as his friend Goldsmith said, "a wit, if not first, in the very first line," he made a formidable adversary. When Dr. Hill, a famous quack, attacked Garrick in the newspapers (presumably because even the talents of the actor could not save from disastrous failure a poor farce written by the empirical gentleman) he was quickly disposed of by one of the cleverest and most cutting couplets that ever graced the English language. It was simply this :

> " EPIGRAM ON DR. HILL.
>
> For *physic* and *farces* his equal there scarce is ;
> His *farces* are *physic ;* his *physic* a *farce* is."

Garrick, who wrote the lines, had administered another shock in verse, some time before, to the same culprit. Hill had published a pamphlet containing *A Petition from the Letters I and U to David Garrick, Esq.,* in which it was contended that the great player misplaced the aforesaid letters in his pronunciation of certain words. To this the guilty man made answer:

> " If 't is true, as you say, that I 've injured a letter,
> I 'll change my note soon, and I hope for the better.
> May the right use of letters, as well as of men,
> Hereafter be fix'd by the tongue and the pen :
> Most devoutly I wish they may both have their due,
> And that *I* may be never mistaken for *U*."

Poor poetry it all may have been, as standards go in these days of naturalism, realism, pre-Raphaelism, and various other isms, but it served its purpose well by contributing to the gayety of nations. Can the same thing be said of much of our modern verse?

Sometimes Mr. Garrick had greater managerial troubles than those associated with the writing of witty epigrams, as, for instance, in the beginning of 1763, when he went through the unpleasant experience of another theatrical riot. There was no obnoxious *Chinese Festival* this time ; the bone of contention proved to be a financial rather than a patriotic one. It appears that the treasurer of Drury Lane, Benjamin Victor, had altered Shakespeare's *Two Gentlemen of Verona*, and when the play was to be given for the benefit night of the adapter, a paper was circulated in public places setting forth the injustice of the management in treating the production as an absolute novelty and charging full prices for what was nothing more or less than a revival. When the benefit evening came (the sixth evening of the performance of the comedy) the head and front of the malcontents, a Mr.

Fitzpatrick, "harangued the spectators from the boxes, and set forth, in very warm and opprobrious language, the impositions of the managers, and with much vehemence, pleaded the right of the audience to fix the price of their bill of fare.* When Mr. Garrick came forward to address the house, he was received with noise and uproar, and treated with the utmost contempt by the orator and his friends. He was not permitted to show the progressive accumulation of theatrical expenses, the nightly charge of which, from the year 1702 to 1760, had been raised from 34 pounds to above 90 pounds."

Whatever may have been the merits of the dispute —and it was argued with some show of justice, in behalf of the patentee, that he had been put to considerable extra expense through the *Two Gentlemen of Verona*—the uproar of the house became so great that Garrick could not make himself heard. As it seemed evident that he had no intention of yielding to the popular clamor the indignant spectators broke out into unrestrained riot, tore up the seats, smashed the lustres and girandoles, and generally behaved themselves like ruffians of the most approved type. And that put a violent end to the performance for the benefit of the unfortunate and unvictorious Victor.

When the next night came, a new tragedy, *Elvira*, was the attraction, but it was plainly to be seen, from

---

* It was demanded that only half-price should be charged after the third act.

the very moment the doors of the theatre opened, that the play was *not* the thing on this occasion. As Garrick made his appearance, several in the large audience, now in tumultuous mood, cried out : " Will you or will you not, give admittance for half-price, after the third act of a play, except during the first winter a pantomime is performed ? " Garrick replied to this demand with a reluctant " Yes ! " upon which there was loud applause.

The episode did not end here, for the house now insisted on apologies from several of the manager's company. It is hard to imagine just what the poor players had done to ask pardon about, but a mob, particularly an English one, is inclined to be brutal, and it was decided that the fun should not cease with the submission of the chief offender. Moody, one of the unfortunates, was called upon to express his contrition for having interfered, the previous night, with a scoundrel who attempted to set fire to the theatre, and thinking that he would get out of the difficulty in a tactful manner the actor said, in the voice of a low-comedy Irishman, that " he was very sorry he had displeased the audience by saving their lives in putting out the fire." But this remark added fuel to the flame, instead of extinguishing it. Fierce cries of " Down on your knees ! " and " Ask for pardon ! " rang through the house with such vehemence that it was plain to see what would have been Moody's fate had he been in the pit, or even in the boxes. But he was not to be frightened into so dishonorable a compliance ; he boldly faced the sea of angry faces and shouted above the din, "I will not, by G—." When he went behind the scenes Garrick, who with all his faults could sympathize with bravery, gave him an admiring embrace, saying at the same time that "whilst he [Garrick] was master of a guinea Moody should be paid his income."

This was a pretty little incident, of course (how charming is the picture of the mighty David unbending in the presence of his company to caress one of his subordinates) but unfortunately the story has a tamer conclusion. What does the prudent Roscius do next but bounce on the stage and assure the howling ruffians that Mr. Moody "should not appear again during the time of their displeasure." The man who so often threw his soul into some of the most valiant and heroic of theatrical personages could not even imitate the manliness of one of his own henchmen.

In the meantime things resumed their normal condition at Drury Lane, but Moody found himself in an awkward predicament. He was unable to appear at that theatre, and yet unwilling either to take one of Garrick's treasured guineas or to leave London for the provincial stage. Finally he took the bull by the horns, or rather bearded the leonine Fitzpatrick in his chambers in the Temple. "I suppose, sir, you know me," said Moody, as he entered the room.

"Very well, sir ; and how came I by the honor of this visit?" demanded the astonished Fitzpatrick.

"How dare you ask me that question, when you know what passed at Drury Lane, where I was called upon to dishonor myself, by asking pardon of the audience upon my knees."

"No, sir, I was not the person who spoke to you."

"Sir, you did, I saw you and heard you. And what crime had I committed to be obliged to stoop to such an ignominious submission? I had prevented a wretch from setting fire to the playhouse, and had espoused the cause of a gentleman in whose services I had enlisted!"

"I do not understand being treated in this manner in my own house!"

"Sir, I will attend you where you please; for, be assured, I will not leave you till you have satisfied me one way or other."

It is pleasant to learn that after much parleying between Mr. Fitzpatrick, who stood very much upon his dignity, and Mr. Moody, who was determined to have redress, the former wrote to Garrick that whenever the actor should be allowed on the stage of Drury Lane he (Fitzpatrick) and his friends would attend and help to reinstate the delinquent in the popular regard.*

* Of this John Moody, who proved a valuable actor in his careful, conscientious way, an amusing anecdote was related some years ago in the *Cornhill Magazine*. Among the traits of stupidity put to the account of actors, by which droll unrehearsed effects have been produced on the stage, there is none that is supposed to convey greater proof of stupidity than that

And now it must be confessed that the greatest actor of his time, the man who had held London entranced for twenty years, experienced a sudden coldness on the part of the public. The theatre-goer has from days immemorial claimed the right to be capricious; he may laud a player to the skies one season and wish him in the subterranean regions the next; and accordingly, when the *Beggar's Opera* had a revival at Covent Garden, he exercised this sacred prerogative by getting madly enthusiastic over the new *Polly Peachum*, rich-voiced Miss Brent,* and turning a cold shoulder on the idol of Drury Lane. All the beauties of *Hamlet*, *Ranger*, *Benedick*, and *Lear*—characters which

which distinguished the actor who originally represented *Lord Burghley* in the *Critic*. The names of several players are mentioned, each as being the hero of this story; but the original *Lord Burghley*, or *Burleigh*, was Irish Moody, far too acute an actor to be suspected for a fool. When Sheridan selected him for the part, the manager declared that Moody would be sure to commit some ridiculous error and ruin the effect. The author protested that such a result was impossible; and, according to the fashion of the times, a wager was laid and Sheridan hurried to the performer of the part to give him such instructions as should render any mistake beyond possibility. *Lord Burghley* has nothing to say, merely to sit a while; and then, as the stage directions informed him, and as Sheridan impressed it on his mind, "*Lord Burghley* comes forward, pauses near *Dangle*, shakes his head and exit." The actor thoroughly understood the direction, he said, and could not err. At night he *came* forward, *did* pass near *Dangle*, shook his (*Dangle's*) head, and went solemnly off.

* Miss Brent was a pupil of Dr. Arne, and had, curiously enough, been refused an engagement at Drury Lane prior to her success in the *Beggar's Opera*.

Garrick resuscitated in a vain endeavor to check the tide that was hurrying the people towards Covent Garden—were as nothing to the attractions of *Polly*. "That bewitching syren charmed all the world, and, like another Orpheus, drew crowds perpetually after her," while on one awful night at the rival house, when Garrick and Mrs. Cibber acted, the receipts were less than four pounds!

Poor Garrick! This was more than human nature, or at least his nature, could stand. *Mens conscia recti* might be a fine old Latin motto, very admirable when used in a classic tragedy, but what was the consciousness of intrinsic merit worth, under such dismal circumstances, to a man whose very existence depended upon the applause of the multitude? What availed it to be the most distinguished tragedian or comedian in the world if you could only draw three pounds, fifteen shillings and six pence per night, with a singing woman piling up the gold at another house? It is quite natural, therefore, that the deserted favorite should temporarily relinquish the management of Drury Lane to his brother, George Garrick, and Mr. Lacy, and take a European tour in accompany with the most faithful and devoted of wives, who during the whole of their married life was never absent from her illustrious husband for so long a space as twenty-four hours.

It was in the autumn of 1763 that the Garricks set out on a journey which proved a decided balm to the soul of the discomfited David. Everywhere he was received with the greatest kindness and consideration ; he had a special audience with the Duke of Parma, before whom he recited a scene from *Macbeth*, and he felt the supreme happiness of being embraced by the fascinating Mlle. Clairon. This French actress saw Garrick represent, in pantomime, the grief of a father over the death of his child ; she was so wrought up by the superb exhibition of power that she caught her surprised colleague around the neck, kissed him fervently, and then politely apologized to the amused Mrs. Garrick.

Garrick enjoyed himself thoroughly for more than a year and then turned his face homeward,* after being careful to send in advance of himself a poem called *The Sick Monkey*. This effusion was written as a satirical account of his travels, something that should disarm the criticism of his enemies, but it proved dull, in wretched taste, and fell as flat as the much-quoted pancake. After he reached London, however, and re-appeared some months later (November, 1765) as the crusty *Benedick*, King George III. applauded from the royal box and the crowded audience showed by its cheers that the idol had been replaced on his well-earned pedestal. " Mr. Garrick has benefited by his wanderings," reported the critics. " Even the great Roscius may learn by experi-

* He had become alarmed, no doubt, at the growing popularity of that brilliant young actor, William Powell.

ence," said one ; "his deportment is more graceful and his manner more elegant," observed another ; and "he has given up all theatrical clap-trap," wisely added a third. In fine, Davy was himself again, so far as public favor was concerned, although physically he was already on the wane. Some of the old-time vitality, a flash of the early fire, might be missed ; the once dainty figure had grown corpulent, and frequent attacks of gout and a more serious trouble warned him that he could no longer tax his strength as he was wont to do. No one was more alive to the limitations which age was fast putting on his genius than the actor himself, who humorously alluded to them in the prologue which he spoke on the revival of *Much Ado About Nothing*.

> "In four-and-twenty years the spirits cool ;
> Is it not long enough to play the fool ?
> To prove it is, permit me to repeat
> What late I heard in passing through the street ;
> A youth of parts, with ladies by his side,
> Thus cocked his glass, and through it shot my pride ;
> *'' T is he, by Jove ! grown quite a clumsy fellow,*
> *He 's fit for nothing but a Punchinello"* —
> 'O yes ! for comic scenes, Sir John—no further ;
> He 's much too fat for battles, rapes and murther,'
> Worn in the service, you my faults will spare,
> And make allowance for the wear and tear."

We next hear of Garrick as hard at work writing plays, one of them *The Country Girl*. It was a free but decent adaptation of Wycherley's *Country Wife*, one of the most filthy plays of the Restoration period, and in spite of its attractiveness in this new dress it suffered from one serious drawback. Miss Reynolds, who played the title character, was too old and homely to look the ideal country girl of sixteen or so. Yet what theatre-goer of to-day has not met with a like anomaly, and become hardened, perhaps, to *Juliets* old enough to be grandmothers, charming but middle-aged *Portias, Rosalinds* of maternal, benevolent aspect, and fine *Hamlets* of fifty or sixty. One of the best modern performances of *Lady Teazle* was that given several years ago by a gifted artiste of seventy, who can still delight an audience as do but few living actresses. We are lenient with such a drawback, for we know that when a woman plays *Lady Teazle* or *Juliet* as she should, she is often too old to look the part. But in the days of Garrick critics and public were not always so philosophical, and the *Country Girl* hardly met with the success anticipated by the author.

Garrick's brilliant career was now drawing to a close. We can leave to better biographers the account of his last professional years, not even halting to describe his participation in the Stratford Jubilee (held ostensibly in honor of Shakespeare but given quite as much in recognition of Garrick), and hurrying on to that tearful night * of June 10, 1776, when this Titan

---

* About the same time Garrick sold his share in the patent of Drury Lane for £35,000. The purchasers were Richard Brinsley Sheridan, Thomas Linley, and Richard Ford, and Sheridan assumed the actual management of the theatre.

of the stage bid farewell to it forever. Before that last performance, Garrick appeared in a round of his most famous characters; and that entertaining *raconteur*, Frederick Reynolds, tells how he saw the great man's final presentation of *Hamlet*.

"On the morning of that day," says Reynolds, "Perkins, who was my father's wig maker, as well as Garrick's, cut and trimmed my hair for the occasion. During the operation he told me, that when I saw Garrick first behold the ghost, I should see each individual hair of his head stand upright; and he concluded, by hoping, that though I so much admired the actor, I would reserve a mite of approbation for him, as the artist of this most ingenious, mechanical wig; 'the real cause,' he added, '*entre nous*, of his prodigious effects in that scene.' Whether this story was related by the facetious perruquier to puff himself, or to hoax me, I will not pretend to decide; but this I can say with truth, that though I did not see Garrick's hair rise perpendicularly, mine did, when he broke from *Horatio* and *Marcellus*, with anger flashing from 'his two balls of fire' (as his eyes were rightly called) exclaiming,

' By heaven, I 'll make a ghost of him that lets me.' "

The narrator was also on hand on the farewell evening. Garrick played *Felix* in *The Wonder* with a fire that made him young again and afterwards addressed the enthusiastic yet sorrowing house, broke down in

the middle of this, the most pathetic Epilogue of his
life, recovered himself, ended his valedictory and then,
solemnly bowing, walked off the stage forever, amid
the mingled tears and plaudits of the brilliant assem-
blage. On this night, continues Reynolds, "my
brother Jack and I, after waiting two hours, succeeded
at length in entering the pit. But the commencement
of the evening was somewhat unfortunate to my brother,
who, during the struggle in the pit passage, not only
had his watch stolen, but so completely lost his temper
that, on the detection of the thief, who immediately
offered to restore the property, Jack, instead of receiving it, with all the fury of an enraged young lawyer determined to have the stolen goods found on him. Accordingly he seized him, and shouted for police officers—
in vain ; the crowd involuntarily prevented a possibility
of their interference. . . . Jack now dragged the
thief into the pit, and again called loudly for police
officers, who at length came, though somewhat late ;
for owing to the increased confusion the bird had at
length broken from Jack and flown !

" The riot and struggle for places can scarcely
be imagined," continues Reynolds, "even from the
above anecdote. Though a side box close to where
we sat was completely filled, we beheld the door burst
open, and an Irish gentleman attempt to make entry,
vi et armis. ' Shut the door, box-keeper,' loudly cried
some of the party, ' There 's room by the pow'rs !'
cried the Irishman, and persisted in advancing. On

this, a gentleman in the second row rose, and exclaimed, 'Turn out that blackguard!' 'Oh, and that is your mode, honey?' coolly retorted the Irishman, 'come, come out, my dear, and give me satisfaction, or I'll pull your nose, faith, you coward, and *shillaly* you through the lobby!'

"This public insult left the tenant in possession no alternative; so he rushed out to accept the challenge; when, to the pit's general amusement, the Irishman jumped into his place, and having deliberately seated and adjusted himself, he turned around and cried; 'I'll talk to you after the play is over.'

"The comedy of *The Wonder* commenced, but I have scarcely any recollection of what passed during its representation; or, if I had, would it not be tedious to repeat a ten times told tale?* I only remember that Garrick and his hearers were mutually affected by the farewell address; particularly in that part where he said 'The jingle of rhyme and the language of fiction would but ill suit his present feelings' and also, when putting his hand to his breast he exclaimed, 'Whatever may be the changes of my future life, the deepest impression of your gratitude will remain here, fixed and unalterable.' Still, however, though my memory will not allow me to dwell further on the events of the evening my pride will never permit me to forget, that I witnessed Garrick's dramatic death."

The physical death of this wondrous player, who

* Would that he had done so, nevertheless.

had so often mimicked the Grim Visitor that now stood
upon his threshold, occurred peacefully and painlessly
on January 20, 1779. Two days after the funeral (his
remains were laid with great pomp and ceremony at
the base of Shakespeare's statue in Poet's Corner,
Westminster Abbey) his brother George Garrick went
over to the great Majority, fitly enough, as it seemed.
George had been David's right hand man at Drury
Lane, a *Fidus Achates* as well as a relation. On his
returning to the theatre after a brief absence he would
invariably ask "Has my brother wanted me?" and
when he was gathered unto his fathers, a friend said
wittily but tenderly, "His brother wanted him."

NEW DRURY LANE THEATRE

OPENED IN 1794 AND DESTROYED BY FIRE IN 1809.   FROM AN ENGRAVING BY W. J. WHITE AFTER A DRAWING BY J. CAPON.

CHAPTER XIV.

" I HAVE been very seriously at work on a book, which I am just now sending to the press, and which I think will do me some credit, if it leads to nothing else. However, the profitable affair is of another nature. There will be a *Comedy* of mine in rehearsal at Covent Garden within a few days. I did not set to work on it till within a few days of my setting out for Crome, so you may think I have not, for these last six weeks, been very idle. I have done it at Mr. Harris's (the manager's) own request; it is now complete in his hands, and preparing for the stage. He, and some of his friends also who have heard it, assure me in the most flattering terms that there is not a doubt of its success. It will be very well played, and Harris tells me that the least shilling I shall get (if it succeeds) will be six hundred pounds. I shall make no secret of it towards the time of representation, that it may not lose any support my friends can give it. I had not written a line of it two months ago, except a scene or two, which I believe you have seen in an off act of a little farce."

Thus wrote a certain young gentleman to his father-in-law, Thomas Linley, in November, 1774. It need hardly be added that the son-in-law was Richard Brinsley Sheridan, who, at the early age of twenty-three, had translated Aristænetus, fought a couple of duels, eloped with and married, the beautiful Miss Linley of Bath, and just completed a comedy which is still considered one of the most delightful in the English language.

This prodigy—for so must have been the man who could produce both *The Rivals* and *The School for Scandal* before he reached his thirtieth year—was the son of Thomas Sheridan, the self-constituted rival of Garrick, and the grandson of Dr. Sheridan, who obtained a sort of reflected glory from his intimacy with Jonathan Swift. Richard's mother, charming woman, had intellectual gifts of a much more than respectable order ; she was the author of several long-since forgotten novels and of a play* which so august an authority as Garrick pronounced "one of the best comedies he ever read." Another comedy of hers, which never saw the light, might have possessed interest even for posterity, since Tom Moore records that it "has been supposed by some of those sagacious persons, who love to look for flaws in the titles of fame, to have passed, with her other papers, into the possession of her son, and after a transforming sleep, like that of the chrysalis, in his hands, to have taken

* *The Discovery.*

wing at length in the brilliant form of *The Rivals.*"
Poor lady! even were this true, you never would have
grudged your erratic son the fame of it all.

As a schoolboy young Richard proved a dismal failure, and he who, in less than thirty years afterwards,
"held senates enchained by his eloquence and audiences fascinated by his wit, was, by common consent
both of parent and preceptor, pronounced to be 'a
most impenetrable dunce.'" At Harrow he was a
sad fellow when it came to study hours, but at play-
time he proved so lovable, manly, and genial that he
suffered less punishment for his indolence than might
otherwise have been meted out to him. The erudite
Dr. Parr, then one of the under-masters of the school,
wrote of Sheridan many years later: "There was
little in his boyhood worth communication. He was
inferior to many of his school-fellows in the ordinary
business of school, and I do not remember any one
instance in which he distinguished himself by Latin
or English composition, in prose or verse. . . .
His eye, his countenance, his general manner, were
striking. His answers to any common question were
prompt and acute. We knew the esteem, and even
admiration, which, somehow or other, all his school-
fellows felt for him. He was mischievous enough,
but his pranks were accompanied by a sort of vivacity and cheerfulness which delighted Sumner* and myself. I had much talk with him about his apple-loft,

* Dr. Robert Sumner, then the upper-master.

for the supply of which all the gardens in the neighborhood were taxed, and some of the lower boys were employed to furnish it. I threatened, but without asperity, to trace the depredators through his associates, up to their leader. He, with perfect good-humor, set me at defiance, and I never could bring the charge home to him.''

This bright young scamp, who could steal apples, neglect his lessons, and yet endear himself to his teachers by his natural charm and sprightliness, soon grew ambitious. He had a soul above apples after all ; he longed for the airy pinnacle of a literary celebrity, and in the year 1770, when he is living with his father at Bath, we find him scheming with an old Harrow chum, young Halhead, now at Oxford, to make the world ring with the sound of their names. They are so boyish about it all, too ; as, for instance, when they determine to translate the epistles of Aristænetus, about whom nobody cares, and especially when done into English by two unknown lads. Then they write a parody called *Jupiter*, which never gets acted ; they issue one number of a rather puerile paper called *Hernan's Miscellany*, and plan half a dozen works whose brilliancy must surely set the Thames on fire.

The only tangible result of this literary partnership is that translation of Aristænetus, which is expected to win so much classical reputation for the apprentices. The first part of the work—alas ! there never was the least demand for the second part—appeared anonymously in August, 1771, and for a time all too brief the ambitious authors deceived themselves with dreams as to its success. Several of the reviews are fairly favorable, and a friend writes to Sheridan : " It begins to make some noise, and is fathered on Mr. Johnson, author of the *English Dictionary.*" Poor Johnson !

Then comes a harsh critic who growls : " No such writer as Aristænetus ever existed in the classic æra ; nor did even the unhappy schools, after the destruction of the Eastern Empire, produce such a writer. It was left to the latter times of monkish imposition to give such trash as this, on which the translator has ill spent his time. We have been as idly employed in reading it, and our readers will in proportion lose their time in perusing this article." Ungenerous man ! Perhaps you enjoyed, later on, the wit and sparkle of *The Rivals* or the *School for Scandal*, and never knew that the playwright who gave you such unstinted pleasure was the aspiring young person whom you had so unmercifully rebuked.

With all their zeal for classic lore and modern fame there was one passion which the translators found much more poetic and enthralling. They had both fallen madly in love with the lovely " Maid of Bath " —Halhead deeply but hopelessly ; Sheridan, as was his way, impetuously and buoyantly. Miss Linley, then not more than sixteen or seventeen, was a fit subject for such ardent heroine-worship. The daughter of an eminent composer, she followed out the musical traditions of the family by singing in oratorio, but no amount of publicity or admiration could destroy the bloom of her girlish sweetness and modesty, or take away one whit of the gentleness and purity of that angelic face.*

" Her exquisite and delicate loveliness, all the more fascinating for the tender sadness which seemed, as a contemporary describes it, to project over her the shadow of early death ; her sweet voice, and the pathetic expression of her singing, the timid and touching grace of her air and deportment, had won universal admiration for Eliza Ann Linley. From the days when, a girl of nine, she stood with her little basket at the pump-room door, timidly offering the tickets for her father's benefit concerts, to those when, in her teens, she was the belle of the Bath assemblies, none could resist her beseeching grace. Lovers and wooers flocked about her ; Richard Walter Long, the Wiltshire miser, laid his thousands at her feet. Even Foote, when he took the story of Miss Linley's rejection of that sordid old hunks as the subject of his *Maid of Bath*, in 1770, laid no stain of his satirical brush on her. Nor had she resisted only the temptation of money : coronets, it was whispered, had been laid at her feet as well as money. When she appeared at the Oxford oratorios,

---

* " To see her as she stood singing beside me at the pianoforte was like looking into the face of an angel."—WILLIAM JACKSON.

grave dons and young gentlemen were alike subdued. In London, where she sang at Covent Garden, in the Lent of 1773, the King himself is said to have been as much fascinated by her eyes and voice as by the music of his favorite Handel."*

Sheridan's courtship prospered, notwithstanding the claims and importunities of more pretentious admirers, one of whom happened to be his brother Charles. The melancholy, love-lorn Halhead took himself out of the lists altogether by going to India, and the now successful suitor gave vent to his poetic muse in several well-tuned love verses, such as

> " Dry be that tear, my gentlest love,
> Be hush'd that struggling sigh,
> Nor seasons, day, nor fate shall prove
> More fix'd, more true than I.
> Hush'd be that sigh, be dry that tear,
> Cease boding doubt, cease anxious fear,—
> Dry be that tear."

Whether the " boding doubt " and " anxious fear " thus referred to had anything to do with the unwelcome attentions of the blackguardly Captain Mathews it is now hard to say, but it is certain that the unpleasant notoriety into which this married *roué* was fast bringing the young singer influenced her sudden determination to seek temporary refuge in a French convent. Sheridan gladly fell in with this rather wild project ; he saw in it the prospect of a wedding rather than a con-

* Leslie's *Life of Reynolds.*

vent, and thus it came about that on a certain evening when Mr. Linley and several of his family ("a nest of nightingales" Dr. Burney called them) were absent at a concert, one of the nightingales flew away. Young Richard appears at her father's house with a sedan chair, takes the fair charmer to a postchaise waiting for them on the London Road, and here, being joined by a woman "specially engaged" to play *Propriety*, they set out on their adventurous journey. Arrived in London, the now cautious lover introduces his intended bride to a wealthy brandy merchant, an old friend of the Sheridan family, as a rich heiress who was eloping with him to the Continent ; the old man is delighted at Richard's wisdom, compliments him, too, on having given up all ideas of marrying "that Miss Linley, of Bath," and enables the couple to make good their immediate escape to France.

It would be going into ancient history, however, to narrate how they were married by a priest at a little village near Calais, how they were finally induced to return home, and how Sheridan fought two duels with that prince of hounds, Mathews, and got seriously wounded in the second encounter. Meanwhile, the respective fathers of the young lovers were deeply chagrined at the whole affair. Sheridan, fearful that an avowal of the marriage would cause Mr. Linley to separate Mrs. Sheridan from him forever, never told of the ceremony at Calais, and the supposed Miss Linley, no less reticent, went on living with her father, singing divinely and looking lovelier and more pathetic than ever. One hears several pretty stories about the shifts to which the two unhappy ones were reduced so as to get a glimpse of each other, one anecdote, the most romantic of them all, picturing Sheridan disguised as a hackney coachman, driving his wife home from a Covent Garden concert. At last, as all the world and his wife know, the stern heart of the paternal Linley relented, the misery, the romance, the stolen conversations, and the surreptitious glances came to an end, and Richard Brinsley Sheridan and Eliza Ann Sheridan, his wife, went through the formality of a duly English marriage, under official license, in April, 1773.

The now twice-married couple settled down quietly in a little cottage at East Burnham, and though their resources were limited Sheridan manfully refused to allow his wife to sing any more in public, notwithstanding the tempting offers of managers from different parts of the kingdom. In so doing he naturally deprived the concert-stage of a rare acquisition, and put an extinguisher on Mrs. Sheridan's professional career; but as she was only too glad to give up her vocation and Sheridan himself had no idea of living off the earnings of his companion, nobody had a right to complain. Such a disposition of affairs might not have suited the "New Woman," but unfortunately, that indispensable personage had not then appeared on the social horizon.

Dr. Johnson, in his dogmatic way, highly approved of Sheridan's decision. "We talked," says Boswell, "of a young gentleman's marriage with an eminent singer, and his determination that she should no longer sing in public, though his father was very earnest she should because her talents would be liberally rewarded. It was questioned whether the young gentleman, who had not a shilling in the world, but was blessed with very uncommon talents, was not foolishly delicate or foolishly proud, and his father truly rational without being mean. Johnson, with all the high spirit of a Roman senator, exclaimed : ' He resolved wisely and nobly, to be sure. He is a brave man. Would not a gentleman be disgraced by having his wife singing publicly for hire? No, sir, there can be no doubt here.' "

Thus we come down on a quick pace to the anxiously awaited night of January 17, 1775, when *The Rivals* was produced at Covent Garden, with Edward Shuter as *Sir Anthony Absolute*, Woodward as *Captain Absolute*, Lewis as *Falkland*, Quick as *Acres*, Lee as *Sir Lucius O' Trigger*, Mrs. Green as *Mrs. Malaprop*, and Miss Barnsanti as *Lydia Languish*. The first performance of the play was a failure, principally because Mr. Lee made so poor an impression as *Sir Lucius* ; he was replaced in the part by a Mr. Clinch, and the false start was soon forgotten in the popularity that attended ensuing presentations of this rare comedy. We who have seen it acted by that incomparable company headed by Joseph Jefferson (the most lovable and humorous of *Acres*), Mrs. John Drew (the inimitable *Malaprop*), and the late William J. Florence (an ideal *Sir Lucius*) may well ask whether *The Rivals* had so fine an illustration on its introduction to the stage. The original cast seems to have been, with one or two exceptions, capable rather than strikingly effective. Shuter, to be sure, was considered by Garrick to be the greatest comic genius he had ever seen, but his humor was broad and inclined to buffoonery, and one can imagine that the choleric *Sir Anthony*, as he played him, must have been more grateful to the galleries than to the critics.* Woodward, versatile comedian that he was, could hardly have been at his best as the ardent *Captain Absolute*, while vain little Quick,

---

* This performer was once engaged for a few nights in a principal city in the north of England. It happened that the stage that he went down in (and in which there was only an old gentleman and himself) was stopped on the road by a single highwayman. The old gentleman, in order to save his own money, pretended to be asleep, but Shuter resolved to be even with him. Accordingly, when the highwayman presented his pistol, and commanded Shuter to deliver his money instantly, or he was a dead man—" Money," returned he, with an idiotic shrug and a countenance inexpressibly vacant—" Oh, Lud, sir, they never trust me with any ; for my uncle here always pays for me, turnpikes and all, your honor! " Upon which the highwayman gave him a few curses for his stupidity, complimented the old gentleman with a smart slap on the face to awaken him, and robbed him of every shilling he had in his pocket, while Shuter, who did not lose a single farthing, pursued his journey with great satisfaction and merriment, laughing heartily at his fellow-traveller.— *Theatrical Anecdotes.*

the first of *Tony Lumpkins*, in whom "noise and extravagance" were substituted for "nature and humor," probably missed not a few of the delicately put on colors in the figure of "fighting *Bob*." William Lewis, no doubt, made a gentlemanly and effective *Falkland*, and Lee Lewes, one of the great *Harlequins* of his time, may have been a suitable *Fag*, but it is safe to assume that Mrs. Green, a droll but by no means great actress, was not the very best of *Malaprops*. The names of Barnsanti, Dunstal, Fearon, Mrs. Bulkley, and Mrs. Lessingham, the other members of the cast, signified little then and nothing now. Can it then be possible that a *fin de siècle* audience has seen a finer performance of *The Rivals* than that vouchsafed the frequenters of Covent Garden on the great initial night? Certainly our conservative old gentleman, who mourns for the "palmy days" of his past, will never admit such a heresy into his theatrical catechism.

A still greater triumph than the ultimate success of *The Rivals* is awaiting the now much be-praised Sheridan. First he collaborates with Mr. Linley in writing the opera of *The Duenna*, which has a run of over seventy nights at Covent Garden during the season of 1775-6*; then he combines with Mr. Linley and Dr.

* "In order to counteract this great success of the rival house, Garrick found it necessary to bring forward all the weight of his own best characters ; and even had recourse to the expedient of playing off the mother against the son, by reviving Mrs. Frances Sheridan's comedy of *The Discovery*, and acting the

Ford to purchase Garrick's interest in the Drury Lane Theatre, and next brings out, in his new capacity of manager, his adaptation of Vanbrugh's *Relapse*, called *A Trip to Scarborough*. Still this is merely preliminary to the greatest epoch in the purely theatrical portion of his life, that 8th of May, 1777, when *The School for Scandal* first sees the light.

The new comedy gave Sheridan much greater concern than did *The Rivals;* he had changed the story, elaborated the dialogue, and polished up the epigrams materially before the final draft was ready for the prompter, nor is it strange, therefore, to find that while it lacks the spontaneity and naturalness of its predecessor, *The School for Scandal* is far more witty and scintillating. It may be artificial—was not the life it pictured artificial—and it is worse than faulty from a dramatic standpoint, yet its sparkle is still undimmed more than a century after the first production. Though the play be merely the champagne of Sheridan's genius, the vintage is a rich one, and seems to improve with age.

The circumstances under which the new comedy first appeared were probably much more favorable, with respect to the cast, than in the case of *The Rivals*, for this was the assignment of characters :

principal part in it himself. In allusion to the increased fatigue which this competition with *The Duenna* brought upon Garrick, who was then entering on his sixtieth year, it was said, by an actor of the day, that " the old woman would be the death of the old man."—MOORE.

Sir Peter Teazle	.	.	.	.	Mr. King.
Sir Oliver Surface	.	.	.	.	Mr. Yates.
Joseph Surface	.	.	.	.	Mr. Palmer. '
Charles Surface	.	.	.	.	Mr. Smith. '
Crabtree.	.	.	.	.	Mr. Parsons.
Sir Benjamin Backbite	.	.	.	Mr. Dodd.
Rowley	.	.	.	.	.	Mr. Aickin.
Moses	.	.	.	.	.	Mr. Baddeley.
Trip .	.	.	.	.	.	Mr. Lamash.
Snake	.	.	.	.	.	Mr. Packer.
Careless	.	.	.	.	.	Mr. Farren.
Sir Harry Bumper	.	.	.	.	Mr. Gawdry.

Lady Teazle	.	.	.	.	Mrs. Abington
Maria	.	.	.	-	.	Miss P. Hopkins.
Lady Sneerwell	.	.	.	.	Miss Sherry.
Mrs. Candour .	.	.	.	.	Miss Pope.

The most brilliant star in this galaxy was the beautiful Mrs. Abington, who had such various claims to celebrity. She was the questionable heroine of several as questionable amours (had not Garrick called her "that worst of women?"), and she came out of the dregs of London life, yet she triumphed over her surroundings, developed into an actress of rare spirit and humor, set the fashions for society,* which even admitted her within its well-guarded precincts, had her portrait painted by the great Sir Joshua Reynolds, and earned the encomiums of Horace Walpole. It was the latter who wrote of her, referring to an unfounded rumor that she had retired from the stage :

* The once popular "Abington" caps were named in honor of this actress.

THOMAS KING.

AS "PEREZ" IN BEAUMONT AND FLETCHER'S "RULE A WIFE AND HAVE A WIFE."
FROM A DRAWING BY DODD.

> " Sad with the news, Thalia mourned ;
> The Graces joined her train ;
> And naught but sighs for sighs return'd,
> Were heard at Drury Lane.
>
> But see—'t is false ! in Nature's style
> She comes, by Fancy dress'd ;
> Again gives Comedy her smile,
> And Fashion all her taste."

This was the Abington who delighted the audience that night, critics and laymen alike, by her performance of the elegant *Lady Teazle*. She had been a kitchen wench, a seller of flowers (did not a few persons with inconvenient memories recall her nickname of " Nosegay Fan "*) and an errand girl to a French milliner, but she could play the country miss turned woman of fashion with a naturalness and sureness of touch that bespoke the Duchess, rather than the cobbler's daughter.

As the *Lady Teazle* proved so admirable, likewise did the *Sir Peter* of Thomas King, the intimate friend of Garrick, and a conservative actor whose epigrammatic, dryly amusing style must have seemed just suited to the part. How could it have been otherwise with a man of whom Charles Lamb wrote so picturesquely : " His acting left a taste on the palate sharp and sweet like a quince ; with an old, hard, rough, withered face, like a john-apple, puckered up into a thousand wrinkles ; with shrewd hints and tart replies."

---

* Fanny Barton was her maiden name. Her father was sometimes a soldier in the Guards, and sometimes a cobbler.

Another of the *dramatis personæ* who must have added strength to the cast was William Smith—

"Smith the genteel, the airy and the smart,"

as Churchill called him. To play *Charles Surface* one had to be a gentleman as well as a comedian, and Sheridan was peculiarly fortunate in having at hand an actor whose distinction of manner and good-breeding enabled him to give such realism to the character. *Charles* represented what would now be vulgarly termed a "dress-suit" part, and those of us who have seen some talented but hopelessly *outré* comedian trying to look comfortable as the hero of a stage drawing-room can understand how difficult it is to procure the necessary combination in this respect. Even men who are gentlemen by birth and education cannot always appear graceful and at ease in so-called society plays. But "Gentleman Smith," with an elegance that never deserted him, either on or off the boards, played the careless *Surface* with a finish and air of fashionable ease that proved a delight to the audiences of his own generation, while it set the model for the players of a future one.

A fine group, these first exponents of *The School for Scandal.* There was Yates, so excellent as an humorous old man, who must have been an unctuous *Sir Oliver;* and we know that John Palmer's *Joseph Surface* was considered unapproachable. "So admirable a hypocrite has never yet been seen : his manners, his deportment, his address, combined to render him the very man he desired to paint. His performance on the stage bore a very strong similarity to that he was famous for in private life. He was plausible, of pleasing address, of much politeness and even of great grace. He was fond of pleasure, which he pursued with so much avidity as to be generally very careless of his theatrical duties."* Then what a life-like *Sir Benjamin* was James Dodd, who has been pronounced the most perfect fopling ever seen upon the stage. "He took his snuff, or applied the quintessence of roses to his nose with an air of complacent superiority, such as won the hearts of all conversant with that style of affectation." Such was the man who was spoken of as "the prince of pink heels and the Soul of empty eminence."

But there is no need to dwell on the individual virtues of the players who lent such *éclat* to the initial performance. It was a triumphant night for all concerned, from Sheridan down to the prompter,† and the applause was frequent and enthusiastic, as though prophetic of the reception this glittering work would meet with in after years. Frederick Reynolds, then a mere lad, quaintly relates how he was returning home from Lincoln's Inn about nine o'clock that evening, and passing through the Pit-passage, from Vinegar-Yard to Brydges Street, he heard such a tremendous noise over

---

* *Life of Sheridan.*

† Hopkins, the father of the original *Maria* (Miss P. Hopkins). Miss Hopkins afterwards became the wife of John Philip Kemble.

his head that, "fearing the theatre was proceeding to fall about it," he ran for his life, "but found the next morning, that the noise did not arise from the falling of the house, but from the falling of the screen, in the fourth act, so violent and so tumultuous were the applause and laughter."

The comedy, as we know, had a talkative beginning, and the action, of which there is not over-much at best, was late in developing, so that one of the spectators exclaimed impatiently, during the scene at *Lady Sneerwell's* in the second act, "I wish these people would have done talking, and let the play begin." As the interest in the slender story increased, and it was seen how witty and delightful became this very "talking," the house warmed to the performance and ended by putting the seal of its most vociferous approval upon the new production. The shekels began pouring into Drury Lane box-office, and even when it ceased to exert the charm of novelty *The School for Scandal* could be revived at this house with the most profitable results. Garrick had taken the greatest interest in the rehearsals, for he was proud of his managerial successor, and when the popularity of the piece was assured he sent his "best wishes and compliments to Mr. Sheridan" and added : "A gentleman who is as mad as myself about the School remark'd that the characters upon the stage at the falling of the screen stand too long before they speak—I thought so too the first night —he said it was the same on the second, and was remark'd by others ;—tho' they should be astonish'd, and a little petrified, yet it may be carried to too great a length. All praise at Lord Lucan's last night.'' If a keen critic such as Garrick could acknowledge himself mad about the comedy, Sheridan might well rest satisfied.

There were several of the author's enemies who refused to rest satisfied, however, and they insisted that he had not written *The School for Scandal* at all. The discussion even assumed the dignity of a controversy of the Shakespeare-Bacon-Donnelly type, and there were several wiseacres who mysteriously hinted that the daughter of a Thames Street merchant was responsible for the play. This young lady, it appears, put the manuscript into Sheridan's hands at the beginning of the season, and then marched off to the Bristol hotwells, where she conveniently died in time to leave Richard Brinsley in full possession of the field—and the comedy. In later years, when John Watkins, Doctor of Laws, *et cetera, et cetera,* came to write his memoirs of Sheridan, he gave particular credence to this rumor, and lamented that the doubt thus raised had never been cleared up, ''because an unfavorable impression has been made, which will become deeper and more extensive in proportion to the lapse of years, and the efforts that may be made for its removal.'' You were a poor prophet, Dr. Watkins. The public of to-day knows as little of the story as it does— saving your memory—of John Watkins, LL.D.

CHAPTER XV.

THE eighteenth century, so rich in its theatrical life and tradition, now sped on the homeward stretch, and the time was fast approaching when the players who had drawn their inspiration from the marvellous Garrick would make their final exits. A new dramatic era, glorious in the possession of the tragic Siddons and the mighty Kean, waited on the threshold of the theatre ; when its knock was heard the great Roscius had departed,* but some of his contemporaries yet remained to bring back pleasant memories of the past, and unconsciously prepare the way for the giants of a different school and age. Before closing these "Echoes" of the old-time theatre, we might therefore linger for a moment among the coterie of entertainers who so gracefully ushered out the ancient regime—one of the most imposing epochs that the historian of the stage will ever chronicle.

There was the statuesque, the *Medea*-like Mistress Yates, a beautiful incarnation of tragedy, whose

---

* It must not be forgotten, however, that Siddons acted in Garrick's company and made a failure as *Portia*. Her genius and her fame never developed until after the great actor's death.

haughty, disdainful looks and noble voice could
command the attention of even the dullest spectator.
She was not what in these days one calls a sympathetic actress; on the contrary, she seemed all fire
and majestic dignity, without that emotion which
one associates with less strong-minded members of
her sex, and Churchill wrote of her that

> ". . . through the region of that beauteous face,
> We no variety of passions trace.
> Dead to the soft emotions of the heart,
> No kindred softness can those eyes impart.
> The brow still fix'd in sorrow's sullen frame,
> Void of distinction, marks all parts the same."

That she could, on occasion, display a fair amount
of *ésprit* and even humor, in spite of all her grandeur
and classic severity, is shown by what William Godwin,
the husband of Mary Wollstonecraft, wrote of her
Violante in *The Wonder.* "What I recollect best of
Mrs. Yates," he says, "is the scene in which Garrick,
having offended her by a jealousy, not altogether without an apparent cause, the lady, conscious of her entire
innocence, at length expresses a serious resentment.
Felix had till then indulged his angry feelings; but
finding at last that he had gone too far, applies himself
with all a lover's art to soothe her. She turns her back
to him, and draws away her chair; he follows her,
and draws his chair nearer; she draws away further;
at length by his winning, entreating, and cajoling, she
is gradually induced to melt, and finally makes it up
with him. Her condescension in every stage, from its

commencement to its conclusion, was admirable. Her dignity was great and lofty, and the effect highly enhanced by her beauty ; and when by degrees she laid aside her frown—when her lips began to relax toward a smile, while one cloud vanished after another, the spectator thought he had never seen anything so lovely and irresistible, and the effect was greatly owing to her queen-like majesty. The conclusion, in a graceful and wayward beauty, would have been comparatively nothing ; with Mrs. Yates's figure and demeanor it laid the whole audience, as well as the lover, at her feet."

One of this imposing woman's great parts was *Lady Macbeth*, in which it was even considered that she equalled the famous Mrs. Pritchard.* The *Macbeth* who assisted her in a notable production of the tragedy was John Henderson, of whom Mrs. Siddons has left it on record that he was " the soul of feeling and intelligence."

* Mrs. Pritchard (born 1711, died 1768) lacked grace, breeding, and gentility of manner, but she acted low comedy characters, such as women of the shrewish, common type, with unbounded humor, while she won great favor in certain tragic parts, notwithstanding her exuberance of expression, and her disposition, as Garrick pointed out, to " blubber her sorrows." This was the actress of whom Dr. Johnson said to Mrs. Siddons that " in common life she was a vulgar idiot." The same critic observed once that "her playing was quite mechanical. It is wonderful how little mind she had. Sir, she had never read the tragedy of *Macbeth* through. She no more thought of the play out of which her part was taken, than a shoemaker thinks of the skin out of which the piece of leather of which he is making a pair of shoes is cut."

The name of Henderson has nothing magical or inspiring about it now, but a century ago it called up sunny visions of one of the most unctuous of *Falstaffs*, who could also, on occasion, metamorphose himself into the far different character of the subjective *Hamlet.* His eye might lack expression, his voice be weak, and his figure wanting in grace and symmetry, but he was a fine actor, for all that. He came of good stock, was a gentleman by ancestry and breeding, and as a youth developed a very ardent ambition for the stage. In 1768 he solicited the interest of George Garrick, who pronounced against the histrionic prospects of the aspirant, owing to the poverty of his vocal equipment. But the young man is not to be daunted ; he procures an engagement at Bath, where he makes a success, and this is but the prelude to an honored career on the metropolitan stage. David Garrick, who seems to have had for him a mixture of jealousy and contempt, writes in 1775 :

"I have seen the great Henderson, who has something and is nothing—he might be made to figure among the puppets of these times. His *Don John* is a comic *Cato*, and his *Hamlet* a mixture of tragedy, comedy, pastoral, farce, and nonsense. However, though my wife is outrageous, I am in the secret ; and see sparks of fire which might be blown to warm even a London audience at Christmas—he is a dramatic phenomenon and his friends, but more particularly Cumberland, has [have] ruined him ; he has a manner of pawing when he would be emphatic, that is ridiculous, and must be changed, or he would not be suffered at the Bedford Coffee-house."

But as the younger Colman well said, although Henderson was many degrees below the standard of Garrick's theatrical genius, he was "many degrees above the mark of his critical detraction." Indeed, with all his physical limitations he made a fine impression as *Benedick*, in which he seems to have imitated the jealous David so well as to almost eclipse the latter in that character—a fairly good showing for an actor who "had something and was nothing," especially if we add this to the list of his other successes, headed by *Falstaff*.

In referring in his *Random Records* to the diplomatic way in which the elder Colman* brought Henderson before the public, the manager's son writes: "There is no denying that he had contracted some bad habits in his deportment, such as an odd mode of receding from parties on the stage, with the palms of his hands turned outwards, and thus *backing* from one of the *dramatis personæ* when he was expressing happiness at meeting. With these adventitious faults, he had to contend against physical drawbacks ; his eye wanted expression and his figure was not well put together. My father was ambitious to start him in characters whose dress might either help or completely hide per-

---

* Colman bought the Haymarket theatre from Foote a short time before the latter's death, which occurred in October, 1777.

sonal deficiencies ; accordingly it was arranged that
the two first personations should be *Shylock* and *Hamlet*,
in which the Jew's gaberdine and the Prince of Denmark's ' inky cloak ' and ' suit of solemn black,' were
of great service. I know not whether *Falstaff* immediately followed these, but whenever he did come, *Sir
John's* proportions were not expected to present a model
for the students of the Royal Academy. By this management the actor's talents soon made sufficient way to
battle such ill natured remarks as might have been expected upon symmetry ; and the audience was prepared
to admit, when he came to the lovers and heroes, that

> ' Before such merit all objections fly.' "

A player of far different calibre was Henry Mossop,*
vehement, vain, and sonorous of voice, who could

> "In monosyllables his thunders roll,"

and who, in spite of his awkwardness and hardness of
expression, was looked upon as one of the best actors
of his time. We read of his quarrelsome disposition,
his checquered career, his envy of Garrick, and cannot
but derive amusement from his altercation with Thomas
Sheridan. It was in the youthful days of Mossop, just
after he had won a remarkable initial triumph in Sheridan's company at the Smock Alley Theatre, in Dublin. He had appeared as *Richard III.*, attired in a
rather dandified and inappropriate costume, and hearing
that the manager had casually commented on the cir-

---

* Mossop was the son of an Irish clergyman of the Established
Church, and first saw the light in 1729. He died in 1773.

cumstance, he sought him out and said in his declamatory, deliberate fashion : " Mr. She-ri-dan, I hear you said I dressed *Richard* like a cox-comb : that is an affront : you wear a sword, pull it out of the scab-bard ! I 'll draw mine and thrust it into your bo-dy ! "

There was no pulling of scab-bards, however, for Sheridan had the good sense to take the challenge for what it was worth. Mossop had a weakness for indulging in heroics off the stage as well as on, and he was not always as impressive in real life as he intended to be. Certainly he could exert no terrors for the Dublin cobbler who refused to leave the actor's boots at home until the bill for their mending was settled. " Tell me," thundered the tragedian, putting on his most crushingly tragic air, " are you the noted cobbler I oft have heard of ? " " Yes," replied the man, " and I think you are the diverting vagabond I have often seen ! "

It was a comparatively short life, but not always a merry one, this meteoric existence of Mossop. There were moments of delirious success, both in London and Dublin, but the cares and responsibilities of management, when he set out for himself in the Irish capital, crushed him in the end. He died in abject poverty, and all the money found in his possession was fourpence. It is better to leave him under more cheerful circumstances, and we may do so by a quotation or two from those chatty *Recollections* of John O'Keefe. " I was one night witness to an untoward circumstance at Smock

Alley Theatre," he writes. "Congreve's *Mourning Bride* was the tragedy ; Mossop, *Osmin,* and a subordinate actor *Selim. Selim* being stabbed by *Osmin* should have remained dead on the stage, but seized with a fit of coughing he unluckily put up his hand and loosened his stock, which set the audience in a burst of laughter. The scene over, the enraged manager and actor railed at his underling for daring to appear alive when he was dead, who, in excuse, said he must have choked had he not done as he did : Mossop replied, 'Sir, you should choke a thousand times rather than spoil my scene.'

"At a period when the payments were not very ready" (O'Keefe continues) "at the Smock Alley treasury, one night, Mossop, in *Lear,* was supported in the arms of an actor who played *Kent,* and who whispered to him, 'If you don't give me your honor, sir, that you'll pay me my arrears this night, before I go home, I'll let you drop about the boards.' Mossop alarmed, said, 'Don't talk to me now.' 'I will,' said *Kent,* 'I will ; I'll let you drop.' Mossop was obliged to give the promise, and the actor thus got his money, though a few of the others went home without theirs. Such the effect of a well-timed hint, though desperate."

A more sedate figure on our eighteenth century canvas was Tate Wilkinson, a phenomenal mimic, a very poor actor, and an energetic provincial manager. Of his imitative powers, there are a number of anecdotes, one of which relates how Tate passed himself off for

Foote before a London audience, which was so thoroughly deceived as to indulge in cries of " Bravo, Foote ! " and such comments as " What fine spirits Sam 's in to-night." All the while the original who was being so wonderfully copied sat concealed in his private box, hugely enjoying the hoax. Perhaps the most interesting of all these stories is the familiar one concerning the seductive Woffington, which John Bernard can give us.

On his first visit to Dublin with Foote, they were engaged by Barry and Mossop to give their entertainments on the alternate nights with Peg Woffington's performances. Foote considered that it would be an attractive feature in the bill, if he announced an imitation of the above lady by Wilkinson ; but the design coming to her ears, she sent Sam an abusive note acquainting him that if he attempted to take her off she had some friends in Dublin who would oblige him to take himself off. Foote showed this epistle to his companion, who, nothing daunted, proposed that instead of an " imitation " they would give a scene from *Alexander the Great* in character, Foote mimicing Barry in the hero, and Wilkinson, Mrs. W. as *Roxana*. Preparations were accordingly made, and their bills published : what gave greater zest to the announcement was, that *Alexander the Great* had been played the night before. Among the flood of spectators came Peg in person, and seated herself in the stage box, not only to enlist the audience in her favor, and silence Foote by her appearance (which was truly beautiful), but if anything occurred to give the wink to a party of young Irish in the pit, who would rise up to execute immediate vengeance on the mimics. Sam and Tate were thus treading on the surface of a secret mine.

When Foote appeared, as he could present no resemblance to Barry but in manner and accent, the surprise was necessarily transferred to the entrance of his companion, a tall and dignified female, something like the original in face, but so like in figure and deportment that the spectators glanced their eyes from box to stage and stage to box, to convince themselves of Mrs. W.'s identity. Peg herself was not the least astonished, and her myrmidons below were uncertain how to act.

Foote commenced the scene sufficiently like Barry to have procured applause, had not Tate thrown himself into one of Peg's favorite attitudes meanwhile, and diverted the attention. Eye and ear were now directed to the latter, and the first tone of his voice drew a thundering response from the lips of his auditors. As he proceeded the effect increased ; the house was electrified ; his enemies were overpowered, and Peg herself set the seal of his talents by beating her fan to pieces on the beading of the boxes.*

Probably no one who ever had to do with the theatrical profession had more personal peculiarities than this same Tate Wilkinson. A sweeping assertion, considering the curious characteristics of many a player

* *Retrospections of the Stage.*

and manager, past or present, but it is at least certain that the intimate friends of the mimic bore eloquent testimony to his remarkable habits and individuality. He had a sweet way, for instance, of going into the gallery of his theatre and there hissing with the utmost vehemence any player who had refused to take his advice on some point of acting, and it is said that on one unexpected occasion he made his sibilant objections so unbearable to the occupants of the upper tier that he was ignominiously hustled out of his own house into the street.

The most amusing of all his eccentricities was a fondness for rambling on in his conversation and going from one topic to another with an irrelevancy that caused the greatest wonderment from those who were not familiar with this little weakness. " Sir," he once wandered on aimlessly to Michael Kelly, " Barry, sir, was as much superior to Garrick in *Romeo* as York Minster is to a Methodist chapel—not but I think that if lobster sauce is not well made, a turbot is n't eatable, let it be ever so firm. Then there 's that Miss Reynolds : why she, sir, fancies herself a singer, but she is quite a squalini, sir ! A nuisance, sir ! going about my house the whole of the day roaring out *The Soldier tired of War's Alarms*, ah ! she has tired me and alarmed the whole neighborhood ; not but when rabbits are young and tender they are very nice eating. There was Mrs. Barry, for example ; Mrs. Barry was very fine and very majestic in *Zenobia ;* Barry in the

FOOTE AS "FONDLEWIFE."

A SCENE FROM CONGREVE'S COMEDY, "THE OLD BACHELOR." FROM A DRAWING
BY J. J. BARRALET.

same play was very good ; not but that the wild rabbits are better than tame ones. Though Mrs. Barry
was so great in her day, yet Mrs. Siddons—stewed and
smothered with onions either of them are delicious.
Mrs. Pope was admirable in *Queen Elizabeth*—a man I
had here made a very good *Oroonoko ;* not but I would
always advise you to have a calf's head dressed with
the skin on, but you must always bespeak it of the
butcher yourself; though the late bespeak of Lord
Scarborough did nothing for me, nothing at all—the
house was one of the worst of the whole season ; with
bacon and green—not twenty pounds altogether, with
parsley and butter."

To speak of the idiosyncracies of actors suggests
an endless string of anecdotes, not the least amusing
of which has for its hero the solemn and sagacious
William Bensley, an ideal *Malvolio* and an impressive
Ghost in *Hamlet.* Bensley had been in the army and
we are told * that when he thought proper to unbend
from his dignified stateliness he was prone to the
relation of his moving accidents by flood and field.
Whenever the name of any foreign station occurred in
conversation Bensley would exclaim, " I was there in
——such a year, and served under (such a General) as
lieutenant," etc. Charles Bannister (against whose
punning propensities Bensley waged war) had noted
down all these assertions for many months, and on one
particular evening, after a coolness for some days be-

* *Records of a Stage Veteran.*

tween the tragedian and himself, proposed his health
in the following words : "Gentlemen, I rise to drink
the health of one who has sought the bubble reputation
even in the cannon's mouth ; who, quitting the field
of fame, bespoke her trumpet to bray forth his eulogies
in the path of the drama. The scenic power of my
friend, Mr. Bensley, you well know, you all appreciate
[loud plaudits, and Bensley, overcome by gratitude,
fervently squeezing Bannister's hand] but, Gentlemen,
it is as a defender of his country that I rise to drink
his health ; he has fought, he has bled for Old England
[tremendous applause, and Bensley bowing his ac-
knowledgments].   He was captain in the —— regiment
at Calcutta —— in ——. He was at —— in ——. He led
the forlorn hope at —— in 17 —— [Here Bannister enu-
merated all the places Bensley had ever mentioned in
his moments of exhilaration, to the tragedian's dismay.]
Gentlemen," concluded Charles, "my friend's age is
but forty-six, he has been twenty years on the stage—
I find, therefore, by accurate calculation that he must
have carried a pair of colors when eighteen months old
—an instance of precocity, power, and courage unex-
ampled in the history of the world." *

Poor Bensley might prose on about his martial experience and act with force as well, and the witty Ban-

* Ralph Wewitzer tells of a country gentleman, who having
fallen asleep while Bensley was repeating a long speech in
"his usual croaking voice," suddenly started up and cried out :
"Hullo ! reach me my blunderbuss this instant ; I thought I
had shot that croaking devil yesterday."

nister could conjure large audiences by the spell of his sweet voice and amusing burlesque of Italian singers, but neither of them held the same warm place in the public heart as did the estimable Mrs. Pope. What a host of associations cluster about her name. The friend and colleague of Garrick, in whose company she figured so conspicuously, and a player at Drury Lane, for many years, she represented all that was best in the school with which she was so pleasurably identified, and when she died in 1797, another link was lost between two great theatrical epochs.

Her maiden name was Younge, and she came of a very respectable but impecunious family. Just as she was preparing to earn her own living, as one historian curiously informs us,* "a dignified Professor of the Long Robe paid his *devoirs* to her. This gentleman being early bred an apothecary, and afterwards pursuing the Law (with whose quibbles he soon became very conversant) it is not to be expected he should be a connoisseur in the mysteries of Cupid." But it seems that "short was the date" of this paradoxical love-affair "where the hearts did not unite." In brief, "the natural moroseness of his temper breaking out, removed the artificial affection she was induced to shew him; and despising a settlement so incompatible with happiness, she really dissolved a connection in which her hand, not her heart, consented."

Miss Younge, now fancy free, determined "to be

* *The Secret History of the Green Room.*

the carver of her own happiness,'' and having a strong liking for the works of the English dramatists concluded that she might do worse than play in some of them herself. She procured a note of introduction to Garrick, who took an interest in her ambitions, and was soon a prominent member of his company. Her salary was next raised to three pounds, and at the end of the season she was disporting herself in comparative luxury to the tune of five pounds a week. She was an attractive woman, with superb neck and shoulders, and a face that had great beauty of expression, although her features were not actually handsome, nor did she lose anything by being frequently compared to the famous Lady Sarah Lennox. Lady Sarah was probably the only woman that honest, phlegmatic George III. ever passionately loved ; he would have married her had he not been unfortunate enough to be a King, and he was himself one of the first to notice the strong resemblance between the actress and his one-time sweetheart. There is, indeed, a pathetic little story as to how, many years later, when the charms of both women were faded, His Majesty attended a performance at Drury Lane and seeing Mrs. Pope on the stage, (in middle life she married Pope, the actor, who was young enough to be her son,) he startled the Queen by muttering in a melancholy, preoccupied manner, ''She is like Lady Sarah still.''

Miss Younge was unusually valuable in that she could play both tragedy and comedy, going from *Lady*

Macbeth and *Juliet* to *Rosalind*, and then descending below-stairs to the atmosphere of dancing chamber-maids, with ease and success. But she shone more brightly in comedy than in the serious roles ; she had a dry humor that proved irresistible, and as Hazlitt said, was " the very picture of a duenna, a maiden lady, or antiquated dowager—the latter spring of beauty, the second childhood of vanity ; more quiet, fantastic and old-fashioned, more pert, frothy and light-headed than anything can be imagined."

She owed not a little of her effectiveness to the training of Garrick, whose temper she could disturb just as well as did several more of his feminine supporters. There is a rather foolish legend that the squabbles of the actresses hastened his retirement from the stage, and that a certain undignified contest over a petticoat, of which Miss Younge and Mrs. Yates were the hero-ines, gave the *coup de grace* to his determination to quit the boards forever. Garrick was too experienced a manager to be driven off by these tempests in a tea-pot, although some wiseacres would have it so, never-theless, and one of them wrote the following epigram entitled *The Manager's Distress.*

> " ' I have no nerves,' says Younge, ' I cannot act.' "
> ' I 've lost my limbs,' cried Abington ; ' 't is fact.'
> Yates screams, ' I 've lost my voice, my throat's so sore.'
> Garrick declares he 'll play the fool no more.
> Without nerves, limbs, and voice, no show, that 's certain :
> Here prompter, ring the bell, and drop the curtain."

Let us drop the curtain on Younge without a thought for petty bickerings, heart-burnings, or prosaic petti- coats. What prettier scene on which to ring it down than that June night of 1776 when Garrick plays *Lear* for the last time. He has acted the old *King* with even more than the customary pathos, as though the part harmonized with his sadness of mood, and when the performance is over he solemnly leads *Cordelia* (Miss Younge) to the greenroom. The veteran knows that he has but one more appearance to make before bidding farewell to the theatre forever, and he says to his companion, with a sigh : "Oh, Bess ! this is the last time of my being your father ; you must now look out for some one else to adopt you." *Cordelia* falls on her knees with theatrical, yet real feeling, and falters, "Then, sir, pray give me a father's blessing." And as the mournful Roscius gently raises her, while the rest of the company look on silently at this never-to-be-for- gotten epilogue, he cries, trembling and affectionately, "God bless you——God bless you all !"——and hur- ries from the room.

It is so characteristic, so like the emotional children of the stage, and withal so sincere ; a charming picture into which, through all the tears, comes a glimpse of golden sunshine. A happy moment, is it not, for the lowering of the green baize on the many scenes de- picted in these *Echoes of The Playhouse?* We can put out the lights, shut up the house, and go home, not in sad- ness, but hopefully, cheerfully. Betterton, Bracegirdle,

MISS YOUNGE.

AS "ZARA" IN "THE MOURNING BRIDE." FROM A DRAWING BY ROBERTS; ENGRAVED BY READING.

Oldfield, Garrick, Woffington and the rest—they have all gone, but the Muse whom they ennobled lives on, richer in memories of the past and strong in promise for the future.   Like some resplendant Cleopatra,

> " Age cannot wither her, nor custom stale
> Her infinite variety."

THE END.